AND THEN CAME *You*

BOOK TWO

THE RYAN FAMILY SERIES

All rights reserved. No part of this publication may be reproduced or maintained in any form or by any means, electronic or mechanical, including photocopy, recording, or any information storage and retrieval system, without permission in writing from the publisher or author.

All characters in the book have no existence outside of the imagination of the author and have no relations whatsoever to anyone bearing the same name or names. They are not even distantly inspired by any individual known or unknown to the author and all incidents are pure invention.

Copyright © 2024 by Dorothy Elizabeth Love
www.DorothyElizabethLove.com
Cover design by Oxygen Covers / Picture art from Freepik

ISBN Paperback Book: 978-1-965437-04-9
ISBN eBook: 978-1-965437-01-8

Library of Congress Control Number (LCCN): 2024917480

Manufactured in the United States
Second Edition

AND THEN CAME *You*

BOOK TWO
THE RYAN FAMILY SERIES

DOROTHY ELIZABETH LOVE

SCENE EXCERPT

Get a taste of what's to come in this book…

After he positioned their bodies for penetration, she inhaled and waited for her fulfillment. He began massaging her with his manhood. Her wetness seeped and ran down the sides of his hardness.

"You want me now?" he asked, pressing an inch or two deeper inside her.

"Ohhh!" she breathed, her senses rippling. "Yes…" She reopened her eyes as his mouth captured her nipple. "Park… Oh, please."

She was hot and wet and tight and wanting. It took massive concentration on Parker's part not to thrust wildly. He licked her breast, and she began to move her hips and squeeze the muscles encircling his manhood. It was too much; he couldn't stop himself. He rammed the remainder of himself inside her quickly and immediately captured her mouth with his to silence her sensual scream.

Hi there, Reader. It's time to cuddle and enjoy! And if you want more, this novel is part of a 3-book series. For details, check out my "**Message to Readers**" at the end of the book.

The Ryan Family Series
- The first novel, WHISPERS IN THE NIGHT
- The second novel, AND THEN CAME YOU
- The third novel, TAKEN BY YOU

Contents

Scene Excerpt	iv
Chapter One	1
Chapter Two	7
Chapter Three	17
Chapter Four	25
Chapter Five	41
Chapter Six	51
Chapter Seven	59
Chapter Eight	75
Chapter Nine	83
Chapter Ten	91
Chapter Eleven	101
Chapter Twelve	113
Chapter Thirteen	129
Chapter Fourteen	141
Chapter Fifteen	151
Chapter Sixteen	157
Chapter Seventeen	167
Chapter Eighteen	179
Chapter Nineteen	189
Chapter Twenty	199
Chapter Twenty-One	209
Chapter Twenty-Two	217
Chapter Twenty-Three	221
Chapter Twenty-Four	229
Chapter Twenty-Five	235
Chapter Twenty-Six	239
Chapter Twenty-Seven	243
Epilogue	245
The Ryan Family Series	249
Author's Message to Reader	251

THE RYAN FAMILY

CHAPTER One

P arker Ryan knew this night would end in disaster.
As he apprehensively looked up from the glass he was holding, another jolt of the unexplainable, eerie feeling seized him, then metamorphosized into a shiver. Parker looked around the crowded banquet room; everything looked normal. He cursed himself for allowing his gloomy thoughts to distract him from this glorious event. This was a celebration of both his wedding engagement and the grand opening of his second restaurant.

Pasting a superficial smile on his face, he glanced around the room again. Teal green, white, and gold balloons with streamers decorated one side of his new restaurant, Parker's Place. Half-finished meals and gifts littered the tables as glasses filled with champagne, wine, and other assortments of drinks were lifted in anticipation of a toast. Parker's best friend began to speak.

"I want to wish Parker and Cynthia all the happiness in the world. Parker, you and I have been good friends ever since I introduced you to Cynthia, and that's the only reason I let you have her." Marcus, the best man, bent and kissed Cynthia's cheek. "If he ever gives you a problem, you know where to find me," he joked. "Okay, everyone." Marcus lifted his glass again. "May the two of you be forever happily married."

Cynthia gently squeezed Marcus's hand before turning to face Parker. Caringly, she stared into his warm brown eyes. "I will always love you," she whispered.

He leaned over and kissed her. That was what he needed to wash away the anxiety. He pulled his fiancée into his embrace. Everything was right; life was wonderful. He closed his eyes and inhaled her fragrance. He had always loved the floral scent she wore. He pressed another kiss against her forehead and reveled in the joy of her.

Pop! Pop!

Parker flinched before whirling around to see where the sounds were coming from. Two of his waiters were opening more bottles of champagne.

Why had he thought it was gunfire? He practiced at the shooting range periodically and was aware of the sound. He didn't realize he was holding his breath until he exhaled.

He shouldn't be this jumpy. What the hell was wrong with him? Was it wedding jitters? He didn't think so. He loved Cynthia; he wanted to marry her. The wedding was in two days.

"Are you okay?" Cynthia asked.

"Sure," Parker said after restoring a smile.

"You aren't planning to change your mind about the wedding, are you?" she asked. His delay took too long. "Well, are you?"

Parker lightly kissed her lips. "I can't wait." He wished he could remove the concerned look on Cynthia's pretty face. His problem was affecting her.

Damn! He didn't want to upset her. How could he tell her what he was thinking?

Parked tried another approach. "I can't wait to make love to you," he whispered in her ear. "Are you sure it's bad luck to make love to you just before the wedding?" Her concern evaporated. He wished his could be extinguished so easily.

A burst of laughter from the end of the table caught Parker's attention. He looked in the direction of the laughter and saw his sister, Patricia, scolding her husband, Mac, for telling a bawdy joke. Parker winked at her, and she blew him a kiss. The merriment was beginning to lessen some of Parker's concern. Besides, everyone else was enjoying the festivities. *So, should you,* Parker scolded himself.

As the party ended, everyone hugged or kissed both Parker and Cynthia as they began leaving. Parker and Cynthia held hands as they walked through the double doors leading outside into the warm summer Atlanta night.

Cynthia pointed at a shooting star. "Make a wish," she insisted.

"Sure." Then he said, pulling her close to kiss. "We've just told God, family, and friends that we want each other. There's no turning back," he said softly.

"There isn't for me," Cynthia said.

"I got you now. And the chase was worth it. I want to walk out of my restaurant thirty years from now with your hand in mine."

She laughed. "That will probably be because we'll be too old to hold ourselves up." Rubbing a finger across his bottom lip, which tipped up in a grin, she added, "Did you forget to wish upon that star?"

"I've already got everything I've wished for." He kissed her again. "But can we go home and play in bed?"

"I think you just may get that wish after all," she winked wickedly.

"So, tonight will be the most memorable ever?" Parker asked.

"No. I'm saving that for our wedding night," Cynthia answered, smiling. "But I've got something planned for you tonight."

"I can't wait. Let's go." They stepped off the curb, heading for Parker's Lexus parked across the four-lane street.

"Hey, Parker!"

Parker turned and saw Marcus calling him.

"Wait a minute," Marcus said.

Cynthia squeezed Parker's hand before releasing it. "I'll wait in the car."

Parker nodded and handed Cynthia the car's key fob. He turned to his friend. "Make it short, Marcus. I'm in a rush." Parker watched as Cynthia moved away. He wanted to hold her, touch her, all night.

Marcus teased Parker about his libido's over-activity. Then he started to ask the question he'd stopped Parker for in the first place. "I wanted to know…" Marcus stopped and stared into the distance, alarmed by something. "What the hell?"

Parker turned and saw a car racing toward them, headlights off, swerving from side to side, barely visible.

Parker's heart plummeted at the sight of Cynthia frozen in the middle of the road. She looked terrified, not knowing which way to run.

"Cynthia!" Parker began running toward her, but Marcus caught his arm.

"You're gonna get yourself killed," Marcus said to Parker. "Cynthia, move!"

Parker shoved Marcus out of the way. As if in slow motion, because he didn't believe his feet were moving at all, he ran toward her, one impossibly slow step after another. Though he willed his strong, athletic body to move faster, it didn't seem to be listening. Fear, heart-wrenching and immeasurable, was what he saw in her eyes as she slowly turned to face him.

Then she screamed his name, terror in her voice, and reached toward him. As the tips of her fingers brushed his, the car slammed into her body, catapulting her into the air.

And then Parker saw nothing. Nothing at all. Nothing real. Because it couldn't be real. It couldn't be happening. Cynthia couldn't be taken from him.

"Nooooooo!" Parker's anguished bellow was louder than the cries and screams from the crowd forming behind him. "No!" He pleaded with whatever savior watched over him. "No!" In a voice filled with anguish, he pleaded for the life of the woman he loved because somehow, he felt God had just turned His back on them. "No! No! Noooo!"

When he reached Cynthia's body, he ignored the blood, her twisted legs, her whimpers of pain. Carefully cradling her in his arms he sobbed, "Don't leave me Cindy. Please don't leave me."

Her pain-wrenched eyes, normally filled with love and merriment, struggled to remain open. Those eyes were the ones that he always saw the best of himself.

Then those eyes closed. Forever.

Parker sat dazed. Everything he held dear slipping away from him. Holding tightly onto Cynthia's lifeless body, he knew the torment he was feeling would only grow, and that he could never be the same again.

Pain, deep and interminable, tore at the core of his heart. It wasn't supposed to end this way, but the unthinkable had happened. He had lost the part of his life that made him whole. And, somehow, he had known it would be this way.

He looked toward a dark dreary heaven and howled.

THE RYAN FAMILY

CHAPTER Two

One year later

It was dangerous to drive the sloping road at the speed he was traveling. If he didn't take the upcoming curve precisely, his black Corvette would go over the edge of the cliff and crash 100 feet down. He had traded in the Lexus for something with more speed and this car satisfied his need.

As Parker Ryan approached the curve, he pulled his foot off the gas long enough to downshift from fifth gear to fourth but didn't apply the brakes. As he sped around the curve, the car fishtailed and skidded backward.

The excessive speed forced the car forward toward the edge of the road overlooking a hundred-foot drop. The back wheels teetered on the shoulder's edge, spinning, unsuccessfully attempting to grip the road. Burning rubber spoke of the heated battle for traction. Parker floored the gas, and the tires finally took hold in the gravel. The car roared back onto the pavement and down the winding road. An oncoming car veered off the road and out of the way as Parker's Corvette raced past.

Parker looked in the rearview mirror and smiled at the other driver's consternation as he also congratulated himself on how he had handled the curve. Still traveling far too fast, his past suddenly flashed in front of his mind's eye. Someone had been driving carelessly the night Cynthia Thomas, his wife-to-be, was killed. The difference to Parker was that he wasn't drunk like that driver who had hit Cynthia.

He didn't want to experience the past from a year ago just now, so he pressed on the gas. Speeding, he had discovered, made him feel as though he was outrunning his misery. At least temporarily. It was a fool's thought, but driving fast somehow allowed him to keep slightly ahead of the twisted game that represented his life. But every time he managed to get ahead; life threw him another curve ball it seemed.

As hard as he tried not to, the memories came back.

Cynthia had loved living in the northern suburbs he was passing through. A drunken driver took away their chance to enjoy what was to be their custom-built dream home located there.

Why did God take Cynthia from me? He wondered.

Why couldn't I run fast enough to save her? "I should have made it," he whispered.

Parker still didn't have answers, but he kept torturing himself with the questions.

Unlike most days, today, he had a reason for driving fast. His mother, Harriett, was visiting when she fell, injuring her knee and hip. She was having surgery on the hip today, and Parker didn't want to be late this time. She had wanted to have the operation at home in Florida, but Parker wouldn't hear of it. He wanted his mother near him. He needed to be there if she needed him. He will be there in time… this time.

Careening into the parking lot of the hospital, Parker wheeled into the parking space closest to the entrance. Again, he had tested fate, and again, he had won. But he felt little satisfaction.

Entering his mother's room, Parker said, "Mom, you look as though you're comfortable here." He smiled, glad to see her looking less nervous about the surgery.

"Hey, baby, come give me a hug." As Harriett wrapped her arms around him, she added, "You didn't have to come back to see me again. I'm going into surgery in a bit."

"That's why I'm here." He sat in the chair next to her bed and scooted close enough to fold his arms on the side of the bed. He put his chin on his hands. "How's room service?"

"Okay, but I'm scared, Parker. I don't know if I want to go through with this or not."

She had no choice if she wanted to walk again. Parker suspected she needed his comfort and was glad to be at her bedside. "Remember how you used to climb into bed with Patty and me when we were kids? We would be scared about something, and you would get into bed with us and tell us a bedtime story."

"Did I do that?"

"All the time," Parker said. "Move over, I'm coming in. It's payback time." As he carefully maneuvered onto the edge of her bed, trying not to aggravate her injured hip, he said gently. "I can't remember any of the stories though. You tell me one instead."

"What are you doing!" That shout came from the doorway.

Parker looked over his shoulder and saw one attractive woman entering the room. She would be even prettier if she weren't frowning at him with her mouth gaping open.

"I'm trying to think of a bedtime story," he said. "Know any?"

The woman ignored his question. "Get out of that bed before you aggravate her hip."

"Look, miss… Or nurse—" Parker couldn't read her name badge from where he was positioned.

As he was about to ask her name, she interrupted him. "It's doctor," she said matter-of-factly.

Harriett hurriedly interrupted their exchange. "This is one of my favorite doctors, Parker. Her name is Dr. Chi Addams," his mother offered. "Her first name is pronounced *Chee* with the 'e' sound although it's spelled C-H-I. Dr. Addams, this is my son, Parker."

Parker, noticing how the good doctor was still standing with her hands on her hip, turned in his charm and flirted blatantly. "If I had known the doctors here were this attractive, I would have gotten here earlier." He lazily crossed his booted ankles on the starchy white bedsheet.

"Parker, behave," his mother commanded.

"Yes, Parker, take your mother's advice." Chi folded her arms beneath her full bustline. She was accustomed to men staring at her chest, but Parker Ryan did not attempt to hide his observation, as other men had the decency to do. "Take my advice as well. Get out of that bed."

"Is that an order?" he asked. He didn't budge as his eyes roamed over every flattering aspect of her figure.

His mother started swatting at his jeans-clad leg again for misbehaving.

"It is," Chi said with finality. This man, son or not, was jeopardizing her patient's well-being. And the way he was undressing her with his eyes was definitely influencing her well-being as well. She was beginning to feel chilly from the imaginary draft caused by the way he mentally removed her clothes. Then his stare caused her body to heat up.

Parker was just about to make a sarcastic retort of *"Make me move,"* but his mother swatted at his leg again. He turned to her and said, "Mom, would you please stop hitting me? You thought this was a good idea, too!"

Harriett frowned at him, embarrassed at how loud her son had made that announcement. Dr. Addams had given her strict orders not to move her hip. Even though she appreciated her son's attempts to comfort and alleviate her fears, her hip was now aching more from his moving on the bed. Harriett also didn't want to upset her doctor any more than she already was.

She whispered to her son through stiff lips, attempting to hide her chastisement from Dr. Addams, "Get out of my bed."

"Mr. Ryan, may I speak to you alone?" Chi asked, turning toward the door without waiting for his response. As she opened the door, she looked over her shoulder to see if Parker was coming. He was, so she said to his mother, "I'll be right back, Mrs. Ryan."

"Mom, don't go anywhere while I'm gone."

"I was thinking about running up the street to get some fried chicken," Harriett teased.

"I'll do that for you," Parker responded, knowing his mother was attempting to soften the tense mood.

"I don't think so," Chi muttered under her breath as they exited the room. "Her cholesterol level is high enough as it is."

"That was a joke," Parker said. "Are you always this serious?"

Standing a few feet down from Harriett's door, Chi leaned back against the wall, ignoring his question. "Look, Mr. Ryan, I can appreciate your attempt to comfort your mother, but I think as her doctor, I know what's best for her." She looked at him pointedly, hoping to hide the way his sexy grin was affecting her. "And jumping into her bed, moving her injured hip, isn't. I would appreciate it if you would…"

Parker had just brazenly placed the palm of his right hand against the wall next to her shoulder, halting her words. Chi looked from his eyes to his hand then back to his eyes. The laugh lines around his eyes deepened, enhancing the warm, enticing stare. Thick, black brows winged soft brown eyes. Their brown coloring reminded her of warm toffee running over the sides of vanilla ice cream. His pupils were slightly dilated, making his gaze even more penetrating. As the toffee stare moved from her lips back to her eyes, a warm tingle bubbled inside her. The corners of his lips tipped higher, widening his lazy grin. He had the straightest, whitest teeth. The black, silky hairs of his facial stubble showed the shadow of a beard on his pecan complexion. It added a rugged, appealing, and dangerously alluring feature. He smelled of musk cologne and manliness. She liked that.

"...follow my instructions without question," Chi finished. She was slightly surprised that it took so long to complete the sentence.

"I'll do whatever you want. As long as I can..." Parker stopped, enjoying her attempt to remain in control, "enjoy it."

His flirtation wasn't working. She obviously wanted to entice him by playing the aloof, serious type. He had experience with this kind of woman. He could handle it. Yet, her slight change in disposition when he put his arm up looked more like an annoyance rather than attraction. But when he flashed his knee-weakening smile, she softened a little.

He liked having her caught off guard. It softened her features and enhanced her attractiveness. His profession required him to know people and how to get a positive response from them. Professional women, such as this one, require a strong approach. Her defiant look and stance when they first entered the hall had relaxed when he placed his hand next to her shoulder, and her authoritative air had lessened.

Now he only saw... How could he describe it? A sensual, delectable, and gorgeous woman. He liked the way she wore her hair. It was short, cropped in the back, and a little longer on the sides and top. Several black strands formed a bang that flattered her forehead. Her eyes were slightly slanted and the color of sienna. Her medium brown complexion was flawless except for a beauty mark about an inch to the right of her full, plum-colored, kissable lips. He almost touched that mole.

"I don't…" Chi had to clear her throat, her voice sounding too husky even to her. She had to stop this. "I don't think your wife would appreciate you leering at me this way." She moved to the right since his arm blocked any movement to her left. She was leaving. This wasn't appropriate behavior for either of them.

Then he touched her, halting her. At first, she wasn't looking at his face because his touch drew attention to the hand on her shoulder. When she did look into his eyes to tell him to remove his hand, the change she saw kept her from speaking or moving. The warmth in his eyes had been doused, leaving a cold, hard look there.

She considered asking him if he needed medical assistance. He looked to be in great pain. She watched him struggle to mask a look she couldn't quite define. Something was wrong with Parker, and she needed to assure herself that he wasn't ill.

Parker had managed not to think about Cynthia since walking into the hospital, but Chi's statement about a wife brought back those haunting memories of Cynthia dying in his arms. Thinking about Cynthia while he stood there lusting after Dr. Chi Addams made him feel dirty.

Then he looked at the wall above Chi's head. The pale blue wall revealed no clues to the senseless destruction of a life. That destruction had torn down the support walls and comforting internal structure that used to hold his life together. Now he felt alone and crushed.

Why me? Parker's question to himself still went unanswered.

He hung his head dejectedly as he stared at her name badge. Looking back into her face, he said, "Dr. Addams, there is no wife, and never will be."

There was a pain in that low muttered statement, a wound that no bandage or medicine could heal. "Oh," was all Chi managed to say. Something bad had happened to him. If she interpreted his statement correctly, it involved a woman.

As close as they stood, it would have been easy to reach out and wrap her arms around him and tell him it would get better. But that wasn't proper, professional behavior, nor did she know if it would ever get better. Whatever *it* was.

Parker, looking back at her name badge, said questioningly, "Chi?" Then he touched her name badge, lightly tracing the 'C' in her name. The pressure from his finger touching the badge pressed the metal latch of the plastic badge against her breast. She had never noticed how low on her chest she wore the badge until the backs of his fingers touched the top of the material covering her right breast. His touch was feather-light yet heavy with arousal. She glanced around to see if anyone had witnessed his blatant and stirring touch. This shouldn't be happening, but somehow, she didn't want it to stop.

Because of his sad look, she convinced herself it was therapeutic for Parker if she remained silent until he was able to regain his composure. Shouting at him and walking away would not help the situation, she concluded. If he wanted to trace a damn letter, let him. It wouldn't kill her. Besides, she already had one Ryan family member to worry about. Upsetting Parker Ryan could bring an unnecessary worry to his mother. After he finished tracing that one letter, she would unceremoniously move away and go back to check on patients.

Parker's whispered question sounded as though he was aching. "Chi? Is that a nickname?"

Her heart wanted to console him, but she didn't know the source of his pain. His question came from nowhere, and she assumed he was trying to rid his thoughts of the awful memory that held him hostage.

He was still looking at her name badge. "It's short for Chinzea," she said quietly.

"Chinzea." He paused. "I like the sound of that."

Parker stood there remembering Cynthia's smile and laughter. She was so giving and so loving. Why did she have to die like that? And why did I have to witness it and suffer from the nightmares of it?

Her initials were 'CT.' Cynthia Thomas. After they married, it would have been Cynthia Ryan. He looked for an 'R' in the letters of the badge.

The badge read: 'Chi T. Addams, MD.'

"Dr. Chinzea Addams," he said softly as he underlined her name with the tip of his right index finger, "take care of my mother."

The internal spark Chi felt from his warm caress caused her to inhale softly. She stood straighter and stared at his strong chin. "Mr. Ryan!" Chi said abruptly, breaking his trance.

"Yes?" He watched Chi stare at his fingers on her badge. Then he noticed the impression of a hardened nipple through the material of the white lab coat.

What the hell am I doing! He thought. "Chi," he croaked, flushed by his actions. He noticed the self-conscious and flustered look on her face. "I didn't mean to touch you like that."

She managed a few more coherent words. "We were talking about your mother's condition."

He'd forgotten about that. *How long had he been touching this woman?* He wondered. "I won't aggravate her hip or bring her fried chicken," he finally said, looking deeply into her eyes.

"I appreciate that. Now, excuse me. I need to finish my rounds." Chi moved away, heading swiftly down the hall.

Parker stood there, wanting to see her hips sway, but the long, white lab coat she wore prevented it.

Chi, he said to himself. Touching her made him feel…feel better. He wanted to do it again. Chi Addams somehow managed to take away some of his pain.

Chinzea. He liked the musical sound of it when she pronounced her name. He also liked the feel of her, too.

Chi managed to go around the corner and make it to the nurses' station before collapsing against the counter and placing her forehead on her hands as they gripped the counter. Her nerve endings were sizzling from Parker's obtrusive massage in the middle of the hall. She prayed no one else saw it. He had looked as surprised as she had felt from his actions. He hadn't realized what he was doing. If he could make her pulse rate increase and her libido do somersaults unintentionally, imagine what he could do if he really tried. The sensual thought boosted her heart rate.

"Dr. Addams?" A deep, male voice came from behind.

Startled, she stood up straight and turned. "Yes?" Thank God, it was the Orderly!

"A guy named Parker Ryan asked me to give this to you."

It was a note written on hospital stationery. She read it and swallowed hard.

It simply read:

I'm sorry about touching you that way.

I don't regret it. I like the feel of you.

CHAPTER Three

Chi woke the following morning slightly aroused and greatly flustered from a dream about Parker Ryan. She had kept her distance from men like him. He was a playboy. Men like that used women and drained them emotionally. She had enough problems in her life. It was foolish to think about a man she had no intention of ever getting involved with.

Chi's morning routine was automatic. Up at six, shower, dress, and transfer the contents of her pockets and her badge to a clean lab coat. Grab fruit or a muffin for breakfast. Have a cup of coffee on the drive to the hospital. Once there, review charts and start morning rounds to visit patients—who more than likely were still sleeping. On days when not on-call or in surgery, she sometimes attended conferences.

She planned to be at the hospital all day, but her morning routine was interrupted by an emergency call. A motorcycle accident victim had been brought into the trauma center. She was paged to do an orthopedic consultation on him. ER needed Chi's expertise if bones were broken or if orthopedic, reconstructive surgery was required.

After arriving at the ER, Chi carefully examined the injured man and studied his X-rays for fractures and breaks. It was a miracle he didn't have any broken bones, only a few fractures. Because he had worn a helmet, he hadn't suffered any skull fractures either when his head hit the pavement. They spent the rest of the morning working as a team mending the man's confusions and abrasions.

Once done in the trauma center, Chi went back to her morning routine. She wanted to check in on the postoperative patients first: Robert Noles and Harriett Ryan.

Chi had just finished visiting with the elderly Robert Noles and stood fidgeting outside the closed door to Harriett Ryan's room. The voices coming from inside the room told her that her patients had visitors bright and early, and Chi hoped Parker Ryan wasn't one of them. She couldn't believe how nervous the thought of another encounter with him made her. He was too arrogant, too self-assured, and too sinfully attractive.

Placing nervous hands inside her lab coat pockets to prevent herself from wringing them together, she felt a folded piece of paper. When she pulled it out and unfolded it, she reread Parker's note about touching her body. His written words revitalized her erotic dream about him.

She should not be this uncomfortable about seeing him. After all, she had spent her morning in the ER, watching those doctors attempt to repack the motorcycle victim's guts back into his body, and that hadn't bothered her. Yesterday she had removed a part of Mr. Nole's gangrenous foot and had examined it less than fifteen minutes ago, and that hadn't fazed her either. But the knowledge that Parker *might* be on the other side of the door made her fidget.

Chi stood straighter, took a deep breath, willed herself to calm down, and entered her patient's room.

Across the room, a man and a woman, obviously a couple, were seated. Parker sat on the side closest to Chi. When Chi walked into the room, she attempted not to notice Parker looking over his shoulder at her. Nearing the bed, she watched him turn his body to face her.

"Good morning, Dr. Addams," Harriett said softly.

Chi planted a warm smile on her face. She wasn't expecting a crowd to be visiting Harriett Ryan. However, upon seeing Parker, she was glad they were in the room. She didn't want to face him with just an incapacitated Harriett to help block her from him. He had been brazened in his actions yesterday, and his note confirmed how much he liked it. She didn't want to take any chances around him.

"Morning, Dr. Chi," Parker said. The politeness in his voice conflicted with the gleam in his eyes. Chi knew he was thinking about their encounter yesterday and wanted her to know it. No one had ever called her Dr. Chi either. She ignored that.

"Good morning, everyone," Chi said, stopping at the foot of Harriett's bed. She wanted to get a closer look at her hip, but Parker was in the way. No matter, she could come back when the visitors had left.

Harriett started the introductions with too much pep for a woman who was on pain medication. Chi assumed it was because Harriett had her loved ones close to her. "This is my daughter, Patricia Carter, and her husband, Mac. This is Dr. Chi Addams."

"Good to meet you." Chi smiled at them both before noticing the baby in Mac's arms.

Mac stood, extended his hand, and greeted her. The baby giggled and smiled brightly. "This is my daughter, Courtney."

Chi couldn't help herself; she walked over and tickled Courtney's sock-covered foot. "You're precious," she said in a soft, mothering voice. "And cute as a button."

Patricia Ryan-Carter noticed the mesmerizing look her brother was giving the doctor. Both her daughter and her brother were very taken with Dr. Chi Addams. "You're my daughter's friend for life now," Patricia said to Chi.

"She's beautiful," Chi said, smiling at Patricia. Then she turned to look at Harriett. "How are you this morning?"

"I'm fine," Parker responded. She wasn't talking to him, and he knew it.

Chi was about to open her mouth and give him a few choice words, all profoundly rude. He had some nerve, she thought. Then she remembered her patient, the two guests she'd just met, and one precious baby who wasn't privy to her previous encounter with Parker. At least, she hoped they weren't. She heard Patricia clear her throat and saw Harriett reach for Parker's arm.

Maybe they did know!

He must have said something to them, Chi concluded. "Nice to hear you're doing well." That was as nice as she was going to be to him. He was intentionally trying to embarrass her, and it was working.

She needed to get out of the room. She would take care of her patient first, though. "How are you, Mrs. Ryan?"

"In a little pain."

"Let me see what I can do about that. I'll come back and check on you later," she promised. She turned to Patricia and Mac. "Let's not tire her out too much, okay."

"Dr. Chi?"

She turned to Parker. No one had ever referred to her by that name. And she wasn't sure how to correct the use without sounding egotistical.

"Did you get my note?" he asked.

She did. But wasn't going to let him know that. She feigned amnesia. "Note? What note?"

"The one I asked the Orderly to give you yesterday." Parker stood and came closer. His stare was meaningful and distracting. When he was a few inches away, he said to her lips, because he wasn't looking into her eyes, "I can tell you what it said, if you didn't get it."

She felt the heat from his body, but it wasn't as hot as the look in his eyes.

Parker's grin widened, and Chi heard a distinctively deep laugh, poorly disguised by a cough, coming from Mac Carter. It snapped her to her senses.

"Oh, that note," Chi said. "I do remember something from an Orderly." She hated being thrown off guard, but he had that effect on her. She remembered her patient. Turning back to Harriett, Chi said, "Mrs. Ryan, I'll have the nurse get you something for the pain." She had to get out of there before Parker launched another assault on her senses. No telling what he had planned. He felt quite comfortable making her uncomfortable amid his family. Quickly turning to the other guests, she said, "Nice meeting you." She stepped past Parker and headed for the door.

As Chi got outside the room, she took a nerve-calming deep breath. The sound of his voice startled her.

"Dr. Chi?"

Surprised, she whirled around to face Parker. "It's Dr. Addams."

"Sure, it is." Parker stopped when he got a few inches away from her. She was declaring orders again, he thought. He preferred the other Chi, Chi the woman, not the doctor. He was hoping he would get a chance to see her this morning. "Thank you for being understanding yesterday."

He had two reasons for visiting the hospital; she was definitely one of them. The mole on her cheek brought on images of his tongue lingering there before kissing her lips.

She was attempting to think of the best words to tell him how she felt about his actions. None suitable came to mind. "No problem. I'm sure your mother's surgery is affecting you."

"Maybe."

"Well, if there isn't anything else, I must go check on my other patients," Chi said, searching for something other than his appealing face to look at.

"There was one other thing I needed to share with you." Parker stepped closer and looked down at her. There was a sincerity, a serenity in her stare that pulled at him. He couldn't, no, didn't want to stop himself. He leaned forward and planted a mind-stirring, passionately soft kiss on her lips.

Chi found herself leaning into it. When he pulled away, she instinctively leaned forward for more.

"I'm glad you see things my way," Parker said, pleased with her reaction. "Thanks for that, too."

Then he smiled arrogantly, turned, and headed back into his mother's room.

She stood there shocked for a few seconds before heading into the room after him. "Parker, I would appreciate you refraining from…" She was about to tell him, "Touching my body and kissing me anymore!" She stopped when she noticed four sets of adult eyes looking at her. Parker's eyes, she noticed, held mocking humor. "Can I speak to you alone?" she asked him. She turned to leave the room, hoping he would follow her.

"I'll call you tomorrow," Parker said to her retreating back.

Chi turned to see Parker heading to the chair he had occupied earlier.

The hell he would! She vowed, leaving the room. No one treats me like this and gets away with it.

"How dare he!" she muttered after closing the door to Harriett Ryan's room. Chi looked down the empty hallway and realized she was standing there alone, fidgeting, and talking to herself.

And it was all his fault.

THE RYAN FAMILY

CHAPTER Four

"Dr. Addams, phone call on line 1. Dr. Addams, line 1." The voice on the intercom system announced. "This is Dr. Addams."

"Good morning. It's Parker Ryan."

She'd been itching to blister his ears since he kissed her and walked away. She took on a stance of defiance, placing her free hand on her hip. The nerve of the man! He feels her up, kisses her, embarrasses her, and then ignores her.

"Let me tell you something, Parker Ryan. I don't appreciate you fondling me and kissing me in the middle of the hospital halls. I…"

He butted in, "Neither did I. But I thought it was too early in our relationship to ask you over to my house so I could fondle and kiss you there."

"Relationship?" she repeated loudly. "Have you lost your mind? We don't have any damn relationship. I'm your mother's doctor. That's all we have in common. Am I making myself clear?"

Silence.

"Hello? Parker? Are you there?" she asked more sanely.

"Yes, I am."

"Good. I have only four words to say to you." "Don't ever touch me," she thought about it, "again!"

"That's five words, Dr. Chi."

She wanted to bang the phone against the wall, several times as if to knock some sense into this stubborn man's head.

"I told you, it's Dr. Addams. Can't you remember that?"

"Are you angry because I call you Dr. Chi?"

"Don't be silly. Of course not."

"Then why are you shouting at me?" he asked simply.

She noticed several nurses and one other doctor several yards away staring at her. She was ranting like a maniac. She wouldn't be surprised if they put her in restraints and took her to a psychiatric ward for closer observation. She couldn't blame them; she was acting like a raving lunatic. None of these people had ever seen her acting this way before. As a matter of fact, she didn't remember ever acting this way before.

And it was all his fault.

She couldn't control her attraction to him and that upset her. Submitting to his charm meant opening herself up to a man. That would be catastrophic.

"Look, Parker..."

"Chi..." They spoke at the same time.

"You first," he said.

She calmed herself. It wasn't completely his fault she was losing control. She just couldn't handle a man barging into her life uninvited. "Parker, this is my place of employment. I have a reputation to protect. It's hard enough being female and Black. Please respect that."

"Have dinner with me tomorrow night?" Parker asked.

She couldn't believe he had asked her that. "I can't."

"Why?"

"Because I don't want to, Parker." She needed to be careful to protect herself, her secrets, and her son from the likes of this playboy.

"That's not a reason."

"Yes, it is."

"If you don't want me to approach you at the hospital, how are we going to get to know each other?"

"That's just it. I don't want to get to know you. You're not the type of man I date."

"Date? Sounds like you're not serious about anyone right now. Neither am I." Parker wanted to better understand his attraction to her. A planned rendezvous would allow him that. He looked at the calendar on his desk. "What about Saturday night?"

She laughed, her voice almost shrieking. She couldn't believe his gall. "I'm busy." She wasn't but wouldn't venture to go out with him. "It's not a good idea. We're two different types of people, and I'm not attracted to you."

"Funny," he said. "Your body is."

She fell silent. He was right about that. Every time they occupied the same room, her senses and emotions went out of control, an internal danger signal warning her that he was a womanizer. Some of the nurses had already speculated about him. She would not get involved with another playboy. The last one almost ruined her life.

No decent man would touch and kiss her so brazenly. He didn't know her from Adam (or Eve, in her case), and she was cautious enough to keep it that way. As a doctor, she ran across diseases transmitted by playboys. If not a disease of the body, then one of the soul. Playboys spread far more misery than joy.

When Parker's mother was first admitted, he had stormed into the hospital demanding to give blood, just in case his mother needed it because of the surgery. He was 'O' positive, a good type to have on hand. The hospital could always use extra blood, so they accepted his. Chi had seen the tests on his sample. He was free of communicable diseases, but she would not expose her emotions to any of his playboy, manipulative tactics. Those tactics were deadlier than any germ lurking and growing in hazardous containers in the entire hospital.

"Chi," he said, and she noticed he wasn't calling her 'Dr. Chi' any longer. "I realized that maybe my actions came across too strong."

She laughed at that, too. "I would say very strong. Much too strong for my taste." She glanced at her watch. "Parker, I'm on my way to see your mother."

"Tell Mom I said hello." To her agreement, Parker said, "It was inappropriate to touch you that way, Chi. My only excuse is that I've been so absorbed," he thought about it then limited his admission to, "with my mother's health that I wasn't thinking straight. I would like for you to think about my offer of dinner, and I hope that we can talk about it later."

She was about to tell him that wouldn't be possible when her emergency pager beeped.

"I've got an emergency call," she said hurriedly, "I must go. Bye." She hung up the phone.

Thirty minutes later, Parker rushed into Peachtree General looking for Dr. Chi Addams. He had called his mother's room, concerned, after Chi hung up the phone. There had been no answer. He had just been to his mother's room, and she wasn't there. He was scared shitless as he raced to the nurses' station. When the nurse there, who had just come on duty, wasn't sure what was going on, he asked to have Chi paged.

Parker hoped he hadn't gotten there too late. What if his mother died? He was supposed to be there for her. What could have happened so quickly that Chi had to rush to her bedside? He couldn't lose his mother. He couldn't lose anyone else again.

As Chi came racing down the hall, Parker ran toward her.

"Thank God you came in a hurry," Parker said, grabbing her by her arms and squeezing tightly. "What's happened to her?"

She saw the fear in his eyes. "Who, Parker?"

"My mother! I can't find her. What was the emergency you were called to? Is she all right?" His voice was shaky.

As realization dawned on Chi, her eyes rounded with surprise. When she had said into the phone, she had an emergency and hung up on him, he had incorrectly concluded that she was talking about his mother.

"Parker, your mother is fine," she said calmly.

"Fine?" He didn't believe her. "But she's not in her room," he said, uneasiness lacing his husky voice.

"Yes, fine." She reached up and touched his chest. "I promise. Come with me." He didn't let go of her arms for a few seconds, and Chi wasn't sure if it was because he was afraid of what he might see if he went with her, or that maybe he didn't believe her. "Come with me," she cooed. Stepping backward, she guided him by the forearm.

Chi led Parker down several corridors and stopped outside a room. "Harriett is with the therapist this morning." Immediate physical therapy was critical with older patients like Harriett Ryan.

From the doorway, Parker could see his mother lying on her back stretching her arms above her head as the physical therapist lightly massaged her leg. Harriett was smiling at something funny her therapist had said.

Parker slowly exhaled and looked heavenward. He quickly turned and swept Chi into his arms, holding her tight, his face buried in her neck inhaling her fragrance. She was his grasp on reality. Until that very moment, his imagination had conjured dreadful scenes. And not until Parker saw his mother, did the visions vanish.

Chi, shocked by his actions and because she didn't know what else to do, embraced him. She felt his heart pounding against her chest, his warm neck against her cheek, his strong arms around her back, and his manly essence and smell all around her. She closed her eyes and allowed him to embrace her as she hugged him.

Loosening her embrace, she whispered, "I didn't mean to upset you. I wasn't thinking when I told you I had an emergency. It wasn't your mother's room I was called to." She felt his arms reclaim his hold. "I'm sorry."

"Thank God she's okay." Parker started to rock her slightly, still holding her tight. His rocking and his words began to relay a meaning: Fear of loss, fear of the unknown, relief, gratitude, and vulnerability. And concern. He was a man who cared. Deeply and truly. She was surprised to find such traits in a man like him.

When he finally released her, Chi looked up at him and said in an anguished voice barely above a whisper, "I'm really sorry."

Parker didn't know how Chi managed to keep doing it, but again she had made his pain go away. "You promised me that she was okay, Chi."

"Yes. Just like I promised." She couldn't believe how terribly afraid Parker had been because of her carelessness. Chi felt awful about how upset Parker had been.

No wonder the man had clung to her the other day. He had been attempting to ward off his fears about his mother. And she had accused him of purposely fondling her body. Her own fears caused that reaction.

People reacted to fear in many ways she knew. All this time, he was pretending to be brave and nonplussed, when he was worried sick, hiding apprehension behind a façade of bravado and flirtation.

Like a frightened child, he needed someone to protect him, console him, and comfort him. Then she thought of her son, who was suffering and needing her even though she couldn't be there for him. That miserable thought added to her discomfort.

Unconsciously, her emotions went into overdrive. Chi didn't realize how emotionally embroiled she was until Parker reached up and wiped away a tear from her cheek. "This is my fault," he said. "I panicked. I got us both worked up for nothing."

Embarrassed, she blinked back more tears and did her best to regain her professional composure. "I didn't mean to upset you."

"Why are you crying?" he asked, rubbing another tear away.

"I don't know," she answered honestly. Thoughts of her father's death, her son's illness, and the guilt from the pain she caused Parker had torn down her remaining resistance.

What was she crying about? This was silly on her part, Chi thought. Everything was fine, except for inside her warped brain. "I guess I can't believe I got you that upset. You were needlessly concerned. And it's all my fault."

He leaned down and kissed a salty tear from her cheek. "It will be okay."

Chi smiled before chuckling. "That's my line. Now, let me go and pull myself together. You can wait here for Harriett if you like."

"Will you come back?"

"I've got to handle another issue. I'll see you two later." Chi began walking away.

"Today?" he asked her retreating back.

Actually, she was thinking about visiting Harriett tomorrow and whenever she possibly ran into him again. Slowly, she turned to face him, hiding her surprise at his question behind a professional mask of control and confidence. He needed support right now. It wouldn't take too much of her time away from her other patients if she visited for a few minutes.

Smiling, she said, "Yes. I'll stop by her room within a half-hour."

Chi walked away trying to understand her unusual behavior. She didn't know what was wrong with her. She had learned during her medical training to disassociate herself from the emotional aspect of the job because it could result in situations like this if one didn't. It wasn't good for her, and it wasn't good for her patients.

As Harriett was wheeled out of the therapy room, Parker gave her a big hug, being careful not to aggravate her hip. He decided not to tell her why he was at the hospital unexpectedly this morning. There's no need to upset her about that. He walked beside her wheelchair on the trip back to her room. There, they sat laughing about her experience with the X-ray technician who took films of her hip.

"So, now that this young, good-looking technician has seen intimate parts of your body, to hear you tell it, is he going to set you up on a date?"

Harriett added laughing, "I think he wants to date me."

Parker roared with laughter.

Once the laughing stopped, Harriett asked, "Why are you here this morning?"

Parker wasn't expecting to get into this. "I wanted to see you. Why else?" Parker hoped that the partial truth sounded convincing.

"It's okay, son. You can tell me the truth." When Parker kept silent, Harriett added, "The only reason you're here again this soon, is that you're feeling guilty about how you insisted I have the operation here in Atlanta, instead of back home in Gainesville, where all my friends are."

"You did fall in my backyard, so I wanted to take care of you. I can't do that and run my businesses with you three hundred miles away," he said. "Besides, the doctor didn't think it was wise for you to travel back."

"Parker, I forgot to ask you about it this time, but you know how you sometimes can feel when I'm in pain. Did you sense the fall in your yard?"

"Yeah."

"What about the surgery and the pain I'm in now?"

"No. The feeling I get seems to relate to immediate danger or unexpected pain, I think. And I must be in a relaxed mood. Not concentrating on anything."

"What was it like this time?"

Parker hated talking about this. It made him feel like a freak. To him, it was another one of life's cruel jokes. He had the innate ability to sense, sometimes *feel*, when someone he cared about was in danger. Depending on the level of impending doom, sensed it before it happened. "I don't know. I saw images of you in my mind. Tumbling images. Then I felt sick to my stomach. I put two and two together and rushed home to find the neighbors and the ambulance at my place."

"That's so strange how you do that with me and your sister."

"I know," Parker said. "Now, can we change the subject?"

Harriett reached over and touched his arm. "You have been overprotective of both your sister and me ever since Cynthia was killed."

"Now, Mom, stop exaggerating."

"I'm curious. Did you have that *feeling* with Cynthia?"

"We are not going to talk about this."

Parker sat back away from his mother's grasp. *Could she be right?* No, he thought. "I don't know. Maybe," he said with a hint of abruptness.

Harriett heard the sharpness but wouldn't drop the conversation. "Cynthia's death wasn't your fault," Harriett insisted.

Parker wasn't going to talk about this. He crossed his arms over his chest. "What time is lunch?"

Harriett looked at the clock on the wall. "Another hour." She turned her attention back to her son. "You should not be still blaming yourself for her death."

Standing, Parker planted a smile worthy of a toothpaste ad on his face to mask his pain. He had gotten good at that over the past year. "Let's not spend the next hour dredging up the past. I came here to spend some time with you and have lunch." He justified in his mind that his statement did hold some truth. Now that he knew she was okay, he was hungry.

"I won't force you to talk about Cynthia. But, I think you need to get this out of your system before the guilt eats you up. You can't hide behind that phony smile forever." She extended her hand to him, and Parker stepped closer to hold it. "You're a good man, baby. Always able to handle anything. This is the first time I've seen you unable to handle something. Promise me you'll talk to someone about this." When he didn't respond, she insisted, "Promise me."

Maybe it was because they were talking about reactions to death, but for some reason, he thought it was a deathbed wish. That awful thought bothered him. "I promise." As he kissed the back of her hand, Chi walked into the room.

"Hello, doctor," Harriett said.

"How was the therapy?" Chi asked.

"Tough. I didn't expect to see you again today. Two surprises in one morning. I was just telling Parker that I didn't expect to see him either. He claims he wanted to have lunch with me. I'm not sure that's the whole story though."

Chi looked at Parker questioningly. He must not have said anything to his mother about the misunderstanding they had on the phone. "I was just headed to lunch and stopped by to check on you."

"You are? Great. Take my son with you to lunch. I'll feel better if he stops pestering me."

Parker winked at his mother. He loved the way she operated. He stood and took advantage of the situation. "That's a good idea. I'm starving. I missed breakfast this morning." He turned to Chi, "Are you going to save my mother from my pestering and save me from starvation?"

"It's got to be cafeteria food. I have a short break and can't leave the hospital."

"Sounds fine," he said to Chi. "See ya, Mom."

"Bye, baby. You take care of him, Dr. Chi."

Chi stared at her strangely. Mrs. Ryan had never called her that before.

"My son calls you 'Dr. Chi' and you smile every time he does. I thought you preferred to be called that."

There was just no winning with these Ryans, they just barged right into your life and took over. Regardless of what you thought about it, they had to put in their two cents. Thankfully, she enjoyed their two cents.

They went down the cafeteria line separately because they wanted different meal items from different areas. Chi was already at the table when Parker got there.

Parker looked down at her meal: a salad, side order of corn, a banana, and milk. He shook his head.

"What?" she asked.

"You're planning on eating that?" He pointed at the mixed combination. His doubts about her choices were obvious.

"It's healthier than that hamburger, caffeine-filled Coke, and cholesterol sticks you call French fries. That stuff shortens your lifespan."

"Yeah, but I'll die a happy man. Be thankful you're in a hospital, because when you collapse from ingesting that mixture, I can rush you upstairs to get your stomach pumped." Parker began drowning his fries in ketchup.

She laughed. "You're impossible," she said, shaking her head.

"And you're wonderful." He was looking her straight in the eyes when he said it.

His declaration momentarily silenced her. Then she said, "You don't know me well enough to say that."

"But I do. Want to know how I know?"

She knew she shouldn't be having this discussion with him. It was dangerous to play with fire. But her curiosity won over common sense. "Yes, I would like to know."

"My mother speaks very highly of you. She doesn't trust most doctors, but she thinks the world of you."

Chi countered his statement with reasoning. "It's typical in cases like your mother's. She needs to trust someone; I'm one of her doctors. It happens."

Parker continued. "The first time we met, I was lying next to her, jeopardizing her bad hip. You immediately came to the rescue. I don't think most doctors would be that conscientious and abrupt."

She defended the actions of doctors attempting to minimize his statement. "Any doctor would do that."

Parker added. "When I touched your badge and..." He paused as she flushed. "And... Uhm... touched your chest the other day, you could have easily slapped me, but you didn't. You recognized I needed someone to talk to."

"It comes with the job. You learn to read people."

Parker stated, "When I needed to hold you today, feel you close, you let me. As a matter of fact, you held me and kissed my neck."

She had nothing to say.

A fitting response eluded her. She looked at him, fork suspended in midair, and remembered how good it felt holding him.

Her kiss had been unintentional. It was more like pressing her lips against his neck. It had been so easy to do with him holding her that way, and with this neck so close to her lips. She couldn't stop herself and hoped he had not noticed it because it was a mistake.

Seconds later, she remembered to put the forkful of lettuce and tomato in her mouth and chew. Both tasks took most of her concentration.

Parker continued, "You didn't have to, but you consoled me anyway. And now, you sit here being modest about it all. That makes you quite a lady."

She reached for her glass of milk, thinking she really needed something stronger. *Why do I enjoy hearing this so much?*

"And you want to know something else?"

She didn't. She wasn't sure she could handle it, but she was swallowing at the time.

Parker must have taken her silence for agreement because he continued talking. "I enjoyed every second of it. You're very soft and fit so nicely in my arms. I didn't know your waist was so small until I put my arms around you. I like the feel of your neck against my cheek. I also love your perfume."

"You're quite ticklish, too. I felt you squirm a little when I released you. I like the feel of you," he finished, nodding slowly. "Oh, but you know that already, I sent you a note to that effect."

He took a big bite out of his hamburger with the calmness of a person who had just finished talking about sunny weather, not the delicacies of her body.

She sat dumbfounded at how easily, and comfortably he talked about her body as though it was his to comment about. Yet it made her want to feel his touch again. He was probably telling her these things because he knew she was attracted to him and was hiding it.

"Oh," he said, starting another question. "Another thing. Do you know…"

Chi interrupted him. She knew he was doing this to get a physical reaction from her. She needed to tell him he could stop now because she was having one. No need to rub her face into her uncontrollable attraction to him.

"No, I don't want to know, Parker. I don't think I can take any more of this discussion about my body. I'm getting sensations just from your interpretation."

He stopped his assault on his meal and sat completely still, looking at her. Then, his grin deepened as his toffee-colored eyes warmed. "I was about to ask if you know who I can talk to about getting home care supplies for my mother when she comes home with me. I could see how uncomfortable you were with me talking about you, so I thought I'd change the topic." He sat forward in his chair slowly, his expression softening. "You just confirmed what I suspected. It's good to know you're attracted to me, too."

This was too embarrassing for Chi. She looked down and studied the details of her corn kernels, wanting the floor to open and swallow her up.

"Hey," Parker said at her downturned head. She didn't respond, trying to think of something to say.

"Chi? Look at me."

When Chi looked up, Parker's empathetic look gave her strength. She thought he would be smirking at her, but he wasn't. He was trying to understand. Still, she was embarrassed and needed to add distance between them by ending their lunch. "This is embarrassing. I think, maybe we should…"

"Finish our lunch." Parker completed the sentence for her. He suspected she was about to turn tail and run. He added more playfully, "Or else I'm going to tell my mother to you. You promised to take care of me at lunch. Remember? So, make good on your promise."

It took her a few seconds to recover, but his threat added a charming, softer feature to him. She relaxed. "Okay, I'll stay. Don't tell your Mama on me." She was shaking her head.

"I won't if you won't."

After the initial discomfort passed, they enjoyed lunch and each other's company. Parker found he liked the way she laughed and tried to keep her laughing. Chi found she enjoyed the sound of his voice; the way he used his hands and eyes to express a point. She kept asking questions to watch him move and to hear his voice.

Too soon the thirty-minute lunch was over. Chi was thankful her pager hadn't interrupted them.

As they walked to the elevator, Parker said, "Thanks for having lunch with me."

"No problem," she said.

"We didn't finish our phone conversation earlier. I had asked you to think about going out with me. Will you do that?"

Earlier, she had thought Parker had asked her out simply to gain another notch on his belt, but after thoroughly enjoying his company, she realized he was a caring, decent man. Her answer had changed in her mind.

"I think we just *had* a first date," she said.

"Will there be a second?" Parker needed the answer now. He didn't want to walk away from her not knowing her answer.

"Yes."

Parker liked the way she smiled when she said that. He nodded before saying, "We both need to go. We can talk more tomorrow when I come to visit Mom. I'll see you then."

Chi thought she smiled too quickly. "Okay. I'll see you then." She entered the elevator and turned, then waved her fingers at him. "Goodbye."

Parker stood there, hands in his jeans pockets and studied the warm look on her face as the elevator doors closed. He continued to stare at the spot where he last saw her smile for several moments afterward. Chi Addams added something to his day that he didn't want to let go of just yet.

Turning, he headed out of the building to his car. Outside, he looked up at the late August sky with an appreciative eye. Fat, puffy clouds, shaped like cauliflower, were painted on a powder blue, sunny backdrop. Inhaling, he remembered Chi's smile.

CHAPTER *Five*

Two flower bouquets were delivered to Peachtree General from Parker Ryan. One went to his mother, thanking her for her wisdom and lack of appetite the day before. And the other went to Chi, thanking her for her kindness at lunch. The types of flowers in both arrangements were the same except Chi's arrangement was much larger and had a bottle of wine with it. The card read:

Chi,

Thank you for your kindness and lunch. I won't forget either any time soon.

Chill the wine and let's plan on having a glass together.

Parker

After reading the card, Chi beamed. The flowers were lovely, the card was sweet, and the wine was expensive. She went to the nurses' station and reached for the desk phone to call and thank him. Then she remembered he hadn't given her his phone number. She would have to wait for his visit today.

She had rearranged her patient visitation schedule to allow her to visit with Harriett later that morning. When she walked into Harriett's room, she was excited to see Harriett in a spirited phone conversation, which meant her patient was feeling much better. But Chi was also disappointed Parker wasn't there.

Harriett was saying, "Georgette, Dr. Chi just walked into the room. I've got to go. Call me back later."

Harriett watched Chi as Georgette asked, "Is she and Parker dating yet?"

"I think I've got some juicy news for you. I'll tell you later."

"Just tell me the mood the girl's in," Georgette said, and Harriett knew it was because the soap operas weren't exciting this week. Therefore, Parker's new love interest was filling in the gaps.

Harriett attempted to whisper. "Disappointed. You-know-who isn't here yet," she hung up on Georgette's scream of excitement.

"Good afternoon, Dr. Chi. You've come late today?"

"Had a few surprises this morning. How are you doing?"

"Fine."

Chi checked Harriett's chart. Nothing to worry about. Chi wished Harriett was in one of her talkative moods. She wanted to know when to expect Parker and didn't want to come right out and ask. "Quiet morning. Not too many visitors?" Chi checked Harriett's pulse unnecessarily.

"Not too many." Harriett shut her mouth after giving limited information. She recognized the look of anticipation in Chi's expression. Harriett was loving this!

Chi noticed the new flower arrangement. Looking for reasons to hang around, she went to get a better look at the flowers. "Two more arrangements?" They were added to the multitude of flowers, balloons, and fresh plants scattered around the room. "You're quite the popular one."

"Baby, I'm old. I've met everybody in this world at least twice. At my age, I know everyone."

Chi recognized the flowers in one of the arrangements as basically the same as the ones in hers delivered today from Parker. "Who are these from?" Chi asked, fingering the small envelope with the enclosed greeting card.

"Oh, just people who love me," Harriett added vaguely.

Damn it, Chi frowned. Harriett was making this hard on her. She wondered if it was intentional. Chi looked over her shoulder and saw Harriett reaching for her crossword puzzle.

"May I read the cards?"

"If you like," Harriett said, trying to hide a smile as Chi snapped the card from the arrangement from her son.

Chi read Parker's card to his mother:

Mom.

Will you ever outgrow the depths of your wisdom? I figured out your ploy yesterday. Enjoy these fllowers. Feel free to lose your appetite for lunch anytime Dr. Chi is around.

Parker

Chi smiled at the last line. She was hoping they would have lunch again today. What ploy was Parker referring to? she wondered. Turning to Harriett she asked, "Did Parker bring these to you today?"

Harriett decided to let Dr. Chi off easy. It was obvious she was eager to find out about Parker. "No, Dr. Chi. My son hasn't come today." She saw the disappointed look Chi attempted to hide behind a smile.

"Well, you rest. I'll stop in later," Chi said, heading toward the door.

"You forgot to read the other card," Harriett teased. When she saw the uninterested look on Chi's face, she added, "It's just my friend Georgette wishing me well."

"Nice friend," Chi said sincerely. Then she headed out of the room to take care of other patients.

Hours later, Chi prepared to leave for the day. Parker still hadn't called or shown up. Of course, she didn't carry her cell phone when on rounds, but he had called the Nurses' station before when he wanted to talk to her. She wondered if this was another game of his to arouse her interest. Annoyed, Chi checked her watch again. Then she went to the Nurses' station to see if she had any messages. She checked her pager to make sure the batteries were still charged. She shouldn't be drooling after Parker this way. He had only touched her breast, kissed her, asked her to get to know her better, and then sent her flowers.

Well, no wonder she was acting like a lovesick fool. She hoped this wasn't all a game because she had invested emotions into this already.

Chi made one last attempt to see if Parker was visiting his mother, although she had stopped by twice already, and Harriett hadn't offered any news about his whereabouts. As Chi opened the door to Harriett's room, she heard voices. Smiling, she walked inside the room.

Parker has finally made it!

"Dr. Chi, you're back again," Harriett announced.

"I was headed home for the day and wanted to make sure you were okay." Chi smiled weakly at Harriett's daughter, who was holding her child. If not for the baby, Chi would have pouted. "Good to see you again, Patricia."

"You too, Dr. Chi," Patricia said. Her daughter squealed and clapped her hands as Chi neared them. "She remembers you. I told you that you're her friend for life." When Patricia saw Chi smiling and waving at her daughter, she asked, "Would you like to hold her?"

"Only for a minute, I really must go… Hi there, pretty girl," Chi said softly. "Hi there, you." Holding Courtney made Chi long to be with her child. Her son was four, and she hadn't seen him in two weeks.

That was another reason to be cautious with Parker. What would happen when he found out about her son? She had been happy with the pregnancy until Douglas, the father, accused her of using the pregnancy to trap him. Everyone, including her mother, urged Chi to have an abortion. She had struggled with her conscience. She couldn't take a life, even though it was conceived for all the wrong reasons. She went to the abortion clinic twice and decided against it both times.

In a final attempt to prove Douglas was the father, she had several tests. They not only discovered Douglas was the father but her son was also diagnosed with a terrible illness, sickle cell.

Now, four years later, she wondered how much different her life would be if she had the abortion. She felt miserable because of the life her son was living.

Courtney pulled at Chi's name badge, bringing Chi out of her dark thoughts. She bounced the baby in her arms remembering how good it felt to hold her son. She wanted to be with him soon, but that wasn't possible.

She found herself longing for attention and hoped Parker was coming to give it to her. The anticipation that started to nip at her once she received the flowers had mushroomed into a full-blown craving.

Parker makes me smile, Chi thought.

Mac Carter entered the room. Although charming, he wasn't the man Chi wanted to see. Trying to mask her disappointment,

Chi plastered a professional smile on her face, one she'd often used on ill patients when giving unfortunate news.

Mac recognized Chi's fake smile. His mother-in-law had been filling them in on all the "juicy details," as Mac remembered Harriett calling it. "Dr. Addams, how are you?"

"Fine, thanks. Here's your daughter." Chi walked toward Mac as he extended his arms to take Courtney. "I was just heading out."

"Leaving so soon?" Patricia asked.

Chi was tired of waiting for Parker. He had gotten her hopes up, then disappointed her. It was bad enough she was uselessly hanging around Harriett's room hoping he would show up. At this rate, the hospital probably would dock her pay for wasting time.

"I've been on my feet since five this morning. I'm going home to relax. Good night, everybody."

"Good night."

"Bye," Harriett said, "I'll see you in the morning."

Chi waved bye to Courtney.

"Momma, you're right," Patricia said after Chi left. "Did you see how disappointed Chi was when Mac entered the room? She was looking for Parker."

"I told you so," Harriett confirmed. "We've got to do something."

"Will the two of you stop with the matchmaking?" Mac said before sucking on his daughter's chubby cheek. "Let them handle their relationship. Parker just met the woman, and you two are planning the wedding already."

"Sweetheart, don't you remember our courtship?" Patricia said to Mac. "The night we met, you stopped by my house uninvited. And you kissed me before you left." Patricia noticed Harriett's gasping mouth. She was sure she had shared that piece of information before. "Momma, I told you about that. That was the night he knocked my purse out of my hands and my wallet fell out. Mac found it under his car and later returned it to me."

"Patricia, for the hundredth time, get the story right," Mac corrected. "You walked into me and dropped your purse. I found your wallet later and was kind enough to return it to you." But no one was paying attention to him.

Harriett said, "I remember the part about the purse, but I don't remember any kiss." Harriett pondered this new piece of juicy information. "You think Parker had kissed Chi?"

"I'm not sure. What do you think, Mac?" Patricia asked.

"I think you two need to mind your own business," Mac told them.

"Party pooper." Patricia's pout was fake. Right then their daughter began to cry. "See. Even your daughter thinks so."

Three to one. It was a losing battle. Mac gave up on trying to win.

That evening found Parker doing what he was great at.

The pretty woman standing in Parker's doorway smiled brightly. "Parker, I can stay if you want."

"Thanks, Sheila. I appreciate you coming over. It was busy tonight at the restaurant. I would've had a hard time without your help."

Sheila Banks, the manager of Parker's other restaurant, was attractive, aggressive, and upfront in letting him know she was interested in him. "You sure you don't need anything else?" Her look and tone promised she would give him anything he wanted.

Any other time, he might have been interested in exploring the possibilities a look like that held, but he had other things on his mind. And secondly, Parker made it a practice not to mix business with pleasure. Dating staff members caused all sorts of problems. And for the last year, it seemed he was ending relationships before they became too involved.

"No, but thanks. I appreciate your coming in to work on your day off," Parker stated flatly, rubbing his fingers across his eye sockets. He was tired from working all day on emergency issues at his restaurants. But that ensured the business's success, and he loved it.

Both restaurants were doing exceptionally well, yet success could be tiring. The restaurant's advertisement read: Come park and play at Parker's Place. Come once, and you'll never want to leave again. Fine dining. Live Jazz bands, Banquet Room Activities, and socializing.

Parker was thankful he had time to send flowers to Chi today. He had promised to visit her, but things had gotten out of control at the restaurants earlier in the day: Hired help got sick, a kitchen fire resulted in minimal damage, the bar ran out of gin and scotch, the kitchen ran out of steaks for today's special. The list had grown longer with each passing hour.

Parker noticed it was past ten o'clock at night. How had the time passed so quickly? He reached for his iPhone, realizing Chi would have left the hospital by now. He couldn't believe he had forgotten to get her number. He went through his contacts, but she wasn't listed. He promised himself he'd get her number later. He would make it up to Chi and his mother for promising to visit and not showing up. Right now, he was headed home to get some sleep. He had an exhausting day and needed to rest.

LATER THAT NIGHT, CHI AND PARKER BATHED AND WERE IN THEIR respective beds. They were resting with thoughts of each other:

> He was glad she agreed to go out with him again.
> She wondered what their next date would be like.

> He thought about the feel of her in his arms.

AND THEN YOU CAME

She remembered how he had pulled her close and caressed her.

He wished he had called her.
She was disappointed because he didn't call her.

He lay on his left side touching where he wished she lay.
She lay on her right side and mentally reached for closeness.

He was aroused and needed her body.
She was turned on and wanted his touch.
Apart, yet together, they slept with thoughts of each other.

THE RYAN FAMILY

CHAPTER *Six*

Never again! Chi's frustration was aimed at one man. She was sitting in the doctor's lounge the following day, sipping her morning cup of coffee. She had thought about Parker all day yesterday and dreamt of him all last night. Chi convinced herself that today, she wouldn't waste any more time with the hopes and wishes of Parker Ryan.

The facts were clearer to her now that she had some sleep. She functioned best in a clear-cut world where everything was as it seemed. Parker's actions were typical of a playboy. She'd met this type too many times before. They told you what they thought you wanted to hear. They made promises they never kept.

Hadn't she learned her lesson by now? Chi scolded herself. Everything in life has a cause and effect. Understand the cause, then you could treat the effect. Parker had sparked her romantic fantasies. The sooner she forgot him, the sooner she could get on with her life. She looked up as the door to the lounge opened, and there walked in the object of her misery, speculation, and dreams.

"So, you finally show up?" Chi said flatly, thoroughly disgusted with herself for liking his smile. She stirred her coffee again, unnecessarily, needing to do something to keep herself from staring at him.

He wore a short-sleeved oxford shirt, a denim vest, and jeans that snuggly molded his legs and cupped his manhood nicely. He stood in the doorway looking as tasty as the muffin she had eaten for breakfast. She was glad he was there but didn't want him to know it. He had disappointed her by not calling, and she would let him know she didn't appreciate it.

"Good morning. I'm glad to see you, too," Parker responded.

"You're a day late," she snapped.

"I was busy," he responded shortly.

"If you're going to promise to visit me, please do so, or at least have the decency to call to let me know differently," she huffed.

"I don't have your contact information, so you're not saved in my Favorites on my iPhone," he commented.

He made up that part about Favorites, she thought. "You could have called me here at the hospital. You've done that before," she countered.

"You could have called me," he returned.

"I don't have your number," she retorted.

"I'm on the list of emergency contacts for my mother." He smiled lightly. "Besides, you could have asked my mother."

"I didn't want to impose," she said softly, then looked into her coffee cup. He was halfway across the room and the closer he got, the more her defenses weakened.

"How are you?" he asked.

"I've had better days."

Parker started chuckling. He closed the distance between them and stood looming over her.

From her sitting position, the junction of his pants was level with her eyes. She looked up at his face so as not to stare at his crotch.

Parker placed his free hand at his waist; the other arm braced a stuffed, crinkled, well-used brown bag. "Let me make sure I got this straight. We're arguing because we didn't exchange numbers. Because we didn't, we couldn't talk last night. And…"

She opened her mouth to say something, and he raised his free hand to silence her. Parker continued, "And I wanted to see you, but couldn't. You wanted to see me but couldn't. So, we are going to spend the time we have together *now*," he emphasized the last word by pointing an index finger at the floor, "bickering?" Parker shrugged and then chuckled again. "Did I get this right?"

Although Chi couldn't find a valid reason to continue being angry with him, she had to say something in her defense. "I waited for you all night." When she saw a sensuous grin flatter his face, she realized the blunder in her statement and attempted to correct the slip. "I meant all day."

"No," he shook his head. "Let's go back to the 'waiting for me all night' part."

He knelt in front of her. Chi's legs were crossed at the knee, her hands holding a cup of hot coffee resting on her thigh. He considered the possibility that her anger might cause her to use the coffee as a weapon. But doctors were into healing the ailing and not inflicting unnecessary pain, weren't they? He took his chances. "Didn't you sleep well?" he asked.

"Sort of."

"Would it have been better if I were there with you?"

She wanted to say "yes" to that but kept her mouth shut and stuck to the facts. "You promised to come by yesterday. If you say you will do something, then you should do it. Otherwise, don't make commitments you don't plan to keep."

He laughed at her.

She didn't find anything funny and told him so.

"Are you always this serious?" Parker asked around a laugh.

She was, but she wasn't going to admit to it. She just stared at him, loving the warm color of his eyes. They always reminded her of a summer afternoon stroll to an ice cream parlor. Toffee. Tasty and desirable.

Parker saw several expressions run across her face. She was angry, but glad to see him. She was pouting and didn't want to give in. Pride, maybe, or stubbornness. Not a problem; he could handle this. At this stage of the game, he would allow it.

"Did you get the flowers I sent you?" He saw joy flash into her eyes as she pulled her lower lip between her teeth to keep from smiling.

"Yes."

"Is the wine chilling?"

The corners of her mouth warred between a frown and a smile. "Yes."

"I brought you something today." A full-blown smile broke out. She has a lovely smile, he thought. The dimple in her cheek flattered the mole just below it. He would work at making her smile more often. "Would you like it?"

She uncrossed her legs, placed the cup on the table her, and extended her hands to him. He smiled for several moments before reaching into the bag and pulling out a pretty, gift-wrapped box.

It was a nice size box, she thought. At least a foot long and half as wide. "You didn't have to," she said, taking the gift and ripping away the pretty paper but gently placing the bow aside to save. Opening the box, she began grinning, "Oh, they're beautiful" she said, lifting one of the two crystal long-stemmed wine glasses out of the box.

"You like them?"

"I love them."

"They work well with chilled wine. I'll let you plan something special for us to use them," Parker added as Chi shook her head in humor. "Say, a candlelight dinner?"

"Okay."

"I take it, I'm forgiven?"

Chi needed to make her position clear. Her emotions were at stake. "Parker, just keep your promises," she said softly. "That's all."

"I'm making a promise to kiss you right now. And far be it for me to make a promise and not keep it." He leaned forward onto his knees and spread her legs. Moving closer inside her legs, his hands traveled up the front of her thighs moving from the inner side to the outer, and the higher they moved.

"Parker…" Her breathing increased as he leaned toward her lips. "We can't. Not here…"

He ended her protest by capturing her lips with his. His head was tilted to the left, hers to the right, as he gently tasted the flavors on her tongue and inner mouth. Changing the position of their mouths, he slowly rubbed his lips against hers, savoring their feel, absorbing their lushness. She moaned softly, as his left hand reached for her neck to pull her closer.

"Parker," she whispered against his lips. Shock waves rippled through her from her lips to the junction between her legs and back to her lips as Parker nibbled at them. She wanted more of him.

"Chi…" he started, and she pressed her lips against his, stopping his statement as her hands slowly caressed his chest.

He wanted more of the kiss, more of her. One hand began exploring under the lab coat, then to the top of her blouse. His fingers went underneath and played with her bra strap as he massaged her shoulder.

"Oh, baby," he said, before deepening the kiss. Chi responded by wrapping her arms around him. He wondered what her breasts felt like. His other hand traveled down her blouse to the middle of her upper chest and rubbed gently. He undid the first button of her blouse, so that he could rub his thumb up and down between the softness of her breasts. "Chi…" His tongue did a stimulating tango with hers.

Unbuttoning another button brought sensual sighs from Chi, sounds that were suddenly overshadowed by the click of the door opening.

"Excuse me," someone said, and Chi froze before trying to hide in Parker's vest.

"Give us a minute," Parker said, never turning around.

"You sure you don't need a few more than that?" The male voice sounded humorous.

"No. But thanks."

The door closed as the intruder hooted merrily.

Chi came to her senses, buttoning her blouse and complaining at the same time. "I told you not to do this." Parker helped her straighten her blouse and lab jacket. She batted at his hands. "It's your touching me that got me in this predicament." She batted at his hand again. "Stop that."

"You are kind of cute when you're angry," he said, and she frowned at him.

"Would you move from between my legs, please?"

"But it feels good here."

"Parker, please!"

"Okay, okay." He rose and extended his hand to help her up.

"Did you see who it was?" That was a stupid question, Chi knew, but she was worried the person would talk about her indiscretions.

"I was undressing you at the time and didn't notice," he reminded her, then added. "Would you stop frowning at me like that?"

"This is all your fault."

He laughed at her accusation.

"Parker," she said worriedly, "I might get fired for this."

He sobered. He didn't believe that might happen based on how the man was laughing, but the desperation in her voice sobered him. She took her job and its responsibilities very seriously. He would have to learn to respect that as much as she did.

"I understand," he said. "Tell you what. When you say 'no', I'll try damn hard not to touch you. But you keep kissing and touching me like you just did, all bets are off."

"I can control myself," she bragged.

"Yeah, right." He walked to get her folders, wine glasses, and coffee cup from the table. He didn't believe she could. "Sure, you can," he said sarcastically. "Do you want any more of this?" He held up the paper cup of coffee. She shook her head, so he trashed it. "Is there a blank sheet of paper in here?" He was flipping through her folders.

She took the stack from his hands and found a sheet for him.

Parker wrote down his contact information including the address to his restaurant. "Have you heard of the slogan 'Park and Play'?" when he saw her confusion, he added, "Don't tell me you haven't. I pay good advertising dollars so everyone in Atlanta knows about my restaurant bars."

She shrugged.

"You must not get out much."

"I'm in my residency. That means I work long hours. I don't have time for parking and playing." He snickered at her play on words, yet she kept talking. "When I'm not working, I'm resting or…" She couldn't tell Parker about what she did on weekends, certainly not about her son's situation. Not until she was sure he could understand.

"Or what?"

"Or studying and stuff."

"Stuff?"

She reached into her pocket for a business card. On the back of it, she wrote her cell phone number. "My pager number is there, too. Use it only in case of emergency," she added quietly.

Sticking it into his vest pocket he said, "Have dinner with me on Thursday? I'm featuring a great jazz group this week. I'd love for you to come by to see them play and experience one of the greatest restaurants in the city."

"Okay. Should I know where your restaurants are?"

"You should, but obviously, you don't listen to the radio or watch TV, or else you would," he teased. "I wrote down the address and telephone number of the one where the band is playing. It's also where my office is. I get there late afternoon if you need to reach me at the restaurant."

"Okay."

They stood there looking at each other for several long moments. Parker reached up and feathered her bangs, and Chi leaned into the warmth of his touch.

She checked to confirm the door was closed. Stepping closer then onto her toes she planted a soft kiss on his cheek after slightly brushing her lips against his.

He smiled at that, and she brightened under it.

CHAPTER
Seven

The golden neon lights across the front of Parker's Place lit a path to the glass, double doors of the entrance to the red brick building. The canopy-covered entryway was flanked with plants that made the restaurant more welcoming.

Chi pulled into the side parking lot. Parker had told her he had a reserved space close to the building. Some of the patrons of Parker's Place were parked across the four-lane street in front of the restaurant.

From the sound of the jazz melodies and merriment coming from the entrance every time someone opened the front door, it was obvious lots of people enjoyed 'parking and playing' there.

Before exiting the car, Chi glanced into the rearview mirror to check her appearance. She rubbed her lips together and feathered her bangs. She was ready. As she rounded the side of the building that led to the sidewalk, she looked down at her dress and prayed it wasn't too revealing. It was one of the few dresses she had saved from her partying days. After the birth of her son, she hadn't gone out much and didn't need these types of dresses. She had plenty of business attire and hospital uniforms, but almost no evening wear.

Earlier, Chi had removed the form-fitting, red dress from the plastic covering and warily checked it for moths. After squiggling into it, she stared at her mirror's image in amazement for a few minutes, surprised to see such a beautiful woman looking back at her. It had been so long since she had worn this dress that she had forgotten how it flattered her generous bustline, flat tummy, and small waist. She had added elegant, quarter-sized round earrings that mixed gold, pearls, and rubies. A pearl choker and red pumps were the finishing touches.

Standing at the entrance of Parker's restaurant bar, Chi was beginning to feel self-conscious about how much the dress revealed and wished she had worn a jacket. But she summoned her fast-retreating bravado and opened the door, entering the merriment within Parker's Place. She stood at the doorway trying to decide which way to go. Parker had told her to meet him at the bar when she refused his offer to pick her up at home. She wasn't ready to invite him to her place, but now she wished she had not refused him. Clutching her small handbag in front of her, she noticed a man walking toward her smiling, too widely for her liking.

Where is Parker? she wondered.

Since the bar area was in the opposite direction of the approaching man, she headed for it. She sat at an empty stool at the end of the bar's long counter, then realized the smiling man had turned and was heading her way.

"Well, hello," the smiling man said. "I bet you're looking for someone," he added as Chi watched him curiously, amazed that come-on lines hadn't improved much since the last time she was in a bar. "So am I. Maybe our search is over."

That's so lame! she thought.

"You must," the man overemphasized, "be tired. You've been running all over my thoughts since you walked in. I just can't get you…"

Chi laughed out loud at that ridiculous line. She couldn't believe a man his age—mid-forties, she assumed—would make such an idiot of himself. He had propped his elbow on the bar and winked.

"Have pickup lines become this fascinating in the last few years? I've never heard that one before." She managed to stop laughing long enough to say, "Actually, I'm looking for someone. Maybe you know him. Parker Ryan?" She saw displeasure flash across his stare and assumed he didn't like to be refused. It was his own fault for being lame and desperate, she thought.

As if on cue, the bartender appeared and rescued her. "Good evening. Welcome to Parker's Place. What can I get you?"

"I'd like a Coke with a cherry in it. Also, can you tell me where Parker Ryan is?"

"You must be Chi Addams?"

"Yes."

"Parker told me to watch out for you, but he forgot to tell me you were this beautiful." He winked. "He's in the back with the band. I'm Kevin. I'll take you to him."

"Thanks, Kevin." Chi smiled at the bartender's compliment and made her way around the bar. She followed him down a hallway paneled with stained wood and African American art. By the time they got to the end of the long hall, she was a nervous wreck.

Why was meeting Parker affecting her this way? Two men within the last five minutes had flirted with her, and she brushed them off like lint. She could handle most men. Then again, Parker wasn't like most men. He told her what he wanted and went after it unrelentingly.

Kevin opened the office door and announced, "Parker, I found the lovely lady you told me to look out for." As Chi rounded the bartender, she saw five sets of eyes checking her out with varying degrees of appreciation and interest.

If it wasn't for the warm smile Parker was giving her and the death grip she had on the Coke, she was sure she would have dropped the glass and attempted to hide her body with her hands. Since Parker's stare provided comfort, Chi concentrated on it.

Parker stood up behind his desk and headed toward her. She never took her eyes off his, and the closer he got, the more she became relaxed. He was wearing crisply starched black denim jeans, a taupe-colored, silk, collarless shirt buttoned to the neck, a well-tailored black jacket, and a very appealing expression.

"Chinzea, you're beautiful," he whispered in her ear.

As if on command, she began to feel that way. He had never called her "Chinzea" before, and she liked the way he said it. It made her feel as if her concerns about him had no importance at that moment.

How could one man have so much control over me? she wondered. No other man would have been able to pull her emotional strings so easily. Was it because of his confidence, appeal, or his open display of emotions? Or, maybe, just maybe, she wanted someone to be in her life that mattered, and Parker, although sexually exciting, appealed to her on another level. Something about him said that he needed her closeness and nurturing. Truly needed it.

Parker leaned down and planted a gentle kiss on her ruby lips. "Hello," he whispered to her mouth.

"Hi." Her whisper matched his.

"Let me introduce you to some people." Turning, Parker said, "Chinzea, this is the band Mellow Moods." He pointed to each band member. "Charles, Bobby, Mr. Cool, Raymond. I'd like for you guys to meet a special friend of mine. You can call her Chi."

They all exchanged greetings.

AND THEN YOU CAME

Parker turned back to Chi. "We're done now that you're here. Hungry?" To her nod he turned back to the band, "I'll see you guys up front. I'm taking my lady to dinner."

His lady. Chi wondered what that title meant. Were they officially dating? She didn't remember having that discussion. Was it said for the men's benefit or hers? Was he serious? If so, what was she to do about it? Didn't she have a say in it?

All those thoughts went unanswered because Parker had just put his arm around her waist and pulled her closer. As they walked down the hall to the restaurant, he complimented her again on how lovely she looked. She reveled in the words and his closeness.

They sat talking in a cozy, private booth next to the back windows. In the navy evening sky, a milky moon peeked through the window shades. R&B music drifted around the restaurant and into the booth.

"This is quite the place," Chi said. "Bar in the center, great restaurant on one side, pleasant lounge on the other."

"You like it?"

"Yes, I do." She studied her surroundings, enjoying the muted colors and greenery. The live plants and soft lighting created a comfortable, romantic feel. "I haven't been out partying... No, I mean parking and playing, for a long time," she said with a smile.

"That's what my advertisement promises. You'll have the time of your life here," he quipped. "Chinzea."

"I noticed you called me that this evening. Why?"

"It sounds sexy. You look classy and very sexy. Like your name. How did you come by that name?"

She picked up her drink. "I'm named after my great-grandmother. She was Italian."

"You're Italian?" thick brows converged over a questioning stare.

"My great-grandmother was half-Italian. She married a Black man. The last two generations of ancestors preferred their African

American heritage." She thought about it. "So, I guess, if you care to count it, I'm a small fraction of Italian."

He liked her lovely African features: high cheekbones, and full lips. "And *all* woman."

She found herself nodding before she could stop herself. She surely felt that way around him. The compliment was sprinkled with a palpable physical need for her. His penetrating looks amplified that unspoken need.

She decided not to respond, fearing that her voice would be a croaking whisper. It was difficult to digest such raw, open attention from this man without a powerful reaction. Every blood vessel in her body was pulsating rapidly under his stare. She also knew that once Parker started talking about her body, he would continue to do so. She couldn't handle his unabashed flattery in such large dosages, so she changed the topic.

"Why did you get into the restaurant business?"

"I've always wanted to have my *own* business. I majored in business and finance in college and played football to ensure I got my tuition paid. I was good enough at it because Green Bay recruited me. I did well for a few years, then retired from the ball and invested in the restaurant business. I've loved it ever since."

She admired the fact that he planned his life and lived his plan. That was a respectable quality to have, she thought. And an ex-football player, no wonder he looked so athletic. Chi bet that his body was probably a sculptor's dream: well-developed muscle tone, firm arms and legs, taut stomach.

Thoughts of his naked anatomy made her chest heave. She placed a hand on the tops of her breasts and willed her heart to slow down.

Parker's eyes followed her hand, and Chi's fingers trembled under his penetrating stare. She placed her hands in her lap.

When she moved her hand, Parker noticed another beauty mole close to the top of one breast. He would have to get a closer look and feel of that one.

Chi's question interrupted his thoughts. "How often do you have live bands here?"

"Weekly." He wanted to know more about her. "Do you have any family in the city?"

Chi decided not to mention her son yet. "No, I don't. The closest is in Macon." She changed the topic. "Now that you have your restaurants, is there anything else you are looking to accomplish?"

Several years ago, if asked that question, he would have said a family of his own. Today, he didn't think that would ever come true. Life had decided he had been granted enough and wasn't going to give him anything else he wanted.

"I have my restaurants, I have mom and my sister, Patty. I have a comfortable lifestyle and all the toys I want. What else do I need?"

She wanted to know his views on family and children. But the waiter showed up with their meals, and her question was never voiced. Chi had ordered a salad with grilled chicken strips, and Parker had ordered a steak smothered in a heavy sauce and a potato topped with everything.

Chi pointed at his plate, "Your arteries will never forgive you for treating them that way."

"But at least my stomach will be smiling," he said jokingly. "I'm giving it real food." He looked at her salad. "Sure, you don't want any of my steak?"

It did look tempting. Dieting had never been an issue until the birth of her son. But working long hours at the hospital and constantly walking the halls had allowed her to get her weight under control and maintain her trim figure. Placing her napkin in her lap, she said, "Give me a bite."

He smiled knowingly, "I knew the smell of my steak would get to you." He sliced her a piece. She watched him blow on it to cool it before he positioned the fork in front of her lips.

Chi was expecting him to cut her a piece and place it on her plate, not feed it to her. She decided she preferred it this way. She opened her mouth, and he inserted the fork. She watched him staring at her lips as they closed around the morsel. She chewed slowly because he was gazing at her mouth, swallowed, and licked the remnants from her lips.

As the pink tip of her tongue moved seductively across her lips, Parker was amazed at how her mouth could be such a turn-on. She kissed well with it, spoke well with it, and said his name in such a sexy tone with it. He liked its softness, its fullness, and its shape. He liked kissing it, too. The mole on her cheek, an inch away from her mouth, drew his attention, beckoning him to kiss it.

He sliced her another piece and fed it to her, wanting the luscious treat of watching her chew once more.

As Chi opened her mouth to receive his offering, Parker felt his mouth opening. As hers closed, so did his. Again, her tongue licked her lips, and he could feel his tongue moving inside his mouth. When she swallowed and smiled slightly, he began to envision all the dishes he wanted to feed her. Sweet dishes, so that he could taste them after each swallow she made. And each delicacy, most definitely, fed to her in the nude. Eating suddenly took on a whole new meaning for Parker. He was mentally grocery shopping for dishes to feed her.

"Want more?" He was slicing another piece.

"No, thank you," she said, and the disappointment hit him hard.

He recovered quickly and placed the suspended fork into his mouth to eat the piece he'd sliced. Although tasty and seasoned to perfection, it wasn't as good as watching her eat it.

They finished eating and talked companionably over wine as music played in the background. Chi asked lots of questions about his restaurants, his mother and sister, his football career, and living in Atlanta. When Parker asked a question too personal in nature, she answered vaguely or changed the topic.

Parker had picked up on her avoidance but didn't say anything about it. His past wasn't the most delightful one to talk about, so he respected her nonverbal request to leave hers alone. He did find out a lot about her medical career and admirable plans for the future.

When the music being piped in from the stereo system lowered, Parker stood and reached for her arm. "The band is getting ready to play. Let's go watch." He helped her up, and they went into the lounge.

The black-and-gold-clad members of Mellow Moods were positioned behind their instruments. Chi remembered each of their names. Raymond sat at the keyboard. His well-manicured beard, short-trimmed haircut, and round metal-frame glasses made him look more like an academic than a musician. But his black baggy pants, oversized matching jacket, and gold shiny vest with a gold pocket watch dangling from its pocket proclaimed him as a flamboyant musician. Mr. Cool was sporting a clean-shaven head and a beard. He wore dark shades, a gold vest, half-buttoned, and black pants. Mr. Cool had removed his jacket and sat at percussion. Bobby wore black suits, black shirts, and garnished gold ties and was holding a saxophone.

Raymond introduced the band and told the audience that he had written and produced all the songs in the first segment and indicated record stores where the listeners could find them.

The first song started with an African drumbeat by Mr. Cool. Then Raymond started a melody that reminded Chi of wind blowing, rain falling, and bird calls. Everything went quiet for a few seconds, and then Mellow Moods began playing a combination of jazz and African music.

During several lively songs, Chi discovered that Raymond and his band were not only excellent instrumentals but great vocalists as well. Raymond's voice reminded Chi of Luther Vandross.

It was quite breathtaking to watch and hear the interpretation of love ballads and R&B songs played with an Africanized, jazzy twist. The ensemble was very talented, and Chi enjoyed every song they played.

Chi leaned toward Parker so he could hear her as she whispered. He immediately wrapped one arm around her and placed his other hand in her lap. His touches were completely unnecessary for listening to her and all too pleasurable, making her feel as though she was the center of his erotic attention.

"I think Mellow Mood is wonderful. I'd love to see them again."

"I'll make sure of it."

Parker had positioned his chair next to hers. He had placed his right arm around the back of her chair and rubbed it up and down the side of her arm. His crossed legs were turned toward hers. The polished shine of his black leather boot reflected the soft lighting in the room.

He stroked the nape of her neck and played with the clasp on her necklace several times. Every now and then, his other hand would massage her arm. He kissed her temple and her ear, and whenever he said something to her, he pressed his lips close to her ear. Not only could she feel his warm breath in her ear, but also his warm lips on her ear. Both were very erotic.

As the band started another song, Chi stole a sideways glance at Parker to experience him without his knowledge; watching him with his guard down. When the music got livelier, his head moved in time with it, as did one booted foot. She turned her attention to his firm, manicured hands. He wore a single ring adorned with an emblem of a football team. The index finger of one hand was rubbing the backs of her fingers, each light stroke sending feathery sensations through her skin, alerting the rest of her body that more sensations were forthcoming. His other hand was massaging her neck and shoulder. His touches were heavenly.

Parker leaned over and said, "I'm glad you do."

Only then did she realize that she had voiced her feelings aloud!

Chi saw naked desire coating his toffee eyes. She tilted her head, offering him a kiss. He bent and opened his mouth over hers. Deepening their kiss, she turned toward him and reached for him. He moaned clearly and loudly. Suddenly, Chi realized the music had stopped, and Parker's moans were the only sound around her.

They were in the middle of a room filled with people, and she had openly and lovingly kissed him. She should be ashamed of herself, but she liked the sensation too much to be.

Parker looked at her searchingly, "What did I do to deserve that?"

"I wanted to thank you for showing me such a nice time," she answered honestly.

"If that's all it takes, I've got more where that came from." As the band started a slow tune, Parker grabbed her hand and led her to the dance floor.

She was self-conscious about dancing. When was the last time she'd danced in public? "Parker, we're the first ones on the dance floor. Maybe we should wait for other people to join us."

"Why? Do you want to dance with them instead of me?"

"I'm a little rusty," she explained.

"I'm a good teacher." He pulled her close and guided her in the dance. Though she stumbled at first, he swirled and moved to the music, carrying Chi with him. It was all coming back to her, and she began to enjoy herself.

"When was the last time you went dancing?"

"A while."

"How long ago?"

"A few years ago."

"You're doing great," he said. "You also feel great."

"Thank you, but I'm dancing well because I have a good teacher." She laced her arms around his neck and pulled herself closer to him.

As Parker rubbed his hands down her sides, his lips caressed her temple. "What are you doing with your nights and weekends that keep you so busy that you can't enjoy a few nights of playing every once and a while?" She stiffened. "Chi…?" He leaned back.

She didn't want to ruin it for them. Not now. She would tell him later about her weekend trips. Right now, she would give an answer to satisfy him. "Medical residency is tough. I guess I work too hard."

"We're going to have to do something about that," he promised. He turned her in time with the jazzy beat. They danced a few more songs before returning to their seats.

Around ten-thirty, the long day began to catch up with Chi. Walking all day, the excitement of spending the evening with Parker, the wine at dinner, and the dancing were all taking their toll. She reluctantly informed Parker it was time for her to go.

His displeasure was obvious, but he complained only once. "Let me walk you to your car," Parker added, standing to help her up. "Did you park where I told you to?" To her nod, he added, "Then we can go out the back way."

As they stepped down the two stairs that led to the back parking lot, Parker slipped an arm around her waist. He seemed to unconditionally give her attention and didn't demand that she react to him. For that reason, it was easy to be affectionate towards him. It had been a long time since she'd enjoyed a man's company this way. She had Douglas to thank for her distance from men.

Parker had entered her life so abruptly that she hadn't had a chance to stop him as she had so many others. Now, the only thing she wanted was more of him. She slid her arm around his waist and leaned her head against his shoulder, more tired than she had realized.

Parker rubbed his chin on her head. He thought another layer of defenses had been removed. Getting to know her required hard work. She had attempted to hide her attraction to him, and she talked very little about her personal life. He didn't even know where she lived. Maybe it added a layer of separation between them that she could use to walk away if this became more than she wanted.

This wasn't the typical response he got from a woman. Maybe that's what intrigued him about Chi. Like now, she was touching him, but not in a flirting way. She wasn't trying to entice him into bed; she was just enjoying his company and allowing him to enjoy hers.

When they reached her car, Chi unlocked the door and turned to face him. "Thank you for tonight. This is a great place. It did exactly what your ad said it would." She reached up and tugged at the lapel of his jacket. "I had a great time."

He leaned down and kissed her gently. "Would you like to do it again this weekend?"

"I can't," she said sadly.

"When will I get to see you again?" he asked.

"I'm not sure. Maybe we can have lunch when you visit your mother at the hospital."

He didn't like that response, but he wasn't surprised by it. She was not going to rush this. The other women he had dated all reacted the same way with their over-eagerness to be with him. He worked on autopilot around most of them. It became the same game, with different players. Chi, on the other hand, didn't play by those rules.

"Want to do lunch tomorrow?" Parker asked.

"I don't normally have lunch on Fridays. I leave early to handle a personal matter," Chi said, opening her car door.

"I'll call you," he said.

"Okay." She leaned her head sideways for a final good night smack on the cheek.

Parker was having none of that. He pulled her into his arms and opened his mouth over hers. Instantly, her arms linked around his neck and their kiss deepened. He liked how passionately she gave to him. He figured she would give as completely during lovemaking. As she suckled his tongue and moaned, he was sure.

He leaned back and stared at her for long moments. One lone finger traced a path from the mole on her cheek to the mole on her chest. It was like drawing a path that connected two separate worlds far away from one another, much like his world and hers. He wanted to find a way to make a connection with her that lasted longer than a lunch or dinner date. He wanted to be with her through the night and wake up with her in his arms.

"Take me home with you," he said quietly. The back of his hand gently rubbed across her nipple. "I want to feel you without this dress on." He stroked the area directly under her breast then his palm opened and tickled the underside of her breast. He leaned forward and smooched her lips. His thumb rubbed circular motions around her nipple. "I want to taste you there," he said, his finger on her nipple. His hand smoothed the material covering her stomach. "And taste a lot of other places. Let's wake up together tomorrow and talk about the fun we had before we finally went to sleep."

He was just too damn sexy for his own good, she thought. And probably too much for hers also. She wanted him to do everything he had just promised to do. But difficult as it was, Chi managed to muster the words of denial. Things had to be right in her mind first. "Parker, it's too soon for that."

He didn't expect that response. "Not even if I promise to be good?"

That was tempting. "Not even."

"Then I'm going to have to get another kiss to hold me over."

His kiss was surprisingly soft and lazily done. She expected a demandingly long kiss, but the passionately soft one she got left her longing for more.

When he asked, "Are you sure you don't want me to go home with you?" She knew his softer kiss was a teasing enticement. It worked.

Clearing her throat and stepping back, she couldn't help smiling at the sensuous smirk on his face. He knew he had won that round of sexual play.

Fine. So, you won! she thought. She could play this game, too. She wasn't as experienced as Parker, but she was no quitter. She placed her hand limply at her throat and then traced it down to her collarbone. Watching his eyes follow her hand, she inhaled and exhaled slowly, causing her chest to extend more. With a breathy whisper, she said, "Yes," then paused for effect.

"Yes?" Parker's hopes rose.

"Yes, I'm sure. I'm going home alone."

He chuckled out loud at her obvious teasing and blatant denial. She had him thinking just the opposite.

You won that one, he thought.

He looked off into the distance and reached for her. Still looking away and speaking more seriously he said, "I tell you what." He looked down at her again. "*When* the time is right, I aim to love your body for hours on end. And you, my sexy lady, will regret waiting as long as you did."

You're too arrogant for your own good too! she thought. But it was quite thrilling to hear him say that. "Is that a fact?" she asked in a mockingly huffy tone.

He stared down at her as if interpreting every expression, every move of her head, every blink of her eyes. Gone was his playful expression, replaced by a deeply thoughtful look. Parker wondered if she realized how mesmerizing, how captivating, she could be. She spoke her mind when it came to her requirements for dating, revealing her expectations, and asking that he respect them. All the while giving affection and attention, without compromising. It was strange having a woman tell him her desires so openly. Again, she surprised him. But one thing he held true; Chi Addams made him feel good. And soon, he would do the same for her sexually.

"It's a promise."

CHAPTER Eight

It was exciting.

The discharge of Harriett Ryan from Peachtree General ended up being a party. Balloons, banners, and signs were everywhere announcing that Harriett was 'Homeward Bound.' The celebration started with Patricia providing cake and punch for the medical staff and nearby patients who were allowed to have them. It ended in Harriett's room with everyone wishing her goodbye.

Harriett's room was crowded by Patricia, Mac Parker, two friends of Harriett's who had driven up from Florida, and an assortment of medical staff members including Dr. Chi Addams. The gathering disbanded as Harriett was wheeled out of her room. Most of the people, laughing and chatting merrily, headed to the elevator, down to the parking lot, and to the van that would transport Harriett to Parker's home in Alpharetta.

One man, another patient in the orthopedic ward, asked if someone had just given birth and if that was the reason for the commotion. When he found out the excitement was over the release of a woman who had just had hip surgery, he hooted. He inquired if his party would be bigger since he had a more complicated procedure done.

As everyone else celebrated, Chi felt like crying. It had been over a week since her dinner date with Parker at his restaurant. Although they were becoming better acquainted over her short lunch breaks, Parker hadn't asked her out again. She believed some of that had to do with her telling him it was too soon for them to sleep together.

Somewhere in the back of her mind, Chi concluded that she would get to spend time with Parker if his mother was in the hospital. Now that Harriett was being released, she wasn't sure if he would come by and visit with her anymore. Her lack of success with relationships in the past caused this insecurity to erupt. But what else could she think? Parker's pursuit had tapered off.

Chi followed the procession of family and friends out of the building. As they reached the automatic doors of the hospital lobby, Chi waved goodbye to Harriett and stopped to watch them leave. Because Chi was on the inside of the automatic doors, she couldn't hear what was being said, but they seemed to be hurrying. All at once, Parker threw his arms in the air to delay them, then jogged back toward her.

"We're headed to my place for a celebration luncheon. Mom asked that I thank you again for all your help."

"Just doing my job," Chi said.

"I want to see you tonight. May I?" Parker asked.

"Tonight?" It was Friday night. Normally, she drove to Macon to visit her son on Friday nights.

Parker nodded his response to her question.

Maybe she could drive to her Mama's place in the morning, but that meant less time, precious time, with her son. How could she choose to spend time with Parker over with Anthony? If she said "no" without an explanation, as she would have to do, he would probably think she didn't want to be with him. She wanted him to ask her out again, but not tonight, any night, but Friday night.

Darn! she thought. She had been missing his touch. "I wish I could. But…"

"Tell you what," Parker said. He had suspected this response. "It was a surprise I was planning to spring on you. I've got tickets to the Music concert this weekend. Let's plan on going together."

"This weekend?" For several moments, she internalized the stinging struggle of having to refuse him again.

To Parker, Chi seemed to be in turmoil. Expressions ranging from excitement to chagrin ran across her face.

"I would love to. But I can't."

"Why not?" he asked.

"I'm going to be out of town most of this weekend."

"Out of town again?" He had never had to work this hard at seeing a woman in his life. "Mind telling me if I should be jealous of these weekend excursions?"

"I'm going to visit my family. I can't spend time with them during the week because they're in Macon. I'm leaving tonight."

"Just family, huh?" Parker looked at her searchingly. "No husband or anyone I should be concerned with?"

Tell him! her brain screamed. She saw Mac stepping out of the vehicle and trotting toward them. "No. No one you should be concerned with," she finally responded.

Noticing Chi staring out of the glass doors behind him, Parker looked over his shoulder at the cars waiting for him. "Just call me before you leave tonight." As she nodded, he leaned down to quickly kiss her. It started as just a small kiss, but when he began to pull away, Chi leaned in for a more enticing kiss.

Her kiss was full of longing, and he stood there momentarily puzzled, yet excited, by her action. Her every touch said she wanted him, but when he made plans to be with her, something always came up. Like these weekend trips.

"Talk to you later," he said.

"Okay." Chi attempted to hide her uneasiness. Chi and Parker had known each other for over two weeks, and she still had not mentioned Anthony to him. The longer she waited to tell Parker about her son, the harder it would get. It humiliated her to know she was keeping the proudest joy of her life from a man she wanted to be intimate with. But she had been abandoned and rejected before because of Anthony.

Chi stood there in the lobby full of patients, staff, and visitors, feeling alone.

Is this the way it will feel when Parker finds out about Anthony? She hoped not.

Chi turned and headed back to work. She would have to tell Parker tonight. It was the only way to end her torment. She had to know how Parker felt. If he walked away from her because of her son, it was best he did so now before she invested any more emotion into this relationship.

"Hi," Chi said when Parker answered the phone.

"Hi, yourself. I guess you're getting ready to leave."

"Yes."

"That's quite a drive. A few hours, I think?"

"Just under two."

She wasn't talkative tonight, and Parker wondered why. "Chi, what's wrong?"

Silence.

Parker sat on his bed. It was obvious Chi felt terrible about something. Just as he was about to ask her what, she exhaled and began talking.

"Parker, I need to tell you something." Nervousness took hold of her, making her hands shake. *Why was this so difficult?* "Something important to me."

"Chi, talk to me."

"I don't know how to say it." She paused to consider the best words to use. "I have a baby."

"Pardon?" No wonder she was being difficult, she was pregnant. He could handle this. "You're pregnant?"

"Not *having* a baby. I have a four-year-old. His name is Anthony."

Parker absorbed that bit of information, wondering why she had taken so long to reveal this. And why it was so difficult for her.

He would have to watch what he said. It was obvious this was a sensitive matter for her. He hid his frustration and surprise. He didn't want her driving in the middle of the night, down empty highways, upset and angry over him saying the wrong thing.

"I like his name. Do I get to meet him soon?"

"Do you want to?"

So, this was where she had been going every weekend he decided. To see her son. He would get the details about that later. Right now, he needed to comfort her. She thought he wouldn't like her son.

"He's a part of you. I want to get to know everything about you."

"I was thinking about bringing him home tomorrow. Maybe the three of us can do something together on Sunday?"

"I look forward to it." He listened to her labored breathing for a few moments, then he said reassuringly, "I have a few footballs around here. I'll show him how to throw."

Chi's joy and relief were evident when she said, "He'll love that!"

"Good. You have a safe trip. Call me and let me know you got there safely."

"Okay."

"And Chi…"

"Yes?"

"If he's anything like his mother, I can't wait to meet him."

"Oh, Parker," she said, full of relief. That was the last thing Chi said before saying goodbye.

So far so good, Chi thought as she hung up. She still couldn't believe how nervous she had been, but Parker had made it easy. If there were a possibility of them getting serious about each other, she would tell him about her past, not before then. She couldn't risk the devastation of rejection again. Also, she couldn't enter a relationship hiding ugly secrets that could bring up and jeopardize her son's well-being.

SITTING ON HIS BED, PARKER LEANED FORWARD AND RESTED HIS EL-bows on his knees. He studied his fingernails as he recalled their conversation. "She has a son," he whispered.

"Who has a son?"

Parker looked up and saw his mother sitting in her wheelchair in the doorway.

Why was she up and moving around with that bad hip? "Mom, how long have you been eavesdropping on me?"

"Don't be snapping at me because you're in a bad mood." Harriett was trying to maneuver the wheelchair into the room. "I asked you first, who has a son?"

"Chi does."

"I thought she had a child."

Parker wondered how long his mother had thought about this. And why hadn't she mentioned it to him? Before he could ask her that, Harriett gave him the answer.

"I've watched her with my grandbaby. She's wonderful with Courtney. I suspected she had a baby of her own."

"You ever talked to Chi about him?" Parker asked.

"No. She's a caring, wonderful doctor. I figured she didn't want to cross the line with personal business," Harriett said. "Besides, I like the effect she has on you."

"I thought we were talking about Chi?"

"We are. I like Chi. I like how she makes you smile." His mother began straightening up the papers, cologne bottles, and an assortment of other things on his dresser.

That annoyed Parker. He liked his things the way that they were. Besides, she shouldn't be doing that in her condition. He walked over to wheel her out of his room and away from his stuff.

"Chi would yell at the both of us if she found out you were working in your condition." He turned her chair and began pushing. "Where were you headed before interrupting me?"

"The kitchen. I want some tea," Harriett answered, then asked, "How old is her son?"

"Four."

"She has a baby that young at home and works the long hours that she does? Must be hard on her."

Parker didn't think about that. Maybe that's why she spent time with her son in Macon. He knew her mother lived out of town, but maybe Anthony's father lived there, too, and Chi was spending time with him as well. Maybe that also explained her hesitancy toward dating him.

Parker didn't care for these thoughts at all. He would have to find out a hell of a lot more about these weekend trips. The last thing he needed was relationship complications in his life. And especially the kind that came with a problematic ex-lover. He hoped she wasn't still sleeping with the father.

Having Chi close to him was like having a miracle healer for himself. When she was around, life seemed brighter and worth living to the fullest. If she had ties to a complicated situation, he would have to consider what that meant for them. Parker didn't know exactly what kind of relationship he wanted from Chi. The only thing he knew for sure was that it felt good having her close. As long as it felt good and was problem-free, he would see her.

When they got to the kitchen, he opened the fridge and retrieved the pitcher of iced tea.

"I want hot tea," Harriett said.

Parker placed the pitcher back in the fridge. He decided his mother needed a home nurse and a housekeeper. He wasn't going to go through this for the next few weeks. "I'm thinking about hiring a housekeeper to be here with you while I'm at the restaurant," he said.

"If you think it's best." Harriett wheeled herself to the table. "I hate to be snooping, but are you dating Chi?"

"Mom, snooping is your middle name."

If Harriett could have reached that far, she would have pinched her son for that sassy statement. "Well, if you didn't keep stuff such a secret, I wouldn't have to."

As Parker got the box of cinnamon-flavored tea out of the cabinet she said, "I prefer chamomile tea at night, son."

He grinned. "Definitely getting you a housekeeper."

"Oh, stop changing the subject. I like Dr. Chi a lot. I'm hoping she'll come by and visit." Harriett tried to hide her joy at seeing Parker smile over her statement. He probably wanted the same thing.

"She might indeed," was all Parker said.

CHAPTER Nine

As Chi parked in front of the old house her mother and son lived in, the dim glow of the porch light showed that the pale-yellow clapboards of the house needed painting. The need for repairs was constant. The roof had been replaced a few years ago. Rotten wooden steps and porch that ran the length of the house had been replaced last year after Anthony had gotten his foot caught between some planks. When the boards were replaced, the workers had found termites eating away at the foundation. That repair had drained most of Chi's savings.

She wished she could finish her residency at a hospital closer to her son, but acceptance into a good residency program was not that easy. On the other hand, she was receiving invaluable training, recognition, and respect where she was. If only she could convince her mama to move to Atlanta, then she wouldn't have a problem spending time with Anthony. Chi knew that topic would fall on deaf ears. Relocation was a topic rarely discussed in the

Addams home because too many bad memories and emotional arguments were tied to the family's financial situation.

A year before Anthony's birth, Chi's father had died of liver disease brought on by the medication he had taken. With all the pain and near-death experiences that her father, Tony, had endured over the years, the end of his life was welcomed. To all but Chi.

Part of the reason she wanted to become a doctor was because she had witnessed her father's tremendous pain and suffering. As a child, she had dreamed of becoming a doctor and curing him. Then as a teenager, she had learned that the blood disorder that plagued his life was not only incurable but also hereditary. She, too, was a carrier of sickle cell, though she showed no signs of it. But she'd passed the disorder to her son, and he was suffering.

Her father had carried limited insurance, which went only so far. The only money he saved was targeted for Chi's college education. On his deathbed, he had asked her not to use the savings to pay his medical bills but to become a doctor.

Keeping her promise to him resulted in the loss of their middle-class home and taking on medical bills she was still paying off. If it weren't for her maternal grandmother leaving Agnes this home, they might not have had any place to live.

Chi spent most of her salary taking care of her mother, repairing her grandmother's old home, paying off her father's doctor bills, and raising Anthony. If not for student loans and grants, she would not have been able to finish school at all.

The Friday night two-hour drive to Macon was filled with thoughts of Parker behind her and her mother and son ahead of her. When she got out of the car and walked up the driveway of the house, joy and sorrow battled inside her.

The screen door of the house opened before she reached it, and Anthony ran out to greet her. He was an excitable boy despite his health. Though small for his age, he looked perfect as he ran toward her. She had seen him only three of the last six weekends because she worked extra hours in the orthopedic center to make money.

Life was good when her son was around. Chi knew her daddy would have truly loved a grandson like Anthony, even though her mama said differently.

"Mommy, mommy, mommy!" little Anthony Addams shouted as he ran as fast as his small legs would take him.

Chi dropped her suitcase and ran to him. "Hi, precious!" She swooped Anthony into her arms and lifted him over her head. Bringing her son back down into her arms, so that she could look into his small, copper-colored, happy face, she spoke in her mothering voice—much softer and more loving than usual. "Mommy has been missing you. Can I have another hug?" To her son's vigorous nod, she embraced him tightly. "I missed you so much."

"Grandma said you were coming home," Anthony said.

"And I couldn't wait to get home to see you."

"Mommy, guess what." When Chi leaned back to look at him, he said, "I haven't been sick even. Not since," he contemplated the time, "since you've been gone."

"I'm so proud of you."

"Mommy, guess what else."

"What, baby boy?"

"I didn't think you were gonna come home."

Chi almost burst into tears. She kept telling herself, *Just a little longer.* But how much longer could she go on not being able to raise her child? It was crushing her insides. Fighting to keep her emotions under control so as not to upset Anthony, she said, "But I did. And I always will."

Looking over his shoulder she saw her mother. "Hi, Mama."

"Glad you made it before it got too late. I kept dinner warm for you." Agnes fixed a smile on her face. "Come on in and get settled. I'll set the table."

Chi looked back down at Anthony and planted several kisses across his forehead. "Anthony, come help Mommy get her luggage." Chi wondered if her mother was giving her son any loving attention at all when she wasn't around.

When Chi found out she was pregnant, telling her mother had been a horrible experience. The memories still haunted her: her mother screaming insults at her, several weeks of not speaking, and the arguments about having an abortion. Chi willed those horrid thoughts back into the dark, eerie corners of her brain that they had come from.

Chi always knew her father loved her more than her mother did. She also knew that her mother gave birth to her because her father wanted a child, not because her mother did. In some ways, Chi understood. The hereditary sickle cell disease was painful to watch in those who had the full-blown disorder. Agnes had spent all her adult life watching her husband's bout with sickle cell and eventual death from it. Doctors had speculated that any children they had might suffer the same troubles. Fortunately, Chi had only the trait, which meant she didn't experience the severe pain and discomfort that accompanied the disease. Unfortunately for Anthony and unbeknown to Chi at the time, Douglas, his father, also had the trait, which resulted in Anthony having a full-blown disease. Now, Chi was asking Agnes to spend her remaining years watching her grandson fight the same battle her husband had lost, something that was extremely difficult for them all.

LATER THAT EVENING, CHI, ANTHONY, AND AGNES WERE HAVING DINNER. The meal was eaten in quiet, like most meals were. Only Anthony's playful actions and questions filled the room. Chi picked up her napkin and wiped mashed potatoes from her son's face. She wiggled her finger under his chin. That was a tickle spot, and he laughed.

"I was thinking of taking Anthony back to Atlanta tomorrow morning," Chi said to her mother. "How has he been?"

"Remarkably well. No pain. No attacks. This month's blood tests came back yesterday. Blood cells look good. No signs of sickling."

"Oh, Mama," Chi said happily, putting down her fork, "That's good to hear."

Agnes smiled. "Chi don't get your hopes up. You, of all people, should know that."

"I can still hope for the best," Chi said, slightly annoyed.

Agnes Addams was an attractive woman in her fifties. Her hair was gray and pulled back into a neat bun. Her black dress had no frills but complemented her small figure. A simple pearl necklace and earrings decorated her outfit. She was a soft-spoken, orderly woman who governed her life with discipline.

"Chi, he's showing the signs, and the older he gets, the worse it will get. This disease won't go away." Agnes reached for her glass of wine, something she always had with dinner. "It will never go away."

"I know," Chi said. "I'm hoping it doesn't get worse. Everyone doesn't get sick. I didn't."

"I find it amazing how you, a doctor, continue to rationalize this disease to fit your needs, Chi. Just about one out of every thirteen Black people is a carrier of the trait. With percentages like that, you knew you should have discussed tests with Douglas before you got pregnant since the only possible way to prevent sickle cell is to avoid giving birth to children when both parents carry the trait, like you and Douglas. It doesn't always mean the children will suffer, but the probability is so high."

Chi couldn't say anything in her defense. She alone decided to get pregnant. She alone decided to give birth. Since discussing this tore at the seams of her emotional floodgates, she decided to change the topic. "Mama, I paid your bills with the money I made moonlighting the past few weekends," Chi explained. "You can come with us to Atlanta if you like. Go to the hair salon. Or get a manicure and pedicure." Chi smiled. "Pamper yourself."

Agnes took another bite of food. Chi was always trying to pay her for assisting with raising Anthony. In actuality, they all needed each other. Anthony needed full-time care from someone familiar with his condition, and Agnes was the most inexpensive way of getting it. With Agnes keeping Anthony during the week, Chi had the needed freedom to work and complete her medical training to financially support them all.

"No. You two spend time together. It will be good for me to just stay here and enjoy some peace and quiet," Agnes said. The day her daughter had told her she was pregnant and was going to have the baby was an absolute nightmare. The pregnancy happened so close to the death of Chi's daddy that Agnes secretly believed Chi's getting pregnant was her way of replacing the close relationship she had lost with Tony's death. Tony had pampered Chi all her life and spent every painless day he had to give her most of his attention. And when he was in pain, Chi had spent most of her time at his side.

Agnes also believed Chi had gotten pregnant as a means of getting the baby's father to marry her. Getting two people to replace the relationship Chi had lost with Tony. To Agnes, youngsters today do that all the time, and Agnes wasn't blind to see it happening with her daughter. It had been a bad decision; one that all were paying for now.

"I think I'm going to call it a night." Agnes pushed her chair back.

"Mama, thanks again for keeping him the last few weekends."

"We have no choice, Chi. As a resident, you don't make the kind of money we need. So, moonlighting is the only way we can make ends meet. Besides, I took care of your father for almost thirty years. I know what to expect and do when Anthony has a crisis."

Chi looked at Anthony then because he had been quiet for the past few minutes. His eyes were straining to stay open. She reached out and touched his hand. "Mama, has he been taking naps during the day?"

"Yes. But today he was so excited that you were coming home, he barely slept." Agnes saw the look of concern in her daughter's eyes. "Chi, he's just tired."

"I'm sorry," Chi said, getting concerned over nothing.

Agnes misunderstood and thought she was talking about Anthony. "It's too late for that. He's going to need your strength. I warned you about giving birth to him. But you didn't listen."

"Mama, why do you do this to me? I can't change the past."

"But you could have controlled this," Agnes said sternly.

"You got pregnant with me. Why is my situation so different from yours?" Chi spoke louder than she needed to.

"I didn't know that I could have prevented having a sickly child by not getting pregnant. *You* did." Agnes felt she was putting the blame where it needed to be.

Chi gave up. "Mama, let's not talk about this now." She wanted her mother to be more understanding, and more forgiving, but she saw no signs that she ever would be. "I'm going to bathe Anthony and put him to bed."

Agnes got up and took her dinner dishes to the kitchen. "Good night," she said over her shoulder.

The strain her mother could be at times, Chi thought. Their relationship was nothing like the Ryans'. Over the past few weeks, she'd seen the loving relationship Parker and his sister, Patricia, had with their mother. She remembered that the first time she'd met Parker, he had been lying next to his mother in her hospital bed, ready to tell her a bedtime story. Though that had seemed odd at first, Chi concluded there was always a loving environment around Harriett Ryan.

Walking to the bathroom, Chi knew there was truth in what her mama had said. It had been her fault. She knowingly had gotten pregnant, but at least she was trying to compensate by becoming the best doctor she could be. One major mistake, yet one major accomplishment. Didn't the good outweigh the bad? All Chi wanted was a chance to make things right. But could she make things right? Anthony would never be healed.

As hard as she tried to prevent it, tears leaked from her damaged inner self and spilled down her cheeks.

"Mommy, why you crying?"

"Because," she managed in a raspy voice, "I'm so happy to see you." It was a small lie, but she refused to reinforce the miserable reminder from her mother.

After bathing Anthony and preparing him for bed, Chi lay next to him until he went to sleep. While she was standing at the doorway to turn off the light, her mother approached.

"What time are you leaving for Atlanta?" Agnes asked.

"Early in the morning. Around seven," Chi answered.

"I guess there's no good time to tell you this."

"Tell me what?"

"Douglas called several times over the last two weeks. I didn't tell him you're living in Atlanta. He wants to see Anthony."

"What?" Chi screamed. "Why?"

"He's the boy's father, Chi." When Chi looked as if that wasn't the answer she wanted to hear, Agnes added, "And you loved him once."

Hours later, Chi crawled into bed exhausted by the Friday night drive, the rehashing of the past with her mother, and the discovery that Douglas wanted back into her life. All she wanted was peaceful bliss.

CHAPTER *Ten*

When Parker opened the door to his home, Chi walked into his arms. This was the peaceful bliss she had dreamt about. She needed his warmth, his touch, his strength.

When she didn't let go of him, Parker eased her out of his arms. Looking down, he said, "How are you?"

She needed his understanding. And his closeness. *Please hold me tight*, her mind screamed. Chi was about to ask him to do so, for just a little longer, but Harriett's appearance changed her mind. At least, she had a few precious moments with him. She gained strength from that. Planting a superficial smile on her face, she willed her misery away.

"Hello, Dr, Chi!" Harriett said from her wheelchair several feet behind Parker. "Where is Anthony?"

"Hello, Harriett. He's in the car. I was just going to get him."

"I'll walk you out," Parker said. Halfway down the sidewalk, he asked searchingly, "How is everything?"

She opened the back door to her car and said, "I'm just glad you invited us to spend the afternoon with you." She unfastened Anthony's car seat and lifted him. "I want you to say hello to Mr. Parker."

"Hello, Mr. Parker."

"I'm glad you could come over, Anthony. Did your mom tell you I have a football you can play with?"

"Yes. Mommy said that I can play." Anthony was brave until Chi placed him on the ground. The closer he got to the ground; the larger Parker appeared to Anthony because he had so far to look up to see his face. He wrapped his arm around Chi's leg. "Do you have kids my size that I can play with? Grandma says I should play with kids my size."

"Not today." Parker walked on the opposite side of him as they headed to his front door. "Maybe next time we'll be able to find a few kids your size to play with. But you can still play with my football if you want."

They had just finished eating lunch when Harriett suggested she take Anthony out in the backyard to practice some of the football throws that Parker had shown him in the middle of the family room. Harriett had cautioned against expensive breakables, but Parker assured her that he had everything under control. He had not wanted to get them both sweaty and dirty before lunch. The air-conditioned inside did nicely for the few playful tumbles and instructions he gave Anthony.

After Chi told Anthony the limits of his outdoor activity as well as reminding him to respect Miss Harriett since she would be watching him, Parker took her by the hand and offered to give her a tour of his home.

"And this is my bedroom," Parker said, closing the door to the room behind them.

"I thought you were going to show me all of your home." Chi wrapped her arms around his waist as he came to stand close to her.

"In a minute," he said in a husky voice. "I wanted to show you this first." He rubbed his crotch across the front of her delicate, erotic zone. "I've missed holding you."

"Oh, Parker," she sighed softly. "You don't know how good it feels to hear you say that." Her bliss was deepening. It had been too long since she could drop her control to allow soothing feelings, relaxation, and enjoyment. "I've missed your touch," she added.

"Those are the magic words." In one adroit movement, he bent to kiss her, as his arms reached around her and lifted her into his embrace. Moving to the bed, he lay her back and stretched atop her. "And I want to touch you. All over."

Delightful shivers swept through her. Chi wrapped her arms around his neck and pulled him into a deep kiss.

Parker reached down and lifted her linen skirt to her thighs. He rubbed heavenly strokes down to her calf as she wrapped her leg around his. As he moved his hand up the sides of her thigh, he rubbed his throbbing manhood against her womanhood. She let out a sigh that pleased him. Lifting her blouse out of the waistband, his fingers stroked her tummy and found her navel. Lightly, he traced around it. Rubbing upward, his hand cupped her breast and squeezed gently. Then, his mouth moved to nip at her nipple through her blouse as he squeezed.

"Mmmmmmmm," Chi sighed.

"Do you like that?" he asked, enjoying the way she so easily responded to him.

"I love the way you touch me," she whispered.

When she moved against his pulsing manhood, he surrendered to her request. He pressed his hardness against her, and Chi began grinding more forcibly against him. He groaned, and she called to him with one of her own. He placed his hands on her waist as a signal for her to be still.

"Chi, if you keep moving like this, I won't be able to stop myself." Parker looked toward the window.

She remembered her son and his mother outside. She could hear Anthony's laughter through the bedroom window.

"And if I continue, I will never hear the end of Mom's complaining." He smiled, "She's old-fashioned."

Chi knew better than anyone about disappointing a mother. "I didn't expect anything. Just you holding me."

He threw his head back and chuckled. "You should. It's for damn sure that I want more of you."

When he looked down at her, she smiled wickedly. "How much do you want me?"

Parker took her hand and pressed it against his hard manhood. "This much."

"Touch me a little longer," Chi asked. With Parker's closeness, she was able to experience the one thing she'd been denied the past few years because of the negative forces tugging at her: the feeling of being wanted. When he didn't respond immediately, she said, "Please." Since her hand was still where he'd placed it a few seconds ago, she began massaging the spot.

He was enjoying her too much to ask her to stop. Her caressing transformed his heated desire into raw pleasure. One of his hands reached under her blouse to pull the bra down, exposing her breasts. Through the cotton blouse, he could see her erect nipple. He had no idea of its coloring or the exact size, so he slid his hand further underneath to find out. At least, for now, he would learn its size.

Perfect! he thought. It was the perfect size to suck and explore with his tongue. He lifted her blouse to do just that.

Chi's exhale of pleasure was ecstasy to his ears.

And also, a little too loud, he concluded.

One of them needed to be in control. Regrettably, he reminded her that there were people outside that they were supposed to be entertaining. Chi almost pouted.

Standing, they straightened their clothing.

Chi reached up and ran her fingers across his lips. "I like what you do with this," she said.

"You haven't seen anything yet."

She smiled. "Are you always sure of your abilities?"

It was a few seconds before he could respond because he was pushing his shirt back into the waistband of his jeans. "What I am sure of is how much you will like my abilities."

She laughed. Shaking her head, Chi thought to inform him about that wonderful flaw of his, "You are just too arrogant."

He turned and headed to the mirror to check his appearance. "Thank you."

"That wasn't a compliment."

He grinned and turned back to her. "You look like you've just had a roll in the hay." He looked for a comb on the dresser. "You better use this." He handed it to her. "If Mom yells at us, I'm blaming you."

Walking with their arms around each other, they stopped when a frightening scream came from outside.

"Parker! Parker!" Harriett cried.

Parker raced toward the patio door. If anything had happened to his mother, he would never forgive himself for not being there.

Harriett pointed to the grassy area in the backyard where Anthony was. He was lying face down in the yard.

"He wouldn't respond when I called him," Harriett explained worriedly.

"My God!" Chi ran to her son. "Anthony!"

"Is he okay?" Parker asked, standing over her as she knelt to gently turn her son.

Anthony was looking at Parker solemnly.

"Where do you hurt, Anthony?" Chi screamed. "Where's the pain?" She was rubbing his legs.

"Chi, I think he's okay," Parker said.

"Anthony, tell Mommy where the pain is," she shouted in fear.

"Chi, he'll be okay. I think he just tripped."

"Are you in pain, baby?" She tried to inject calmness into her voice but failed. Her heart was racing. Numb feet and dizziness indicated a lack of blood circulation due to sickling cells. It might be the onset of an attack.

"Mommy, I'm not hurting," Anthony finally said.

"Chi?" Parker was kneeling in front of her. He'd called her several times, but it was obvious she hadn't heard him. "Chi, he's okay. Let me take him."

"Parker, you don't understand." She checked Anthony's pulse. "We need to take him to the emergency room."

Parker picked Anthony up as Chi protested, sitting helplessly on the ground with her hands clasped together.

She looked up at Parker holding her son. "But…"

Parker held Anthony so that he could look directly at his face. Speaking softly but casually, he said, "Say, Anthony? My Mom said you were tossing the football pretty good. What happened?"

"I was trying to kick it," Anthony said dejectedly. "Like the… the…" Anthony struggled for the correct word. "The NL punner."

"NFL punter," Parker corrected.

"Yes, the NFL punter," Anthony repeated merrily. "But I fell." His merriment vanished.

"The punter is great at kicking the ball. So, why didn't you get up and kick the ball again?"

"Cause I can't hold it by myself. You said the ball had to be still. It kept rolling and rolling. I couldn't do it." Anthony finished just above a whisper, frustrated with his failure.

Chi sat listening quietly. Anthony wasn't having an attack, after all, she realized with relief.

"You know what makes the punter great?" Parker asked softly.

"Yes, I do!" Then Anthony thought about it and frowned. "No. What makes him great?"

"He never gives up." Anthony looked confused by that less-than-helpful explanation, and Parker smiled at him. "He just finds something to put the ball on, so it doesn't roll away. Then he kicks it." Parker tickled Anthony's tummy, and the boy squealed in laughter. "Let me hold it for you. Then you can practice kicking it."

Anthony put all his might into kicking the ball. It rolled maybe three feet, but one would have thought it went the length of a football field the way Parker carried on about it. The subsequent kicks traveled a puny distance farther, but the accolades and shouts from Chi, Harriett, and Parker spurred Anthony's confidence with each kick. After about five more kicks, Anthony's ego was well-stroked, and he decided he had enough practice for one day.

Anthony grabbed the ball from off the ground as Chi was holding it for him to kick and announced he was going to tell Miss Harriett that she too could learn to kick like him after her hip stopped hurting.

"Miss Harriett, guess what?" Anthony yelled. "Mommy says you can't kick the ball like me right now!"

Parker turned to Chi. "You doctors take your careers too seriously. Boys are tough."

"He's a baby," Chi explained, attempting to refrain from allowing her eyes to tear. "My baby."

Parker knelt in front of her. "I'm beginning to think there's more to this story." He remembered her reluctance to tell him about her son. "Wanna fill me in?"

"Yes," she said quietly.

When she didn't add anything, he stood and helped her up, then said, "Mom, why don't you take Anthony inside? We'll come inside in a few minutes." He took Chi by the hand and headed around the side of the house.

When he stopped and looked down at her, Chi tried to find the right words.

"Have you ever had a time when everything wasn't going as planned?" she finally began.

He pondered that question. It wasn't what she said, but the pensive look that accompanied it. "Too many times. And I didn't like any of them."

"Our lives, mine and Anthony, have been that way for all of his life." Chi looked into the distance. The warm afternoon and sunny sky didn't lighten her mood. It just added more contrast to her current situation. Life around her always looked better on the opposite side of her position. It was like looking into an amusement park from the outside gates. Wanting to go inside to enjoy the festivities, but not being allowed to.

This was the moment she had dreaded. The moment Parker would find out the truth and abandon her. She exhaled pieces of her fear and then looked up at him.

"He's sick, Parker. And the older he gets; it seems the worse it gets."

"What caused his illness?"

"I did."

Parker frowned in confusion. "You accidentally exposed him to a germ from the hospital?"

"No. Nothing like that. He inherited it from me."

"So, the both of you are sick?"

"No. It's a blood disorder I carry but it doesn't affect me. My father had it. Some people are severely affected. Some mildly. And some not at all."

"What is it?"

Chi wanted to get this conversation over with. It always started the same way. People who didn't understand the disease asked a lot of questions, in the beginning, to discover whether it was a transmittable disease that they could catch. Once they found out they were safe, they immediately ran in the opposite direction. It wasn't a problem they wanted to deal with.

The warm sun did nothing to ward off the chill of apprehension she felt, so she wrapped her arms around herself. Less than thirty minutes ago, Parker had told her how much he'd wanted her. She figured in less than half that time, he would tell her that he never wanted to see her or her sick son again.

"Sickle cell anemia." When Parker just stood there, not saying a word, only staring, Chi began rattling off all the scientific definitions and theories she'd committed to memory. She told him how sickle hemoglobin differs from normal hemoglobin. And that normal red blood cells effectively carry life-giving oxygen to tissues, where sickled cells stop the oxygen from getting through blood vessels. This, in turn, led to severe pain and damage to organs.

She told him about the origin of the disease. The history of the blood mutation was strangely fascinating to Chi. Centuries ago, in swampy areas of Africa, Greece, Italy, and parts of the Middle East where the disease malaria was prevalent, the body's defense system started to create sickled cells to protect itself against the malaria parasites. People with a sickle cell trait were less likely to die of malaria. However, having two sickle cell traits could result in a painful life like that of her father and her son.

"You're fine, but Anthony isn't?" Parker asked.

She looked away from his penetrating stare. "I don't know if he'll get any sicker or not. Anthony's last few tests were good. He's doing great. But I still worry."

Parker crossed his arms across the chest.

In Psychology, Chi had learned that such an action communicated a closing-off, defensive posture. His actions were clear to her. It was the beginning of the end.

"My father died a year before Anthony was born. He would have enjoyed seeing how well Anthony is adjusting to it." Parker turned his back to her. "He's so brave, Parker." Chi hurriedly explained how wonderfully her son was doing. She needed to make sure he understood all of it before he walked away from her forever. "I won't stop loving him," she almost screamed. "Not for anyone." Chi bit back tears. She looked down to hide her fear, her disappointment, her having to watch another man leave her. She would not cry this time.

Because Chi was looking down, she didn't see it coming.

Parker wrapped his arms tightly around her. He pulled her so close, so quickly that she didn't have time to think about it.

"I'm here," was all he said. Then her eyes flooded with tears.

CHAPTER *Eleven*

"So, why are you smiling so much lately, Chi?"

Chi was surprised by the question because the unspoken part of that statement suggested that she had not been smiling as frequently as she could have been.

"What are you talking about, Sarah?" Chi responded as they walked down the corridor.

Nurse Sarah Rogers was not only a good friend, but also a good observer. She grabbed Chi by the arm and the walking stopped. Sarah stared for long moments into Chi's face. When Chi beamed, Sarah said with surprise, "You're having sex!"

Chi looked around, hoping no one overheard that declaration. "Oh, please, Sarah. Sex isn't the answer for everyone."

"No. But good sex is," Sarah said. "Who is he? Tell me everything!" Then she thought about it. "It's that sexy hunk whose mother was in here for hip surgery, isn't it?" When Chi didn't respond right away, she added, "Well, isn't it?"

Chi started walking down the hall, and Sarah fell into step.

"His name is Parker Ryan. And we've only gone out a few times. Nothing serious."

"Yeah, right," Sarah huffed. "And Christmas comes twice a year. You don't expect me to believe there's nothing between you two."

"Friends? Yes. Sex? No," Chi explained.

Chi entered the cafeteria with Sarah on her heels. As they went down the food line, Sarah continued to grill Chi for details.

"So, he was the guy who sent you the flowers and wine that time?"

"Yes."

"Is he the guy that's been calling here for you?"

"I don't know about all of that." Parker had called her a few times. "He knows how busy I am here, so he respects my time."

"And?"

"And we enjoy each other when we're together."

Chi sat at the table thinking about the first and last times Parker had kissed her. The first was surprisingly thrilling and the last, just two days ago, was deeply penetrating.

She and Parker had stood for several long moments embraced in his backyard after she had told him about Antony's illness. His kiss that followed held so much understanding, so much emotional support that it was as if he had breathed a part of his warm strength into her and it steadied her insides. Parker hadn't pulled away as she had thought. When she took Anthony back to her mother, to resume his weekday stay, Chi had driven the route in absolute delight. She had been smiling ever since then.

"Look at you!" Sarah said before laughing again. "You're practically drooling."

"Oh, please." Chi had enough of Sarah's exaggerated outbursts. "He's very understanding. And we're enjoying each other right now."

Sarah, the consummate realist, dealt strictly with the here and now. And just then, Dr. Chi Addams had a dreamy air about her. This was not the case several weeks ago. Something had changed in Chi's life recently, even though Chi chose not to acknowledge it.

"Well, if you aren't going to give me any details now, I hope things go well. If nothing else, have sex with him just to experience that body firsthand. And once you do, give me the details," Sarah added, sitting at the table.

"Lord, Sarah." Chi munched on a grape. "As many people as you treat with sexually transmitted diseases, one would think you would be more cautious."

"But I'm also human. With plenty of human desires." Sarah reached over and took one of Chi's grapes. "No need to deny myself either. Besides, this guy I just started dating is the king of wild sex. Can't get enough. That's all he wants."

Chi looked seriously at her. "Oh, Sarah, please be careful. Don't be one of many women in this man's life."

"Don't preach to me, Chi. I know about Douglas and all his women."

"Douglas said he loved me," Chi said defensively.

"But you got pregnant while he was dating someone else," Sarah said.

"A big mistake. I've learned from that."

"Remember," Sarah confessed, "I always ask the guy if it's okay that I use him as my plaything. It's what we both want."

"And don't fall in love either, Sarah," Chi pleaded. "Not with a man who doesn't plan to commit to you."

"Objection noted," Sarah said. "What happened with Douglas?"

"I'm sure you'll protect your heart. I didn't with Douglas," Chi said. "I desperately wanted him in my life. So desperately that I got pregnant. I was foolish and vulnerable. It was right after the death of my daddy. I didn't want to lose Douglas, too. He saw the pregnancy as entrapment. It didn't make him want me. That's something I wish women would learn that just doesn't work."

"I must admit that I fantasize about real relationships," Sarah shared. "But I don't want that right now. I want great sex and a man physically close to me every now and then."

"I won't preach," Chi said. "But I've been where you are. It doesn't pay."

"At least, you've admitted it to yourself," Sarah added, realizing the truth about herself. "And you *do* preach it enough." They both smiled.

They started eating again, silencing the conversation about infidelity and entrapment, two topics Chi had regretfully mastered. But she had one last thought she wanted to voice about her past.

"Sarah, you know the worst part. I know that I must be careful about pregnancies. I'm a trait carrier of sickle cell. I'd watched the emotional and financial devastation it caused my family all my life, and I still got pregnant without testing or simply asking Douglas if he were a carrier." Chi shook her head. She'd learned a big lesson. "That was my first mistake. Being ignorant and callous about having a child was my second."

They were silent again.

"How's Anthony doing?" Sarah asked, breaking the silence.

"No crises for some time. Anthony is such a champ about it all. And Parker is great with him."

Sarah stiffened. She knew the reaction that men had to Chi's announcement about Anthony's sickly condition. "When are you going to tell Parker about his illness?"

"I already have," Chi said. "It was tough, but I had to deal with it."

Sarah looked up suddenly. "And?"

"And I'm still smiling, aren't I?" Chi explained how and why she told Parker. One of the things Chi enjoyed about Parker was the way he reinforced his desire to make her smile. He managed to always say and do what she wanted him to do. Since their weekend together, it was hard for her to think about anything other than his willing acceptance of Anthony. That touched her deeply. "I can't believe how frightened I'd been. I guess you never really heal from rejection. But Parker's different, Sarah. He cares. And understands."

Sarah smiled widely. "I'm so glad. I knew there had to be something good between you two."

"I know how I can get sometimes when it comes to love. Desperate to get it right. I must remind myself to just enjoy Parker."

"We all make mistakes, Chi. You just have to learn from them."

"You're so right," Chi agreed. "But it's much easier to say it than live it." Chi smiled wickedly. "He's so damn sexy that it's hard to refuse him."

"Then don't. That's probably why he calls all the time."

"He doesn't call me that often," Chi scolded.

Sarah changed the subject. "I have an idea. Why don't we plan a double date? We can get to introduce our 'playthings' to one another. I've heard so much about this Parker, I feel I know him. Marcus travels a lot with his band but will be in town next week."

"You're dating a musician! Since when?"

"Yes," Sarah confirmed. "Not too long. And we do make great music together… in bed."

Chi rolled her eyes. "Oh, please…"

"Hi, y'all," Nurse Mary Meadows said as she walked up to the table.

"Hi, Mary," Chi said, "Want to join us?"

"Actually, I just ran down to grab a snack. I saw you and wanted to let you know that some guy has called here several times today."

"Just friends, eh? Not that often, huh?" Sarah goaded, but Chi didn't respond.

"He wouldn't leave a message," Mary added. "Nor did he want me to page you."

"Respect your time, all right," Sarah editorialized. "More like wanting your time. That's why he calls."

Mary looked at Sarah, then back at Chi. "Something's wrong?"

"No," Chi stated before Sarah could put in any more of her teasing comments. "No big deal. Probably a patient's relative wanting an update."

"He didn't ask for you as 'Doctor'," Mary said. "Sounded more like a personal call."

Sarah gave Chi a knowing look.

An hour later, as Chi neared the Nurses' station, one of the nurses called to her.

"Yes?"

"You have a phone call."

Chi lifted the phone, smiling at her remembrance of the way Parker had responded to her touch. If only they had been alone.

"Hello. This is Drs. Addams?" Her voice was almost sing-songy, but she didn't care.

"Chi? I'm glad I finally caught up with you. I was hoping we could talk tonight."

Chi frowned. "Who is this?"

"Douglas. Who did you think?"

Time froze. Chi was transported back six years earlier. To the time when she'd first met Douglas Edward Carlson. Then, he was *Douglas the Soother, Douglas the Giver, Douglas the Nurturer*. Chi had learned a little too late that he was more like *Douglas the Pretender, Douglas the User, Douglas the Playboy*. And she had loved him throughout all those roles.

Douglas had stood by her during her father's illness. But she had learned it had been because she had helped him with his college homework throughout the evening and his sexual needs throughout the night. Unfortunately, she was one of many emotionally weak women he had given comfort in return for whatever he wanted from them.

"Douglas, why would I think it would be you?" Chi finally responded, wishing she had just hung the phone up. "You aren't supposed to know where I am."

"That's not because I didn't want to be in touch, Chi," Douglas said. "I never wanted to lose contact with you. Things happened. We made mistakes. But I'd hoped we could talk about that. We always had good times together. No matter what else happened between us, we had that."

Chi exhaled slowly. One thing that was a constant: He was always *Douglas the Inventor*. Good times were few and far between. Where in the hell did he get the "always had" part?

"Chi, why don't I come by and see you? I'll be in town in a few weeks and hope that we can spend some time together."

She got to the point, "What do you want, Douglas?"

"You, Chi," he said softly. "I want you again. We can't deny what we had. Or have."

"Excuse me?"

"Our son," he offered. "We have our son."

That did it! Her temper flared. "As I recall, we didn't have a son together! Or at least that's what you told me. I recall you demanding that I have an abortion. And when I refused, I recall you vehemently stating you would not serve as the father, not even if the courts tried to force you."

"Chi, please listen to me."

"Why?" Chi said loudly. "You never listened to me when I begged you to be a part of our lives. Why now?"

"I don't want to get into this over the phone. Please, let me see you," he asked. "I didn't mean to upset you. Not seeing my son is killing me." Douglas paused and exhaled slowly. "Surely, you know how devastating it was for me to hear from your mother that you had the sickle cell trait. I knew I had it. It was just too much. I'd thought your father died from liver damage. I didn't know the liver problem resulted from the medicine he'd taken for sickle cell. How else was I to react to knowing that we risked destroying the chance of a healthy life for our child?"

You could have loved us anyway, Chi thought.

When Chi didn't respond, he finally said, "I felt like I was given a prison sentence to watch our son suffer like your father had. I didn't want that. Not for us. Let's get together and talk about us."

"Douglas, it's too late for us."

"But it's never too late to forgive."

"If you are trying to clear your conscience, feel free," Chi said. "I don't plan on making you pay child support."

"That's my point. I want to discuss that. Think about meeting with me. I'll be in town in a few weeks."

Chi was ready to hang up. She didn't want to deal with the significance of Douglas' statement. All he'd ever preached was not wanting to have anything to do with them. Now this. She didn't know how to react.

"Is there anything else?" she finally said.

"Just one thing," Douglas offered. "Anthony wanted me to tell you hello."

Fear gripped her heart. Had Douglas stolen her son? She could barely get the words out. "Where is Anthony?"

"When I talked to him, he was with Agnes," Douglas replied. "He's smart. But what else could he be with our genes?" He laughed lightly.

Angered and frightened by his contact with her son without her permission, she said flatly, "Sick. That's something that happens when two traits are passed onto a child. Remember?"

"What?" Douglas questioned. "Agnes said he's fine."

"For the moment," Chi said, straining to keep her emotions intact. He'd had long discussions about Anthony with her mother as well without her permission. What was he up to?

They both fell silent for long seconds. Chi heard her pulse throbbing in her ears and wondered if Douglas heard it. This was painfully stressful for her.

"I won't keep you, Chi-Chi," Douglas said, and Chi remembered how she had loved hearing that nickname so many years ago. "I just want you to consider my being a part of Anthony's life."

"Hello?"

"Hi, Parker."

"Chi? This is a surprise." Parker took a seat at his desk at the restaurant. "But I like it when you surprise me," he finished in a husky whisper.

Hearing his voice minimized the frustration from her encounter with Douglas. "How's your day been?" she asked, wishing he wouldn't inquire about hers. She'd never discussed Douglas with Parker and wasn't quite sure how to tell him the latest development.

"The restaurant is always busy during the dinner hours. And Mellow Mood is performing here again this week. They always pull in a nice crowd."

"I would love to see them play again," Chi said, wanting to be near Parker.

"You know you can come by anytime," he said.

"But, of course, you have to promise to see me."

"Seeing you is the part that I'm looking forward to."

Parker paused. "I like it when you say things like that."

"I enjoyed Sunday," she said.

"So did Mom and me."

Chi paused to consider the gravity of her next statement. *Don't use him to forget old memories, Chi,* she warned herself. *Be with him to create new ones.* "I want to see you."

"I think I can arrange that," Parker said teasingly. "The band will be here playing Thursday evening. Since Patricia and Mac will be in town visiting Mom, we can all have dinner here."

Chi liked both Patricia and Mac. They had the kind of relationship she had always wanted: a loving, caring one, even though they were two professional people cut from the same cloth. Patricia had taken an extended leave of absence to raise their daughter.

Chi had tried to find love with someone in the medical profession because she thought the person would be more understanding of human nature and her dedication to making a name for herself. How utterly wrong she had been about that. Douglas was a doctor and had about as much compassion for her and Anthony as a spider had for a fly trapped in its web. He was again trying to trap them in his web. He was planning something. She just knew it. Douglas never did anything without a reason.

In a heated argument over her pregnancy, she had told Douglas to forget about her and her baby, and that she would raise the child herself. As she had left his apartment, Douglas had practically thrown her down a flight of stairs. He had claimed it was an accident while trying to stop her from leaving, but Chi always wondered if it was Douglas' way to cause a miscarriage.

She had picked herself up off the steps, tended to the scrapes she had received, and gone to class. That stunt had made her more determined to become a good doctor and make enough money to take care of herself and her child without him.

Chi needed to prove to herself, and when she honestly thought about it, prove to her Mama as well that she could do it. Agnes had always said, "Chi, life will disappoint you." In some ways, life had disappointed her, but Chi managed to overcome those disappointments.

Chi mostly understood her mother's negative reaction to the world. Sometimes it hurts too much to love. True love also requires that you find the right person, despite the conditions they might have.

The call from Douglas returned to the surface a lot of the hurt she had managed to keep at bay. Pain was pain, whether it was watching someone you love suffer physically or emotionally.

But Parker seemed different. He had a carefree attitude always in search of pleasure, and once finding it, figuring out a way to extract it all while returning that same pleasure. Sometimes, however, she noticed a faraway look in Parker's eyes, as if he were thinking about the past, about some sadness and pain, the kind of pain resulting from a nagging deep, open wound. The kind that only time, understanding, and God's will would heal. That aspect of Parker spiritually called to her, and she wanted to help him.

Parker, please want me, she wished. *Take me with all my flaws, and I'll heal you.* She had almost given up believing any man would openly and willingly want her; then Parker had come along.

Parker was saying, "Then it's a date. But I want to see you before Thursday."

"Okay," Chi agreed easily. "I have a bottle of wine that I got as a gift from this great guy. It came with two wine glasses. We can savor it over dinner… at my place?"

"That'll make me feel special. Want me to bring something?"

"No." She thought about the dishes she wanted to make for him. "I'm thinking about seafood."

"Seafood? Did Mom tell you that I love seafood?"

"No."

Chi would have never considered talking to Harriett about Parker, but that was how Harriett and her mother differed. Harriett probably knew everything about her son's life and the role Chi played in it while her mother, Agnes, didn't even know Parker existed. Only when Chi was sure of her relationship with Parker would she mention him to her mother.

"Chi?" Parker had asked her a question, and she hadn't answered.

She willed her unpleasant thoughts away. "Oh. What were you saying?"

"I asked when you were planning to cook for me?"

"Around seven tomorrow?"

"Sounds good." He paused. "Is something the matter?"

Silence. Then the clearing of her throat.

"No, I just swallowed wrong." She lied, not wanting to talk about what was troubling her. "Well, I'm not going to keep you any longer. I'll see you tomorrow at seven." Chi smiled despite the unpleasant thoughts she had been having about her past ever since Douglas had called.

"Okay. Goodbye."

"Bye."

Tomorrow, she thought. Chi hung up the phone wondering why wanting love from people who wouldn't give it gnawed at her insides. Let tomorrow be a change for the better. She needed to feel wanted. And she would show Parker just how much.

CHAPTER
Twelve

Wednesday evening came faster than Chi could prepare for it. In the one day she had, she managed to grocery shop, give the apartment a quick cleaning, shop for casual summer dress, and still get dinner cooked–grilled salmon, a pasta dish, and sautéed vegetables. A chilled bottle of wine sat in the center of the dining table.

Chi considered putting candles out to give the room a more romantic feel, but the dim lighting in the dining room cast enough of a soft warm glow into the living room. The remainder of the house was dark. Knowing Parker preferred jazz, she put on one of her favorite jazz musicians.

Satisfied, Chi went to the sofa and sat while sipping wine from one of the glasses Parker had given her.

Chi's dress was a soft, rose-colored, spaghetti-strapped sundress that had twenty pearl buttons running from bust to calves. Sitting there with her feet resting beneath her, she thought about all she could do to please Parker tonight. It felt good waiting for his arrival. The anticipation of his expert touch, his knowing caresses, and his wonderful warm lips against her skin had her longing for him.

Maybe tonight would be the night for them to make love, Chi thought. That idea sent a warm thrill through her. She needed him physically. And in so many other ways.

Don't rush this, Chi told herself, just enjoy him.

The soft rap on her front door heightened her anticipation.

When she opened the door, he politely said, "Thank you." Taking the wine glass from her hand, he leaned into a pleasure-seeking kiss. "Thanks for that, too."

She stepped back and smiled up at him. "I hope you're hungry." To his devilish grin that said his hunger wasn't only for food, she pulled her bottom lip between her teeth, then smiled. "For *dinner*," she emphasized. "It's ready."

"Then I guess I'm starving."

All through dinner, Parker noticed another side of Chi he liked. Very sexy and alluring, but also attentive to his needs. It was as if she knew that attending to his most trivial needs, like refilling his wine glass or serving him more pasta, was important to him. Her laugh had the lilt of alto sax, throaty, real, and somewhat musical. On a few occasions, she reached over and touched his hand as she talked. That sent a signal to Parker's brain that she was devoting herself to him, that he was indeed the center of her attention. He didn't know it until he felt it, but he needed to feel as though he was becoming important to her.

"My girlfriend, Sarah, wants to meet you. She says she feels as though she already knows you."

"I take it, you've been spreading rumors about me," Parker joked.

"But all good ones," she said. "A friend of hers has tickets to a concert at the FOX playhouse. Game?"

AND THEN YOU CAME

"When?"

"Sunday night. I'll come home a few hours early from Macon if you're interested in going."

"I'm interested."

"Good."

After dinner, Chi grabbed both of their partially filled glasses of wine and led the way into the living room.

"Join me," she said.

Parker grabbed the wine bottle and followed.

The screened, enclosed patio allowed a fresh breeze to filter inside and be circulated by the ceiling fan. Parker sat comfortably on the sofa. Chi stood directly in front of him. She put down the glasses and took the bottle from Parker. Facing him, she stood between his legs and began rubbing his hands up her legs. That action sent tantalizing chills through her that the gentle breeze, from the ceiling fan above, amplified. She inhaled deeply, tingling from his warm touch.

"Thanks for a great dinner," he said, looking up at her. Because of the soft lighting, he couldn't make out the details of her lovely face. He wished he could because he wanted to gauge her reaction to his next statement. "Chi, I want you to know that I am very attracted to you. It's been a long time since I've felt this way about anyone."

Chi felt a gentle squeeze of her calves. The surprise of his statement and the way he possessively held her stunned her into momentary silence. Then she said, "I wish I'd met you a long time ago."

"Why?" he asked.

"Because life wasn't so complicated," she responded softly.

"Why do I get the feeling you would have preferred I not have said that?"

"No. Not at all." She caressed his face. "We're just so new..." Chi wanted to make sure she wasn't chasing false hopes again.

"New? Interesting choice of words."

"I've noticed something about us."

"Like?" he asked.

"Like I didn't want you to reject Anthony, so I was reluctant to tell you about him."

"I noticed."

"So," she softened her voice because she didn't know how to say it.

"So?"

"So, I wonder if there's something I've missed about you because I didn't ask." Chi paused, then asked, "Do I know all I should know about you, Parker?" *Like do you want me for something serious?* she silently asked.

He released her and sat back.

She sensed resistance. This was going down the wrong path. Maybe she should back off. She thought that maybe it was too soon for this discussion, but a part of her needed to know now. She couldn't assume as she had with Douglas. She had to know, so she just stood there quietly giving Parker time to consider his response.

"Someone I cared about was killed in an accident."

"I see," she said, not knowing where this discussion was headed.

"And it almost tore me apart," he added.

"I understand how you must have felt. It can be quite hard dealing with post-traumatic stress."

Parker took comfort in her genuine concern. "It was a while ago. I survived. I didn't think that I would."

"It's never long enough when it involves someone you care about," she said.

"What makes you say that?" Parker asked, grateful that she understood.

"I lost my father about five years ago. I watched him die. It still hurts even now. I still wonder if I could have done something differently to have saved him. It's an irrational thought because his death was inevitable."

"Sometimes you do have control over the outcome," Parker said.

"As a doctor, I probably should agree. But I've seen medically unexplainable miracles. Sometimes we just can't control the outcome."

Parker had never thought about it that way, nor was he sure if Chi was right. His situation wasn't like hers. If he had run faster or had checked the streets before letting Cynthia cross, or had ignored Marcus, who stopped him as Cynthia stepped into the street, then she would be alive today.

He had remembered crying the night Cynthia died. He had cried the day they committed her body to the ground and several nights that followed as he had lain in the darkness staring at his bedroom ceiling. With every tear came pain. So, he started to dodge thinking about it.

"Was it someone in your family that you lost?" Chi asked.

"No," was all he said before leaning forward and wrapping his arms around her legs. "Cynthia was someone I'd hoped to marry. But I lost her. That caused me to have doubts about relationships, Chi."

He closed his eyes to shut the window to the past. Parker wanted to change the topic. He didn't want to talk about this anymore and shouldn't have brought this up. "That was the past. Let's enjoy the present." Parker leaned back and pulled her down to straddle his lap. He needed to feel, to forget. He wrapped his arms around her waist as Chi placed one hand next to his head and the other on his chest.

"Come here," Parker said, and Chi leaned closer to his awaiting kiss.

If pleasure was the medicine he needed, she would administer several doses. Chi pressed her lips against his. He didn't move his mouth and neither did Chi. She opened her mouth and exhaled warm desire into his slightly parted lips. Then she dipped her tongue into his mouth and licked the tip of his tongue before suckling its tip. She moved against him as their kiss intensified.

That was exactly what Parker needed. His hand moved to the back of her neck as his mouth ravished hers for several long, intense minutes.

His stiffening manhood soon pressed against the juncture of her legs. She moved again slightly.

"That's good," Parker said, and she stopped moving.

"Feeling better?" she asked. Her diagnosis was correct. He needed affection.

"Feeling horny."

"Then we need to stop this." Chi sat up.

"So soon?" Parker realized how good she made him feel. His arms looped around her back and pulled her into a strong embrace. She smelled fresh and floral, and that made Parker wonder how much of that was her soap and how much of that joyous smell was actually Chi. She seemed to make things fresher in his life. "I'll feel a lot better if you stay right where you are."

Smiling, she removed his arms and stood facing him.

Parker reached out and enveloped her thighs. The intimate feel of her softness rekindled sensations in him. The skirt of her dress was long and wide enough so that his hands could easily move up her legs. He reached under her dress, its folds draping over his arms, never revealing anything more than her knees. Leaning forward, he pressed a kiss on the material covering her stomach before rubbing the side of his face against her.

"Before we go any further, I need to know if this is real between us," Chi said warily. Did he only want a *plaything*, or could she depend on having an emotional involvement? "I need to know what to expect."

Parker paused. "Being with you feels good. I haven't felt good in a long time. If you want to talk about expectations, I expect it to continue to feel good. I expect that the more I touch you, the more I'll want to touch you." His teeth played with the buttons above her navel until he loosened them. Dipping his tongue inside, he tasted the soft skin surrounding her navel and within it. Her soft intake of air caused his manhood to tighten even more. "I expect that making love to you will be like a taste of heaven. And until recently, I was beginning to doubt if there was one." The fingers of his right hand were drawing massaging circles on her thigh. He kissed that spot on her thigh through the material.

Moving his hands higher, he felt the change from soft skin to the silk of her panties. His index finger traced the elastic in her panty leg from the front of her thigh to her hip. He leaned around and kissed the spot he touched. His hand went back to the front of her thigh, passing its original spot, and heading to her inner thigh. Her legs parted. Parker felt silky hairs, then moistness.

Unable to see where his fingers were, he closed his eyes and imagined what it looked like there. His imagination was just as erotic as seeing her, but he also wanted to see the real thing.

He moved closer to her. He wanted to taste more of her skin, too. He unbuttoned the buttons to reveal her legs. Leaning forward, his tongue licked; his lips kissed softly, passionately. Higher, he kissed the part of her panties covering her womanhood. Then his hand parted her legs before gently rubbing back and forth. Her signs of joy motivated his actions. With her dress unbuttoned, he continued to enjoy the softness of lace against his lips as he pulled her closer to his mouth.

"I don't know about you, but this does feel real to me, Chi."

"Is sex what you want?" Chi asked quietly.

The side of his fingers grazed the moist center. Back and forth. Chi grabbed his shoulders to brace herself against the sensual shock waves coming her way.

Her moans and moistness told him she needed him physically as much as he needed her. He would have to take care of that. He reached for the waist of her panties. It would be easy to remove them and pull her down into his lap and finish what he had started. But, as that sexual fantasy began to dance around in his brain, he stopped himself.

Her readiness and desire were obvious, but he wanted to savor this, not rush it, or her. She had asked him a question he wanted to answer. "It seems we both want sex. But that's just a part of the many things I'm looking to enjoy with you."

"I'll accept that," Chi responded, caressing the side of his face, his hair.

Looking up at her, he said, "I do expect to make love to you tonight, but I want you to want that." When she didn't respond immediately, he asked, "Am I going too far?"

Chi was sizzling with desire and wanted more. When she originally brought up the topic of "expectations," she was thinking of her past, his past, and how they would dictate their future. Now she only thought of the fire in her body. It was silently screaming for him to continue stroking her flames into a smoldering passion.

"Wait." She stepped away from him.

Parker, overflowing with desire, but not completely surprised, watched her turn and walk away. She still wasn't ready for this. He hoped like hell she would be soon. Cold showers weren't working for him any longer.

He walked out on the balcony to cool himself off. He looked out over the brick ledge of her third-story balcony up at the star-filled sky. Looking down, Parker noticed the grassy fields lined with tall trees. Then his eyes passed over it to a park area inside the gated complex, a nice, safe area for Anthony to play, he thought.

As his eyes adjusted to the darkness, he looked to his right and saw an oversized, cushiony, outdoor lounge chair. To his left, he saw the workbench and barbells Chi used for workouts to maintain the physical strength required for her job. She'd told him that she worked out on the Nautilus equipment three times a week. He liked the feel of her taut muscles but preferred the feel of her soft, smooth skin.

"Pretty quiet out here at night," he said when he heard her approaching.

Chi stood between him and the chair. "I sometimes sit out here and fall asleep. It's so peaceful." Parker turned his head to look down at her. He was still leaning on the ledge. She reached into her dress pocket and handed him a condom, silently asking him to make love to her.

Parker turned and took the square, handy packet. With the back of the other hand, he reached to touch her cheek. A finger gently rubbed across her ruby lips. He leaned down and kissed the mole next to her cheek.

"I want you, Chi," he whispered to her lips.

She leaned up and kissed him softly in response. "I want you, too."

Parker stepped backward and moved to the end of the workout bench. He held out his hand, silently calling her to him. When Chi moved up next to him, he placed his hands on her shoulders and gently pressed her down to sit on the end of the bench.

He knelt so he was at eye level with her. Something had sparked her questions tonight, and he wanted to make sure they were talking about the same thing. "What is it that you're expecting from me?" he asked.

Though it was a question she had thought about often, she wasn't sure she could voice her multiple answers right now. She knew she wanted a decent man in her life; she knew she wanted a father for her son; she knew that she needed honesty and loyalty in her relationship. But was the timing right for voicing those thoughts now?

She wasn't sure. "Be honest with your feelings," she finally said. "I need something real between us." She had no doubts about that. The rest they would continue to discuss later. But for now, she said, "And I want you to make love to me."

He waited for more, but the longing in her voice told him she wanted him now. As his index finger feathered the shape of her lips, his thumb massaged the mole on her cheek. Her eyes closed as the tip of her tongue licked the side of his finger. He moved his hand, and when only their lips were touching, he felt her quick inhale, as if surprised yet greatly pleased by having his mouth on hers. His tongue began to enjoy the flavors and contours of her mouth's warm interior.

Chi moaned as Parker's hands moved to her breasts. He unbuttoned the remaining buttons of her dress and exposed her bare breasts and stomach. His hand trailed along her clavicle to her shoulder, adding sensations as he pulled the strap of her dress down. That same hand, which she greatly appreciated, retraced its path to the center of her chest, and then it went downward, passing her fast-beating heart to the soft area between her breasts. He leaned forward and kissed that spot. Parker gently seized her left breast, sensuously kneading and squeezing before his mouth joined in the sensual exploration of her breasts. As she tilted her head back and moaned, his tongue licked and sucked a hardened nipple.

Chi reached for him and began caressing his chest, back, and shoulders. "Mmmmmm. Oh, Parker," she gasped when his mouth captured the other nipple, sending lightning through her body.

She leaned forward, holding his head with both her hands and planted kisses on his temple and ear. Her tongue traced the outer ear as she exhaled warm air into his inner ear. She liked the way he groaned when she did that. She wanted to touch more of him in more sensual places. Her legs were parted, and Parker was on his knees between them. She slipped one leg between his legs, so she could apply long, slow strokes against his manhood with her shin. Chi was rewarded with another deep and moving groan from Parker as his hands reached around and grasped her buttocks, pulling her closer to him. The sound and movement were so deep, so carnal, so captivating, Chi opened her eyes to see all that she felt.

On the darkened balcony, she saw Parker looking at a hardening nipple. It ached with pleasure and beckoned his mouth. She moved the nipple close to his lips as she pulled his mouth closer to it. He took it into his mouth and suckled hard, then licked gently.

Chi opened her mouth and leaned her head back, imagining his tongue moving across her womanhood, which was aching with anticipation. She was about to call out to him when she opened her eyes and saw a midnight sky spotted with twinkling stars.

They were still outside on the porch! No one could really see them, but anyone walking by was sure to hear them even though they were three stories above ground, especially since Parker's moans were getting louder.

"We're outside," she whispered, her voice laced with arousal.

Parker's response was immediate. "And I want to be inside… inside of you." That was said loudly and demandingly. Then he reached up and pulled off her panties.

Chi wanted to make love and had asked him to, but she had assumed that it would take place in the hidden comforts of her bedroom. But the hunger in his eyes, the growl in his voice, and the strokes of his fingers along the opening of her womanhood told her he would make love to her right there, right now, with no questions asked, and no denials voiced.

Parker gently pushed her back into a lying position on the cushioned bench and placed her feet on his thighs. He moved the flowing material of her dress out of his way and began planting kisses across her stomach and around her navel, her hip.

All of it–his sounds, his statement, his actions, his touching her, coupled with the fact they were on an open balcony, sent erotic jolts through her body. Every inch of her was tingling with anticipation. It was different from anything she had ever experienced. Too bold, too risky, too erotic. Making love that everyone could see, but with no one watching.

As his mouth moved lower, Chi reached up and grabbed the weight bar two feet above her head. Parker's hot mouth opened over her womanly moistness, and his tongue expertly executed an erotic dance that set her mind spinning and body writhing. Chi bit back a cry of joy and held on tight to the bar as her body trembled.

Standing, Parker unzipped his pants and removed them. His underwear and his shoes and socks went next. Then, he pulled his polo shirt over his head. Naked, he knelt and slid several fingers to her pleasure spot as his mouth reclaimed her clit, giving more pleasure than she thought possible.

He moved backward to sit in the chair behind him and pulled at Chi's hips for her to join him. She got the message and released the bar, going with him. Straddling Parker's lap, she looked down into his eyes. His stare told her how much he wanted her. Then he said to her, "Touch me."

As she kissed him, her hands caressed his chest, stomach, and manhood. Her teeth played with his small nipple as her hand marveled at his size and stiffness. *Oh my*, she thought. And it was hers for the night, but could she handle all of him?

"It's been a while for me," she whispered after kissing her way back to his mouth where she nibbled at his lips.

He reached for the foil packet. "Then go easy on me." His voice, laced with desire and hunger, matched hers.

After he positioned their bodies for penetration, she inhaled and waited for her fulfillment. He began massaging her with his manhood. Her wetness seeped and ran down the sides of his hardness.

"You want me now?" he asked, pressing an inch or two deeper inside her.

"Ohhh!" she breathed, her senses rippling. "Yes..." She reopened her eyes as his mouth captured her nipple. "Park... Oh, please."

He placed his hands on her hips and braced her for their ride to ecstasy. He pressed her downward to intake more of his stiffness and laid his head on her chest as she tightly gripped his shoulders.

She was hot and wet and tight and wanting. It took massive concentration on Parker's part not to thrust wildly. She was too tight. He gave her another few inches, then paused to give her time to adjust to him. He licked her breast, and she began to move her hips and squeeze the muscles encircling his manhood. It was too much; he couldn't stop himself. He rammed the remainder of himself inside her quickly and immediately captured her mouth with his to silence the sensual scream she uttered.

Moments later, she returned the kiss and began moving up and down, around and around. That was his signal to start the sexual onslaught again. He did. And her soft moans of delight were sensual music to his ears. The mating dance continued in rhythm with the sounds of need, hunger, and ultimate pleasure until they peaked and embarked into the abyss of ecstasy.

Chi's body began to spasm with release again, and Parker gave her the remainder of his desire as he reached their sexual apex. Both were breathing laboriously as she fell limp against him.

When Chi could finally speak, she said to his neck, "That was so good." His facial muscles moved against her, and she knew he was smiling. "Will it always be this good?"

Parker took her shoulders and lifted her, so he could see her silhouette in the darkness. He wanted to turn on a light to see her reaction to what he was about to say.

"Chi, he kissed the underside of her chin. "I didn't think I would ever enjoy giving again to a woman as I've just given to you. I've missed sharing myself like this."

The women he'd slept with over the past year were simply a means of physical release for him. This time, it was so much more than that. This time, he wanted them both to experience the best they could have. Not until Chi came along had he been able to give so completely, so meaningfully again.

"Parker, I love it a lot." She smiled wickedly. "Thanks for sharing."

He laughed at that.

She leaned forward and kissed him lovingly as they sat there with him still inside her. Positioned the way they were made the kiss more bonding; like the conclusion of a play; the last chapter in a book; or the last stanza in a poem. Their kiss was the closing moment of their lovemaking. It was the part that made all the rest that much more enjoyable. It finished the experience so, so wonderfully.

Later, they showered together. Parker brought the remaining bottle of wine into the shower and poured wine over her body and licked it off. Then he poured it on his body and watched her enjoy him. He wet his finger with it and inserted it inside her, then licked his finger, declaring it a sexual delicacy.

After stepping out of the shower, he rubbed her body down with a coconut lotion and took her to bed, saying the only thing she would be allowed to sleep in was the lotion. As she lay in bed, Parker atop her, kissed her passionately as he began massaging a breast and the junction between her legs. He wanted more of her, and she was more than willing to give herself to him again.

Much later, completely sated and very exhausted, Chi snuggled up to Parker's warm body, reveling in joyous thoughts. And Chi knew then, that their lovemaking–Parker's lovemaking–was like no other experience she had with a man.

"You're very, very good at this," she soothed breathlessly.

He turned his face to her. "Believe me, it's because of you."

"I'm glad you enjoy me," she said. Chi hadn't known it was possible to enjoy a man as much as she had enjoyed him. And this time it *was* right. The logic as to why it felt right was simple, Chi thought.

She was sure that she was falling in love with him.

THE RYAN FAMILY

CHAPTER
Thirteen

Thursday evening started with Chi rushing to get dressed. She had managed to leave the hospital on time and decided to soak in a bubble bath at home instead of showering at the hospital.

She stood in her bathroom massaging lotion onto her freshly bathed body. Looking into the mirror, she wondered if Parker could see all the unpleasantness, she sometimes saw in herself. He kept telling her she was beautiful, but at thirty she felt as though she had lived twice the number of years. The devastation of the past few years and the completion of her medical residency were taking a toll.

Not until Sarah had jokingly mentioned her smiling more had she truly reflected on the changes in herself. She liked the happier image she saw in the mirror and then realized how important self-love could be. Too often, people let the world around them dictate how they see themselves. And, until recently, the world that surrounded her wasn't that pleasant.

In anticipation of Parker inviting her out again, she had purchased two nice dresses. The one she would wear tonight was a simple black dress with a low-cut neck that fit without hugging her body. It ended just about her knees. She complemented the dress with a long black-and-gold scarf that she knotted at the back of her neck. From the front, the scarf looked as though she were wearing a thin cloth choker. Gold earrings with a matching bracelet, black stockings, and black pumps finished the ensemble.

Taking one last look in the mirror, she feathered and teased her bangs, and double-checked the minimum makeup that complemented her skin tone. She rubbed her ruby-colored lips together and smiled. She liked her appearance. She was sure Parker would, too.

Glancing at the clock, she realized she needed to hurry if she was going to get to Parker's Place on time. Locking her apartment door, she looked up into the night's comforting sky. It looked the way it had when Parker had made love to her underneath its glory.

The front of Parker's Place had a welcoming look about it. Maybe she should go and see his other building. It was probably just as attractive and welcoming. Pulling into the side of the parking lot, she slowed next to the space where Parker had told her to park. Another car was in it. She circled the lot and found one in the back corner, several hundred feet from the entrance. She wasn't going to park that far away. She remembered a space across the street from the front of the restaurant.

She parked at the streetside and opened the door as a car sped by. She had to close it quickly to avoid having it hit by the passing car. She got out and waited for other cars to pass before quickly walking across the street.

Entering the restaurant, Chi headed straight for the dining area. She heard people clapping in the lounge area as the music from Mellow Moods stopped. She looked forward to the band's performance after dinner.

The hum of people chatting, dishes clanking, and jazz mixed nicely as Chi made her way through the restaurant. She spotted Parker standing next to a woman near the entrance to the bar area.

"Hi," she said as she walked up and stood next to him.

Parker stopped talking and turned to face her. "Hi, yourself." He reached for Chi's elbow as he turned back to the woman he was talking to. "Thanks, Sheila."

"I think you should go with me," Sheila said to Parker and Chi wondered where.

"I just might," Parker responded before turning to Chi. "Chi, I'd like you to meet Sheila. She's responsible for keeping my restaurants and me sane. Sheila Banks, this is Chi Addams."

They greeted each other and Sheila added, "Taking care of you is the hard part. We've had these restaurants running like clockwork for a while."

"You have a point." Parker smiled before turning to Chi, "Mac and Pats are here. Let's go say hello."

As they began to walk away, Sheila reached for Parker, "One more thing before you go," she purposefully stepped back pulling him away from Chi to add privacy to their conversation.

Until a few minutes ago, Chi didn't think anything could deflate her soaring mood. But watching how intimately Parker was talking to the attractive Sheila Banks made her re-examine herself.

It was the way Sheila carried herself that stood out to Chi. The way she tilted her head up. Touched Parker's arm, and smiled at him were all indications that she was attracted to Parker.

Chi lifted her head as if to keep her spirits from dipping. Why was jealousy nipping at her? There was no reason for this. Sheila was an employee that Parker respected and trusted with his businesses. When Parker headed toward her, Chi smiled.

"Hello, again." Parker leaned down and brushed the mole on her cheek with his lips. "Now, let's go and say hello to Mac and Pats."

"Okay," Chi responded, but before she could stop herself, she added, "I don't remember meeting Sheila the last time I was here."

"Probably not," he said. "She manages my other restaurant, but often helps me out when things get busy at this one."

"As busy as you are, it's great you have someone to help like that."

"She's a lifesaver," Parker said. "I don't know how she always finds time to be here when I need her."

Because she too is infatuated with you, Chi said to herself. Refusing to waste more time on the interest of another woman, Chi said, "You kept me up too late last night."

Parker grinned when he looked down, and said, "I was about to say the same thing."

"Next time, we need to start earlier," she said.

"So, we can end earlier?" he asked, slowing his walk to a stop.

"I didn't say that," Chi said leaning forward and kissing him.

"I like the way you think," he whispered to her lips before kissing them again, "Did I tell you that look great in black?"

She made a mental note of that. "No, but thank you." She stood there looking up at his inviting smile while she enjoyed the feel of his hands on her waist.

Parker led the way to where his sister and brother-in-law sat in a booth along the windows. As they neared, Mac stepped out of the booth. He extended both his hands to her. "I guess I can call you Chi instead of Dr. Addams." To her nod, he pressed his cheek against hers. "Good to see you again, Chi. You look lovely."

"I'm glad Parker invited me to have dinner with the two of you. I was hoping to see you both again."

Patricia scooted out of the booth to stand. "Hi, Dr. Chi." As Mac released Chi's hands, Patricia took hold of it. "I love that dress!"

"Thanks," Chi smiled warmly and glanced at Parker. "You are going to have to call me Chi when there isn't a hospital anywhere close by." Parker winked at Chi who exchanged smiles with Patricia. "How've you been, Patricia? Or should I call you Pats?"

They all laughed.

"That's Parker's favorite nickname for me. No one else calls me that, but I've grown used to it. Momma told me to tell you hello, and that she'll see you on her next checkup." They released their hands.

"How's Courtney?"

"A handful. Mac's spoiling her."

"That's right," Mac said proudly.

"I'd enjoyed her so much. She's such a sweet baby. Is she with your mom?" Chi asked.

"Yes," Patricia said. "And let me tell you, Momma is loving it. She's been harassing us to give her more grandkids." Patricia looked at her brother. "Parker told us you have a little boy."

Chi responded, "He's a joy. But you can dress little girls much prettier than boys. I saw the perfect dress at…"

Parker injected, "Are you two going to join us?"

Chi looked up and noticed Parker standing next to the booth with his hand waving at her to sit down.

She looked up at Mac standing behind Patricia. He was nodding, too. Chi was enjoying Patricia so much; that she'd almost forgotten she was here to eat. "I guess I'll tell you later," Chi finished, then moved toward Parker.

"Stop rushing us, Parker," Patricia scolded playfully.

As Chi and Patricia scooted to the inside seats, Patricia said, "Parker said your son is four. Courtney is going on a year, and I can't wait till she starts talking. At least more than two-word sentences." She leaned against Mac and said, "Right, sweetheart?"

Mac responded, "She mastered saying 'Daddy.' I'm happy."

Everyone chuckled over his obvious pride.

Chi saw so much love and happiness between the couple sitting across from her. *Maybe one day,* she hoped, *I'll have that, too.*

Just then Parker slipped his arm around her shoulders. "Anthony is such a great kid," he said to the group. Looking down at Chi, he added, "You did a good job in raising him."

I like hearing that, Chi thought.

The waiter appeared, and they placed their orders. The meal was filled with conversation, and Chi learned a lot about the man next to her. Parker kept the discussion lively, and she liked his affectionate gestures. Whenever he talked, he used both hands to express a point, but soon after, the hand nearest Chi would find its way back to her. Either her thigh, which he rubbed sensuously; or her neck, which he massaged; or her hand, which he sometimes held in his lap and squeezed, all the while talking merrily.

He told several stories about how refreshing it was to have his mother currently with him. "It's like old times, Pats," he said, and she smiled warmly as if remembering those times. "She's the best." Parker then added jokingly, "Of course, I'm constantly reminding her I'm an adult who doesn't need a full-time mother. I think I have a curfew!"

Everyone laughed again.

After dinner, the group moved to the lounge.

As they reached the table, Patricia turned to Chi. "I've got to go to the ladies' room."

"I'll join you."

Mac looked at Parker and said, "It's always a group activity for women. I've never seen one go to the ladies' room alone."

"Oh, hush," Patricia fussed playfully.

As they entered the colorful, elegantly designed restroom, Chi said, "How cozy. I've never been inside here."

Soft yellow lights gleamed from antique fixtures. A sitting room was furnished with Queen Ann chairs and tables and an enormous mirror trimmed in antique gold graced a wall. Complimentary designer colognes and hair care products sat on gold trays for visitors. The counters were marbled, and the sink fixtures had a gold finish. The soft, paisley-printed wallpaper completed the elegant atmosphere.

Patricia, standing at the marble counter, said, "I told my brother he'd better spend money decorating the ladies' room. We spend too much time in here for it not to be nice." Patricia checked her makeup and applied more lipstick from a pink container. "Want some?" Patricia held out the lipstick.

Chi checked her appearance. "I think I'm okay." She re-fluffed her bangs.

"Chi, Parker is taken by you." They were looking at each other in the mirror. "I think he likes you a lot. So does Momma."

"I feel the same way."

"I can tell. But he's still hurting from his relationship with Cynthia. Be patient with him, and I'm sure he'll come around."

"Come around?" she said, hoping to spark more conversation.

"Pain of the past."

"I'm not interested in stirring up bad memories," Chi said.

Patricia thought about that statement. "Maybe not, but if you want a future with him, you need to understand his past." Patricia saw vulnerability and disagreement in Chi's expression. "It's a two-way street, Chi. I can tell you from personal experience that Mac and I wouldn't be together today if we…" Patricia looked directly at Chi, "hadn't come to terms with issues in our personal lives."

"You seem pretty sure of that."

"I almost lost Mac because we failed to communicate. And I know Parker has an issue with that."

Chi couldn't help asking, "How so?"

"Mac and I broke up once because of a major misunderstanding. Not until we began to communicate our true feelings and fears and were able to work it out. I had thought Parker was afraid to open his heart again, but I've reconsidered now seeing you two together." Patricia explained. "But he may not tell you when or why he hurts. It's too painful for him. Please, be understanding."

"He means a lot to me," Chi responded.

"I don't mean to pry like this, but I just don't want my brother to be hurt because of something in the past that wasn't dealt with."

Chi wasn't sure if she could control that. "I'll try."

"That's all I can ask for." Patricia had washed her hands and was drying them. She liked Chi and knew she would be good for her brother. Everyone had already noticed a pleasant change in Parker. He seemed to have found a reason to enjoy life again. Before Chi, he was just existing. It had to be because of Chi. "Do me a favor. Just continue to be good to him."

"I plan to," Chi responded.

Patricia walked over and hugged Chi before they left the ladies' room.

"What took you two so long?" Parker asked.

"We're women," Patricia answered. "Which means we must please you men. That takes time and work."

Parker laughed at Patricia and turned to Chi as she sat next to him. "Is that true?"

Chi leaned forward and kissed him gently. "Just trying to please."

Enjoying her open affection, Parker said, "Feel free to do that as often as you like."

As the band started its third selection, Raymond, the lead singer, sat at the keyboard and played. He spoke into the microphone, "Our next selection is a special one. Parker's Place's very own Parker Ryan has asked us to play a special song. It's an old cut from the days when music was music. It's called 'You Make Me Feel Brand New.'" Raymond played a classical piano introduction, rapidly running his fingers across the keyboard before starting the slow, melodic tune.

"Come dance with me." Parker stood and led Chi to the floor. "You're beautiful. Do you know that?"

"I know that you make me feel that way."

Reveling in her nearness, Parker closed his eyes as he inhaled the floral fragrance from the soft skin of her neck. He tightened his grip. Holding her was a pleasure in itself. Mac, Patricia, and a few others joined them on the dance floor.

They danced several more songs before returning to their table.

An hour later, they began saying their farewells. Chi hugged Mac and Patricia before they left.

As Parker and Chi approached the door, Sheila walked up to them. Speaking directly to Parker and overlooking Chi, she said, "I need to talk to you. It really can't wait."

"I'll be right back, Chi," Parker said. Chi noticed Sheila's hand was still on Parker's arm.

When he returned to Chi, he led the way to the back entrance. Stepping out of the back door, Chi remembered her car was parked across the street in front of the building. "I'm around here." Chi reached for his hand and headed down the sidewalk that led to the front of the restaurant. "Thank you for a great evening, Parker," Chi said as they walked.

"You're welcome. It's late, and I've had you out past your bedtime," Parker said.

"You'll just have to make it up to me," Chi informed him.

"I would love to take you home tonight."

"Thank you, but no. Sleep is critical for a doctor. I haven't had enough of it lately," Chi said.

"I thought you liked staying up late with me," Parker said with a lecherous grin.

Smiling, Chi said, "I do. But I have a big day at the hospital tomorrow."

"I know a turn-down when I hear it."

"It's worth the wait."

"I know," he said meaningfully, and Chi's insides warmed.

Chi looked both ways. No cars were in sight. She stepped off the curb and was abruptly pulled back.

The action was so quick, so surprising, that it startled her. Turning quickly, she looked up at Parker and was shocked at his expression. There was a cold, distant glaze in his eyes.

"Parker, what's wrong?"

Pulling her back was an unconscious gesture. Not until he saw Chi step into the street did he realize how haunting the memories of the past could be. It was Chi, not Cynthia. Chi wasn't in danger at all. When he saw her wincing in pain, he realized how tight he must have been holding her.

"Where are you going?" he snapped.

"To my car. It's across the street." She pointed across the four-lane highway. "What's… What's wrong?"

He grabbed her tightly by both arms and said coldly, "Don't ever park there again!" He saw dismay in her eyes, but he didn't care. It wasn't safe crossing the street. Didn't she know the danger? Then he realized that he had never mentioned the circumstances surrounding Cynthia's death.

More reasonably, he added, "This street is dangerous."

"I'm a big girl. I can cross the street all by myself." Chi didn't care for his behavior or rough handling. She saw a look of something she couldn't quite describe cross over his features.

Parker released her and looked at the ground, silently counting to ten as he willed his racing heart to stop beating so fast. He looked both ways down the street. Nothing was coming. But when he looked straight ahead again, flashes of Cynthia's accident assaulted him. Cynthia's accident with Chi in it. It was maddening.

What the hell is wrong with me? he said to himself.

Looking back at her, he ordered, "Use the side of the parking lot from now on."

Was this another side of Parker? An unpleasant, chauvinistic, controlling side? One that liked to dictate. She had known of men who used brutality to boost their ego. But she had never seen any sign of that type of behavior before with Parker. Was it because she'd refused to sleep with him tonight? Sheila had made it clear that she was there for him.

Stop it, Chi! That's jealousy! she thought. *Calm down, Chi.*

Chi wanted to ask him what the problem was. His behavior change concerned her. Something had destroyed that wonderful mood they were in, and she wanted to know what.

"Sure," she said. "Is everything okay?"

"Yeah," he said tightly. "Let's go."

Parker held onto her arm and walked fast across the street. She was practically running to keep from being dragged.

When they reached the car, Parker said, "Where are your keys?" As she produced them, he rushed to open the door and deposited her into the safety of the car. She saw him visibly relax as he closed the door. She had to roll down the window to talk to him.

"Thanks, Parker."

He felt better with her in the car. He bent slightly with his hands braced on the door. Looking her in the eyes, he said, "I hope I haven't spoiled your fun just now. It's just that this road isn't safe, that's all."

"I understand." But she didn't understand any of what just happened.

"Kiss me goodnight," he said, and she leaned out of the window. He gave her a quick kiss.

As she drove away, Chi found herself gazing in her rearview mirror to make sure Parker got across the street safely. She had never seen that side of Parker before, and in a way, it frightened her. It seemed as if he didn't know who she was. She rubbed her arm where he'd grabbed her. It was stinging.

Parker stood there remembering as he watched Chi's car drive away. The brake lights lit up several times as the car crept along into the distance.

He didn't like the aching that had erupted within him. Chi was to help him forget, not remember.

She wasn't supposed to bring him pain.

CHAPTER *Fourteen*

The evening following the dinner date, Chi drove almost mechanically to her mother's house. When she had left the hospital, she had avoided her friend, Sarah, because she had not wanted to admit she'd followed Sarah's advice to sleep with the hunk. The handsome hunk, Parker, had transformed into someone she didn't recognize. And Chi didn't know what to tell Sarah about everything that had happened over the last forty-eight hours, nor what to say about their upcoming double date to the FOX Theater on Sunday. Parker had said that he would go, but he hadn't returned any of her calls, only texting that the restaurants needed his attention and that he would call her later. Had she made another mistake with Parker after preaching to Sarah to avoid making one with Marcus?

Chi had replayed the scene over and over in her mind, trying to figure out why Parker reacted like that toward her. Had she done something to offend him; said something wrong? But what? Nothing made sense to her.

Sarah had been wrong, Chi concluded after thinking about it. While it had seemed so right to get physically involved with Parker, she now had doubts. Unlike Sarah, Chi couldn't engage in being physical with a man without attaching her heart. Again, she had let sex enter the friendship and again, she was sorry that she had. All was great between her and Parker until the day after lovemaking.

Chi felt as if she was now doing the one thing that she vowed never to do again: run after a man. She was making a fool of herself again by calling and hoping for him to be a part of her life.

Looking out onto the winding highway that headed toward a dark blue sky, she prayed softly. "I just want someone to love me." Closing her eyes, she sent up another silent prayer, "And to have my son living with me."

Anthony, she thought. *Just a little longer.* She had to maintain her mental strength to continue to make do with only the weekend visits. Money and his health wouldn't allow anything else.

As Chi entered her mother's driveway, she saw a dark-colored sedan parked there. Her mother had a visitor, and Chi regrettably concluded, Agnes would want her to join them for dinner. She always expected Chi to participate in any activity she planned. Agnes had mentioned a gentleman friend she had met at a church function; maybe it was getting serious. Chi silently hoped that her mother wanted privacy tonight because she wasn't in the mood to entertain. She just wanted to collect her son and take him back to Atlanta for the weekend. She didn't want to endure her mother's scrutiny either.

As Chi opened the front door, she heard the distinct sound of a male's voice. Her mother and her guest were in the living room; she could avoid them by cutting through the kitchen to get to her bedroom. She stopped in the kitchen for a glass of water.

"Chi, is that you?"

"Hi, Mama. I'm in the kitchen."

"*We* have company." Agnes' tone suggested refusing to help entertain or visit with their company wasn't an option.

Chi grimaced at the thought of having to feign joy. She didn't think she had the strength or inclination to smile. Her strained emotions, lack of sleep, and exhausting day at the hospital had drained her. She knew she must look as bad as she felt.

Mustering all the strength she had and plastering a pleasant look on her face, she called, "Coming, Mama."

Chi took one step into the living room. The visitor's face sent chills down her spine, and massive, debilitating dread gripped her body. The glass crashed on the hardwood floor, splashing cold water.

Oh my God! her mind screamed.

"Hello, Chi," Douglas said.

"What are *you* doing here?" The words were forced because parts of her lungs were caught in her throat.

Douglas, Anthony's biological father, the only man on the planet she wanted most *not* to ever see, stood up, reminding Chi of just how short he was.

Although a nice-looking man, his displeasure with her stunned reaction was obvious. Douglas took several steps toward her. Managing a smile of indifference before stating the reason for his visit.

"I'm here for my son."

It took all of Chi's will to keep her from rearing back and smacking Douglas in the face for making that ludicrously impossible statement. She bit her tongue to prevent a flow of obscenities from escaping her mouth.

"It only took you four and a half years to figure out you had a son!" Chi finally shouted. She had to take several deep breaths to regain a tone that wasn't offensive to her mother.

"That wasn't the way I wanted it."

"That's the way you requested it!" *You S.O.B!*

"I've finally dealt with the idea of subjecting a child to a lifetime of pain." He reminded Chi of the facts since Chi worked the best with them. "You told me you were on birth control."

"I also told you the pill was making me sick," Chi said harshly.

"You never told me you'd stopped taking them," Douglas countered.

"You knew you had the sickle cell trait; you should have used protection!"

"I didn't know you were going to purposely get pregnant," Douglas said just as loudly, "The last thing I expected was to be forced into fatherhood while in college."

That hurt, and Chi wanted to inflict pain back. She was about to use her purse to knock some sense into the man's thick skull. If only he had been committed to her.

"Don't speak to me about being threatened. I told you then, and I'm telling you now: He's my child, and I don't need you!" Chi screamed.

"Enough!" Agnes had all she could take. Frankly, she didn't want to hear any more details of their torrid affair. At the rate they were going, Agnes was sure that in less than five minutes, they would be arguing over the sexual position each was in during the conception. "Douglas, I will not tolerate this behavior in my home."

Douglas apologized.

"Chi, you caused this. You *cannot* continue to blame Douglas for something you took part in. And regardless, Anthony needs us," Agnes looked at Douglas. "All of us now."

Chi looked blankly at Agnes. She was in total disagreement. "Mama, how could you invite Douglas here without my permission?"

"Someone needed to think reasonably, Chi."

"It's not your responsibility, Mama."

"I've been taking care of Anthony from the day he was born," Agnes said. "He sees me more days in the week than he sees you." Agnes saw that Chi was about to comment, but kept talking, "I've sat back and watched. I hoped that the two of you would resolve your differences for the boy's sake, but you can't get past your pain to help Anthony with his." Agnes reflected on her own husband's bout with severe sickle cell. "And, believe me, I know better than anyone how important it is to have a support system. So, Chi, that gives me the right to ask Douglas to help us."

Agnes turned and walked away, leaving Chi and Douglas to deal with their differences alone.

Chi bent and started to pick up the broken pieces of glass. Her emotions were out of control and part of that had to do with the uncertainty she felt about Parker, as well as the fact that Douglas had shown up unannounced to discuss being a part of her life. She would deal with the immediate issue of Douglas.

Lacking the right words to start the discussion, she reflected on what her mother had said. In so many ways, Agnes was right, but in many ways, she was wrong. It wasn't her mother's responsibility to force Chi into making Douglas a part of their life.

The pieces of glass Chi held represented her fragmented life. Like the broken glass, she could bring all the parts of her life together, but would her life look as it did before? Or would the seams and damaged pieces be visible, like the glass glued back together? Would the damage still show? Mended but imperfect. The question that plagued Chi was whether she could still function if she did blend all the pieces of her life together.

Standing next to the trashcan in the kitchen, Chi considered how the six pieces of glass symbolized the pieces of her life: her relationship with Parker, her career, weekend motherhood, her needy son, her financial struggles, and now, her life with Douglas. Opening her hands, she dumped the glass fragments into the trash.

No more! It was time she mended her life.

She knew Douglas had followed her into the kitchen. Turning to face him, Chi said, "I shouldn't have been so defensive. A lot is going on right now."

"I'm to blame," Douglas offered. "I showed up unannounced."

"This could have happened differently if you had just given me more time to figure out some things, Doug." Chi sat at the table. "You were supposed to come to Atlanta in a few weeks to discuss this."

"I changed my schedule after talking to your mother. I went to Agnes because you didn't seem to care that I wanted to see Anthony," Douglas said, joining her at the table.

"So much is happening right now in my life. You know how it is being a doctor-in-training. And I'm constantly worrying about Anthony." Chi purposely left out the parts about finances and Parker. "I need more time to think about how to incorporate you as well."

"You were always strong, Chi."

"It was because I had to be. Not because I wanted to be."

"Either way, you are." Douglas added, "I spent some time with Anthony before you got here. He talks about you non-stop. You've done a great job raising him."

Chi smiled weakly. She'd forgotten how tired she was. Now that her burst of energy from the shock of seeing Douglas had subsided, she was feeling drained again. She rose to get another glass of water.

"Would you like something to drink?" Chi asked.

"Yes. Do you have anything stronger than water?"

Chi poured him a glass of wine.

"How much time do you want to spend with Anthony?" The mending had started. Chi would start working to repair this piece of her life right now.

"Right to the point," Douglas smiled. "That's new."

"I've changed a lot since we last saw each other. I'm not the needy, gullible girl you once knew."

"I can see that you've changed. But I never saw you as gullible."

Chi knew she should slowly open the door to the past, but she wanted to know what Douglas had seen in her. She had realized she never understood his attraction. "What were my flaws then?" Chi asked.

Douglas took several sips of wine. After placing the glass on the table, he said, "You were vulnerable."

Chi straightened her spine in defense. She hadn't expected that answer. But she kept silent in order for him to continue.

"Let me tell you why," he offered. "We had known each other for almost two years before I found out the real reason your father had constantly been in the hospital. And even then, I found out from your mother. I remember how secretive you were as though afraid of rejection from anyone who discovered the truth."

"That's because my family had been criticized and ridiculed about Daddy's illness for so long. I remember Daddy being called a drug addict because he kept going to the hospital for painkillers. He would refuse to go to the hospital during some of the bad attacks because he didn't want to deal with the accusations. If not for Mama, he probably wouldn't have gone at all.

"But when we got involved," Douglas said, "you owed it to me to tell me. Especially since you have the trait."

"Would you have stayed with me if I had?" Chi asked openly.

"Honestly?" Douglas thought about it. "I'm not sure."

Chi massaged her temples. "A lot of other people were sure. I lost lots of friends because of it."

"Chi, you walked away from me back then."

"You made it impossible for me to trust you," she said.

"You didn't want to."

Douglas the Disputant, Chi thought. "Douglas, after Daddy died, it was rough. Your answer to it was to date other people. I had to move on."

"So, it was easier to do it without me?"

"It wasn't that way at all. See it from my side. You had already begun dating someone else and had made it clear to me that you didn't want to be a part of Anthony's life. The more I asked you, the more defensive you got. I felt like I was stalking you."

"I hear you," he said, but Chi didn't think he did. Douglas preferred an easier outlook on life. He wanted to believe in the gold at the end of the rainbow. He would rather slow down the search for gold than deal with the reality that a rainbow was only sunlight refracted through raindrops.

Crossing her arms, she rubbed her shoulders. "I need to think about your request to spend time with Anthony. If you can tell me what you were hoping for, it will help me decide. Then, we can talk about the details later."

"Does Anthony always stay with your mother during the week?"

Chi became suspicious. "Why do you ask?"

"Agnes indicated that you sometimes work the weekends and when you do, you don't travel to Macon. So, I assume you rarely come home during the week."

Chi felt guilt eating at her. "I come home to Macon as often as I can. I miss Anthony during the week."

"I'm just asking a question, Chi."

"I'm trying to understand *why* you are asking, Douglas."

"I've come to terms with some things in my life. So, I've decided to correct my mistakes. I want to know about Anthony's life."

"What do you want from us?" she asked, looking for clarity.

"I'm hoping to not only get to know Anthony but also get reacquainted with you. I'm planning to move to Atlanta. I've gotten a great job offer there. When I found out that I'd be moving back to the South, I started to search for Anthony." Douglas reached for her hand. "You and Anthony."

Chi blinked several times before pulling her hand from his.

"And," Douglas offered, hoping to win her over, "if we both live in Atlanta, then we have our son's living arrangements to consider. Not to pressure you; just think about it."

"Think about what?" Chi asked.

"Us living in the same city and you having Anthony there full-time."

THE RYAN FAMILY

CHAPTER *Fifteen*

As Chi re-entered her apartment Sunday morning after a visit to the part, her iPhone rang. She gently placed Anthony on the carpeted floor to answer it.

"Hello?" She saw Parker's name displayed

"How are you?"

"Just walking into the apartment. I wasn't expecting your call today." She sat down on the sofa. "I mean, I thought... oh never mind that. Anthony and I just got back from the park. We're doing okay. How are you?"

Chi was forcing herself to keep the conversation light. She wasn't sure what to say to Parker after the incident outside his restaurant. But since her surprise visit from Douglas and the argument that followed, she didn't want to discuss troublesome topics.

Agnes was convinced Douglas was the solution to their problems. Chi had attempted to explain that his barging back into her life with a ridiculous plan for them to raise their son together was a part of the problem. Didn't she have a say in the matter? Or even an opportunity to think about it before decisions affecting her were made? Chi didn't want to discuss problematic situations right now. Not even with Parker. She wanted peace.

"Are we still on for tonight?" Parker was saying.

"Tonight?"

"Yeah. I somehow recall being invited to the FOX Theater with you and your friend Sarah."

"Do you still want to go?" Chi shook her head trying to rid herself of her insecurities. "When I didn't hear from you, I just assumed you didn't want to go."

"I got busy."

"Okay," she said, although she wanted to ask, *"Busy doing what?"* She didn't, however, want to hear the response just yet. *Peace. Give me peace.* "I'll meet you at the theater at seven since I'll be coming from Macon."

"Sure," Parker agreed. "We'll meet in the lobby."

PARKER WAITED IN THE LOBBY OF THE FOX THEATER. HIS TAILORED chocolate suit and cream collarless shirt set off his lean form and toasted skin tone quite nicely. As he looked about, he noticed a pretty Black woman he recognized from the hospital. She was talking animatedly to a man whose back was to him. He was sure that the woman was Sarah, so he headed that way.

Sarah was looking his way, and she must have said something to the man she was with because he began to turn around.

There was something familiar about the man's profile, Parker thought. Then Parker went numb.

There stood Marcus Allan, the man who was to have served as the best man at Parker's wedding a year ago. He was also the man who had contributed to Cynthia's death. They had parted ways because seeing him brought too much pain and prevented Parker from forgetting. After managing to squash the memories of Cynthia's cries and whimpers for so many months, they were coming back in a rush as Marcus, the man who used to be his friend, stood before him.

"Hey, Parker, man!"

Parker could barely hear Marcus over the memory of the sounds of screeching tires followed by a sickening thump of the car hitting Cynthia and her subsequent screams of pain. He fought back the desire to shout and flexed his hands, hoping to calm himself. For several seconds Parker stood there trying to read Marcus's lips because he couldn't concentrate on listening to the words over the noises in his head. He only caught portions of statements.

"Sarah said…coming…excited to see… you'd forgiven… Brother, I've missed you…"

"Marcus?" Parker finally said as his one-time friend threw his arms around him. Parker stood frozen. When Marcus stood back, he asked, "Marcus, what are you doing here?"

"I…" Marcus looked at Sarah in bewilderment. "I thought you knew I would be here," he said in a rush. "Sarah said you knew I was her date."

"Didn't Chi tell you?" Sarah asked.

Before Parker could respond, Chi walked up.

"Hi, everybody. Sorry, I'm late." Chi saw the concerned look on Sarah's face first.

"No, Marcus," Parker said, "this is a surprise to me."

"Parker, man, I'm sorry. I wouldn't have come if I'd known. I should have called."

"You're Marcus?" Chi said smiling, "I'm Chi Addams. So, you two know each other?"

Marcus and Parker both looked at Chi.

Dread descended on her when she saw the painful look on Parker's face and the look of shock on Marcus's face. Parker's look reminded her of the one she'd seen the night she had left his restaurant. Stepping toward him and placing her hands on his chest, she asked, "Are you okay?"

For moments, they just stared at each other.

Finally, Chi asked, "Parker?" His stare remained cold, his body rigid.

In the background, Marcus said, "Maybe we should leave, Sarah."

"Please, Parker, talk to me." It was a plea.

"Sarah, let's go." It was an entreaty from Marcus.

"Marcus, we have tickets." It was a complaint.

"Forget the tickets. Baby, let's go." It was a demand.

Parker spoke so softly Chi barely heard him.

"Chi, you knew about this?"

"I'm not sure if I understand what's going on." It was forgiveness looking for hope.

"Oh, Chi." Parker bent his head, but before he closed his eyes, she saw wetness forming. It was courage fading behind a troubled soul, and she knew it. "Let's get out of here," he whispered.

"Let's go." Chi quickly looped her arm through his and headed toward her car. "Sarah, I'll call you later," she said over her shoulder. "Goodbye, Marcus."

Peachtree Street in downtown Atlanta was crowded with people and held cars headed in both directions. Chi worked her way through it all while holding Parker's hand. She didn't know where she wanted to go, but any place was better than where they were. Something had happened back there, and she needed to get Parker away from it.

Suddenly, he stopped, causing her to stop.

Chi turned toward him. "I'm sorry," she said, reaching up to touch his cheek. "I'm not sure what happened, but I think I caused it."

The intensity of his stare held her hostage. "Chi, I don't know either. But thank you for getting me out of that."

"Who was he?" Chi asked. "Sarah left me a message telling me to make sure you knew he was coming, but that was the extent of the message. Is he a business rival or something?"

"He helped kill my fiancée."

"Oh, God." Chi reached for him. "I thought you said it was an accident."

"I could have saved her if Marcus hadn't stopped me."

"Let's go somewhere quiet and talk about this." She turned to walk away.

Parker stopped her again. "I don't want to talk about it. But I want to get out of here."

"Then, let's go home." Chi started walking toward her car.

Parker stopped her again. "One day, we'll talk about this. But not now. Or tomorrow. Not even the day after that."

Chi stood stunned, not sure what to say. "Okay. Please, let me hold you tonight."

THAT NIGHT AS THEY LAY TOGETHER IN CHI'S BED. CHI WAS ON HER back and Parker resting atop her, his head on her breasts. They had lain there for almost an hour in silence. Chi held him as she rubbed loving strokes over his hair.

Parker, eyes closed and mind full of thoughts attempted to forget what had happened tonight. He couldn't deal with this now. He needed to rid the memories again. Forget the pain. At least this time he had Chi to help him. He felt protected while in her arms, even though the memories hadn't completely gone away.

He should have dealt with Marcus differently tonight, Parker thought. Possibly punched him in the face as he had done the last time. It wasn't the best reaction, but the anger he felt when he had previously attacked Marcus had served to keep him from concentrating on the memories. He would have to figure out a way to push the memories back into their hiding places. Then he could function again.

As sleep took hold, Parker hoped the demons of his nightmares wouldn't close in on him tonight.

CHAPTER Sixteen

P arker knew Chi was in pain.
　　He had to do something. He felt he was going to lose her, too. Parker called her, but she didn't respond. She kept moving away from him. It was dark and murky in the fog. Parker turned left, then right, looking for her as she disappeared. Then the dream changed. Now, Chi was running. No, it was Cynthia who was running. Why was Cynthia there? Then Cynthia spoke to him. She was telling him to go after Chi. But before he could get to her, there was blood.

　　Chi! he yelled, but she couldn't hear him. He saw red flashing lights; and heard beeping; then out of the darkness, a sharp knife appeared. Chi was screaming. He shouted to Chi again. The knife was aimed at Chi's lovely throat, but she got out of the way just in time. Someone was trying to stab her as she tried to get away! Who? Why? There was more blood as Chi struggled.

　　He was watching and unable to assist. The fog swirled, and he saw little Anthony crying. He couldn't get to her…or Anthony. Out of nowhere came a truck that slammed into them.

And he couldn't do anything to stop it. Help them! Someone help them! Help me, anybody…please.

"Chiii!" Parker's screams woke him from his nightmare. "Chi?" he whispered, looking around as the eerie visions faded into the comfortable surroundings of his bedroom. Sweating and breathing hard, he rubbed his hands across his damp forehead. A glance at the clock told him it was five thirty-eight in the morning.

The last time he had seen Chi was about a week ago when he had awakened in her arms. The sound of her voice had pulled him from a nightmare in which he relived the accident. To push his bad memories back into the crevices where they belonged, he began cramming extra work into his schedule. It was the cure that had worked the last time. So, he found a restaurant convention in Florida. Each morning for the last five days, he had taken a forty-five-minute plane ride to Florida, then had flown home each evening to see his mother and work a few hours at the restaurant. He would crash in bed and pass out until the next morning when he would leave town again. He didn't tell Chi he was flying back each night, because he didn't want to be with her until he was sure the memories and accompanying nightmares were under control.

He had filled his time with work and travel up until yesterday, so he concluded that was possibly the reason for his new nightmare. Maybe seeing Chi crossing the street in the same spot Cynthia had been killed, followed by seeing Marcus again, had caused it. Unsettled, he reached for his iPhone.

"Hello?" Chi's sleepy voice filled the phone, and Parker's concerns began dissipating.

"Are you okay?"

"Parker?"

"Yes." Less desperately he asked, "How are you?"

"Asleep, but fine thanks." She looked at the clock. "I can't believe your timing. My alarm would have gone off in a few minutes. Why are you up this early on a Tuesday morning?"

"I woke up thinking about you." He feigned calmness, although his heart was still racing. At least he told a part of the truth, he thought. He couldn't shake a sense of impending doom, but he wouldn't upset Chi over some strange and crazy dream.

"How was the convention?" she asked.

"Longer than planned," he said, still not revealing that the business trip was arranged at the last moment because he needed some way to keep himself busy until he felt he was back in control of his thoughts and, therefore his life. "But it's over. Brought me and my luggage home for good last night."

"I'm sure you're glad to get back so that you can practice some of those helpful tips you learned," Chi joked.

"Exactly," The pleasure in her voice eased his worries a little more. "I would have called you this weekend but knew you had planned to stay the weekend at your mom's. Besides, I'm not even sure where in Macon you live."

That was on purpose, Chi thought. She didn't want Agnes interfering or talking with Parker until she could deal with the issue of Douglas. Especially considering Parker's situation.

Chi was relieved to hear that he wanted to get in contact with her over the weekend because she hadn't been sure if he was avoiding her or not. They had spent the night after the encounter with Marcus together, but Parker had been traveling on business ever since. Yet that had also given her time to concentrate on her issues: Agnes and Douglas.

"I made a promise to my son that when I was with him, there would be no other interruptions. My cellphone is never on." She reminded him. "By the way, Anthony wanted me to tell you he's been practicing kicks."

"That's my boy," Parker said jokingly. "How is he?"

"Doing okay," Chi offered.

"Good." He paused, then said, "I want to see you." Desire mixed with desperation was in his voice. "I've missed my dose of Chi."

Something in his tone pulled at her. "And I've missed giving it to you," she said softly.

They sat for seconds in silence, enjoying the pleasant thoughts of each other coupled with the sounds of breathing.

"Keep your evening open for tomorrow night," he said.

"Okay," Chi agreed. "What do you have planned?"

He didn't know; he would think of something, though. "You'll like it," he said.

"It's a surprise?"

"It's a promise." His creepy dream had gone the way of her sleepiness. "You'll enjoy yourself."

"I always do, with you," she said.

"Wear comfortable clothes and shoes."

"I will." Chi's alarm clock started chirping. "I guess it's time for me to wake up now," she said playfully. Leaning, she turned off the alarm. "How's your mother's therapy going?"

"She's complaining about the pain. You should come over and talk to her. She won't listen to me. I keep telling her if she doesn't follow the therapist's routine, her muscles are going to lock up."

"I'll call her later today." Chi stood up and stretched. "I'm glad you called. It's so good to hear your voice."

"You sound sexy in the morning. I might end up calling you every morning."

"Stop being bad," she teased.

"You want bad? Wait 'til tomorrow." He was feeling a hell of a lot better. He found himself imagining what she had slept in and was just about to ask her when she claimed time was getting away from her, that she had to go. Though he didn't understand why, he needed to say something more. After a long pause, he said, "Be careful today."

Hanging up the phone, Parker sat on the edge of the bed, staring at the carpet, his mind a jumble of questions. Why that creepy dream?

It was all related to Cynthia's car accident, he reasoned: the red lights, a beeping sound, the darkness. Except for the part about the knife. He rubbed his hands across his hair attempting to dismiss the nightmare from his mind.

Stop thinking about this, he scolded himself.

Since he was awake, he decided to get up and do something. Walking into the master bathroom, he turned on the shower and stepped into a watery massage. He needed to relax.

It was true that he had traveled on business over the last few days. It was also true that he didn't have any way to contact Chi at her mother's place on the weekend, but he had Chi's pager number. Parker had convinced himself that he should only use her pager in emergency cases; something that involved his mother's health, he reasoned. But that was an excuse. He was consciously adding distance between them until he could gain control of his pain again. It had been good with Chi thus far, and as long as it was, he would enjoy it.

AN HOUR AFTER CHI ARRIVED AT THE HOSPITAL, SHE WAS PAGED TO the emergency room. Finally, things had slowed down, and Chi had a chance to talk to Sarah.

"Is Parker back from his trip?" Sarah asked.

"Yes," Chi said. "He got back last night."

"Have you two talked?"

"He called me this morning to say hello."

"Chi, that's not what I'm talking about, and you know it."

"We haven't talked much about the incident since the night at the FOX," Chi admitted.

"I think you need to be careful with Parker," Sarah said.

"Why the big change in heart?" Chi asked. "You were his biggest fan."

"I finally got Marcus to tell me the whole story yesterday." Sarah glanced around and lowered her voice. "This is your business, I know, but Marcus told me that Parker changed after the accident. Until the FOX meeting, they hadn't spoken since the funeral. Marcus said Parker tried to save Cynthia and was less than two feet away when the car hit her. She died in his arms."

"Oh, my God!" Chi whispered raggedly.

"I didn't think he'd told you the whole story," Sarah added. "It happened right in front of his restaurant. I can't believe the man goes to work every day and sees the spot where she was killed and doesn't go crazy. We're trained to deal with that, and it still gets to me."

Chi stood there thinking how remarkably adjusted Parker had seemed. No wonder he'd reacted the way that he had when she stepped off the curb in front of his restaurant. It was a protective gesture.

"Parker is harboring a lot of hurt. That's why I'm suggesting you go slow with him," Sarah was saying. "I know you have strong feelings for him."

"My poor Parker," Chi said. She needed to go hold him just then.

"They were to be married two days after the accident," Sarah said.

"I need to talk to him about this," Chi said.

"He hasn't brought it up yet," Sarah reminded her. "And you're not supposed to know about this."

"I know," Chi defended, "but shouldn't he and I talk about this? We're dating."

"I think you should…talk," Sarah said pointedly, "…about a lot of things." She paused, giving Chi time to consider the secrets she was keeping from Parker. "I still think he's a fine brother and a nice guy. I'm just giving you your own advice. Don't get hurt, Chi. Parker may not be over her."

"Thanks for telling me, Sarah. This only makes me want him more."

"I know, Chi," Sarah said sadly, reaching out to touch her friend.

"Dr. Addams?"

They turned to face nurse Mary Meadows.

"Yes?" Chi asked.

"Dr. Wilburn needs you to check out a patient since you're down here."

Chi slipped into her professional mode. "What's going on?"

"A bad guy the police brought in. Attempted robbery. He's in Room 5. Gunshot wound to the shoulder. Entry and exit wound. The other arm with a possible bone fracture. Here's his chart." Mary handed the chart to Chi to review.

"The loser should've been shot through his cold heart. Save us and the taxpayers both time and money," Sarah said, coming around the desk.

Chi looked up from the chart and said, "And you consider yourself a member of the healing profession?"

"I consider myself a realist. You want money, you get a job. Not rob someone." Sarah didn't like people who thrived on other's weaknesses. "I'll go with you."

Chi shook her head at them. "There goes my peaceful morning," Chi said.

"What peaceful morning?" Sarah said, "It's been hellish all day."

"It was a poor attempt at a joke," Chi said. "Let's get some X-rays. Possible sutures for the lacerations."

"I say let him bleed to death."

"Sarah, the merciful," Chi quipped as they walked down the hall together. "And before I get too busy and forget, Sarah, thanks for sharing what Marcus told you."

"Call it friendship," Sarah replied. "Now, let's save the world."

As they entered Room 5, they stopped, surprised that it was empty.

Chi had expected to see the felon handcuffed to the gurney. "Are we in the right room?" Chi said.

"I'll check down the hall." Sarah turned and left.

Chi went to the cabinet to obtain the necessary supplies. Then she heard a noise coming from the connecting room. *That room is supposed to be empty and locked.* As she approached the connecting door, she noticed blood smeared on the doorknob.

"What's going on?" Concerned, Chi opened the connecting room's door and stepped into a dark room. When she reached for the light switch, someone grabbed her arm and pulled her inside the room. A foot kicked the door closed.

Startled, she stumbled several feet and fell against a machine, wincing as its metal edge jabbed her in the side. It started beeping, and red lights flashed when she accidentally turned it on while attempting to brace herself.

Chi whipped around to see a man towering over her. "Who are you!" she whispered.

"Shut your damn mouth before the cop hears!" Chi realized this must be the felon.

She could barely make out his features in the darkness. Her first thought was to calm him. "You're bleeding and need medical attention. I'm a doctor."

"You're my hostage, and I'm getting the hell out of here."

Faint red lights reflected off the sharp object he held. It was a scalpel! She had to get out of this room. "Okay. I understand. What do you want?"

The criminal stepped closer to her, and she could see he was a white male, tall, wearing a tank top smeared with his blood.

He moved the scalpel close to her face and spat out, "Get me out of here!"

"Okay." Her mind was calculating her options to get to safety. "The stairs are close. We go through the room I just came out of, and they're just down the hall."

"Go!"

She started to squeeze past him. His foul odor filled her nostrils, and she held her breath. Suddenly, Chi swung at him, hitting his injured shoulder. He yelled, momentarily incapacitated.

Chi made a run for it! She dashed toward the door, hearing him shouting at her to stop. Looking back, she stumbled and fell onto a machine. The previous jab to her side shot new bolts of pain through her, fear motivated her to get out of the dark room.

Reaching for the doorknob, her hand slipped. It was wet and slick from his blood. Glancing over her shoulder, she saw the scalpel slicing through the air. "Don't!" she screamed, fighting with the knob. The door gave way as the knife sliced through her upper sleeve, just missing her flesh. She fled.

Chi saw Sarah first. "He's got a weapon. Run!" Behind her, she heard the criminal curse as he crashed through the door. Then, Chi saw the police officer.

The cop grabbed his gun and aimed. "Freeze, punk!"

"Whoa! Don't shoot me again." The criminal skidded to a stop and raised his hands, cringing against the pain in his arms.

"Drop it or I'll drop you."

The scalpel hit the floor with a clank. The officer said over his shoulder to Chi and Sarah, "I'm sorry about this. He was whining about the pain so badly I guess I relaxed my watch. I only took my eyes off the room for less than a minute, and he disappeared. I didn't know the room had another exit."

"He needs to be cuffed until we can treat him," Chi said angrily. She could have been killed because of the officer's carelessness. She looked at the criminal with disgust. He didn't look so menacing without a weapon and in a brightly lit room. "This time, I'll have the sharp scalpel. Let's see how it makes you feel."

He smirked at her.

Chi didn't care. "Sarah, let's get to work."

Chi couldn't believe what had just happened. When the scalpel cut through the air, she didn't believe she was going to get out of its way in time.

I was lucky, Chi thought.

CHAPTER
Seventeen

"You look great," Parker said when Chi opened her front door. "Ready to go?"

"Yes," she grabbed her purse off the sofa as Parker stood in the doorway. She didn't feel at all underdressed with her peach shorts and matching blouse because Parker wore shorts and a pullover shirt. "Are you going to tell me where we're going?"

"You'll see."

Parker carefully backed the car out of the parking space. The evening sky blanketed the open roof of the car. He drove slowly through the apartment complex until he reached the small park at the back of the property.

As Parker pulled off the road into a grassy clearing, Chi looked at him. "Are we here?" she asked jokingly, knowing Parker was too old to take her "necking" in a dark lot. The last time she had done that, she was a teenager.

"Yes."

"We're nowhere," she corrected.

"We're here."

She laughed, hard and loud. Looking at him with humor tearing her eyes, Chi said, "We're still at my complex."

"Yeah." Parker reached down and pulled the release for the trunk.

"You forgot where we're going?"

Parker figured he would have the last laugh on this. Getting out of the car, he closed the door on her laughter. He reached into the trunk and pulled out three tall citronella stick lanterns, a picnic basket, AND several blankets. He heard rather than saw Chi getting out of the car. She was still snickering.

When Chi rounded the back of the car, she sobered instantly. "What's all this?"

"You'll see." He handed her the blankets. "Bring these." Parker walked toward the field as Chi followed in bafflement.

He planted the first insect-repellent stick in the grass and lit it. The lantern cast a dim light on the area. He repeated the task with the other two. "These should keep the bugs away." He took one of the blankets from her and laid it on the ground between the lanterns. He knelt on the blanket, using his phone to find classic soul music to play. Reaching into the picnic basket, produced an unsliced loaf of freshly baked bread, a chunk of cheese and meat, a container of sliced fresh fruit, two wine glasses, and a bottle of wine. "Here," he said, handing her a smaller bottle. "You might want to put on some bug repellent."

Chi just looked at him in astonishment. He had thought of everything. This was more enjoyable than anything she'd thought they might be doing tonight. "Nice date idea." Her voice was laced with surprise and appreciation.

"Join me," he said softly.

Chi sat on the blanket as he poured her a glass of wine. "A late evening picnic. This is different and rather romantic," she said with a grin.

"Thank Mom. I wanted to do something completely relaxing."

"Harriett suggested a picnic?" Chi asked.

"No. She suggested dinner at an outdoor restaurant. Luckily she's my mother, or else I might have thrown her out of my house for such a ridiculous suggestion. I own a restaurant!"

She scooted closer, then leaned forward and kissed him passionately. "Parker," she whispered as she kissed the side of his mouth.

"Yes?"

"I love the way you entertain me. I enjoy you." She kissed his neck.

"I enjoy you, too," he said.

"Why?" Chi asked, looking into his eyes.

"Because I remember the 'good' when I'm with you." He was looking off into the distance when he said that but turned back to her. "You make me believe again."

That statement touched her heart. Chi would not have been so moved if Sarah had not told her about Parker's past. "Believe in what, Parker?"

"In me."

They fell silent, just staring at each other.

Parker leaned over and rubbed his lips from side to side against hers. Then he kissed her softly.

That was more than Chi had expected to hear or feel. She wasn't sure if she was prepared to deal with the raw emotions welling inside her.

"Are we getting serious now?" he asked, based on her expression.

"You're always giving to me," she said. "Making me smile. Showing me a fun time. I'm touched."

"Good." Parker reached into the basket and pulled out an envelope. "This is for you."

Taking it, Chi asked. "What is it?"

"Something… fun."

She carefully positioned her wineglass so that it wouldn't tip over. The soft glow from the candles provided just enough light to read the pamphlet she pulled out of the envelope. "This is a cruise brochure." She read the destination, "to Barbados!" She looked up quickly. "For us?" When he nodded, she asked again, overwhelmed, "You and me?"

Parker smiled at her. "Yeah. At least, I hope so."

"When were you thinking about going?"

"I haven't figured that out yet. How about as soon as your schedule allows."

She sat there staring into his warm eyes, always comforting, always penetrating. If the eyes were the mirrors to the soul, his were erotically appealing and profoundly explicit. In them, she saw a man who was centered in his identity and didn't mind showing the world that he was. She wished she could be like that and replicate that part of him in her own life. But she had doubts about herself at times. Her world wasn't as solid when it came to relationships.

Yet more importantly, she had also seen his willingness to show his vulnerability. She could see the pain that sometimes illuminated his eyes. Even when he smiled, she sometimes saw it. Not many people would have noticed it. But she had learned to identify it, relate to it, and wanted to cure it not knowing what it was until she had talked with Sarah. Now, she knew that it was: sadness from guilt.

What else was in his engaging stare, she wondered. Could it be trust? Could she trust him with her feelings? With her heart? With the problems?

Maybe the dim lighting made it difficult to tell. She didn't know, but she had doubts. "Oh, Parker, this is too much."

"It's a trip that will allow us to get away for a week. To enjoy each other. Just fun. And just us."

It was time to talk. Remove her final doubt. "I want you to know more about me. And I about you." *But not on a ship hundreds of miles away from home,* she thought to herself.

Parker was about to make light of her statement, but her tone and serious look stopped him. "I take it, you want to talk about something." He hoped she didn't want to talk about the incident with Marcus.

"I'm so scared I'm not going to get to see Anthony grow up. That I might lose him."

"I can understand that. I know the fear of loss very well."

Yes, Parker, you do. "Are you talking about Cynthia?" Chi asked, hoping to make him open up to her.

"Yeah," he said quietly. "But I'm healed."

She didn't think he was. She stroked his chest. "Time does that."

"Time," he gently touched that hand rubbing his heart, "and second chances." There was a longing and need in his statement that was amplified in his gaze.

Chi smiled warmly, allowing his openness and the raw look in his eyes to motivate her to ask, "What's the most important thing in a relationship to you?"

"Great sex." He kissed that hand. "Willingness to enjoy each other. Great sex," he said again.

"I think you mentioned that."

"But did I mention the 'great' part?"

She smiled, and he continued.

"And trust." It was blunt and to the point.

That jabbed her like a knife. To Chi, trust meant honesty, and she hadn't been honest with him. They both had secrets, but at least his secrets weren't the kind that walked up and caused problems. Douglas had called her today and left a message to call him.

When she had gotten home after work, her mother had called wanting to know when she was going to contact Douglas.

Too many problems, too many secrets.

Parker reached around her waist and leaned forward to nibble on her lips, cheek, and ear. "Give me that, and I'm happy."

"I want you to be able to trust me," Chi said. It was time to tell him about Douglas, her mother, and her fears. That might give him reason to trust her enough to talk about Cynthia. She didn't want to force him to talk about it. She could start by telling him she already knew, but that was forced.

Their relationship was good, but it didn't deal with all the real problems in their lives. Didn't being with someone include sharing the good and the bad? Sharing failed dreams, real pains, and unshattered fears. Showing and giving a person to want to open up and talk without having remorse. Creating a haven for each other.

Was she ready? Was he?

Chi felt his arms tighten around her waist and she winced. "Parker, not too much pressure on my injured side."

Parker loosened his hold. "I'm sorry. What happened?"

"I fought with a machine and lost," Chi explained.

"Pick on something your size the next time."

"Actually, if not for the criminal hiding in the closet, I wouldn't have had to fight at all."

He stopped laughing. "What are you talking about?"

Chi explained the incident at the hospital.

"You're kidding, right?" he asked worriedly.

Chi turned, placing her back against his chest. It took some of the pressure off her injured side.

"Nope. I'm serious. The police got back before anything happened."

"I guess that classifies it as a big day at the office," he said. "But I would think they'd take precautions against arrested criminals running loose in hospitals."

"Don't worry. They do. This wasn't any big deal. And I'm fine." Chi wanted to get back to their earlier conversation. "Let's talk about us again."

"That's a better topic." Parker sat up and reached for the bread. "Mom baked this for us." He reached back into the basket. "Let me get the knife to slice it. Want some?"

She looked over at him. "A small piece," Chi said.

He sliced two pieces, gave her one, and lay next to her. "You were talking about us," he said.

They were talking about untouched territory for them both, she thought. She would broach the discovery now. "I need to share something about myself. About my son's father."

He didn't say anything.

"I hadn't seen Douglas in years, but now he's back. He was the first man I truly cared about. I guess it was love. And I wanted to prove it to him."

This was harder than she realized. Chi sat up and reached for her glass of wine, slightly embarrassed that her past actions still bothered her. A lot of pain and disappointment could have been avoided if she had made better decisions. "I knew I had the sickle cell trait and never told him."

"You only have a trait."

"So does Douglas," she said. "That's why Anthony is suffering. Our two traits made a whole one in him. After he found out I was pregnant and a trait carrier, he left us. He unexpectedly came back several weeks ago, offering financial support."

"I read a little about this. It seems the financial and emotional devastation on a family could be as devastating as the disease itself."

Chi realized this was the opening she needed to finish her story. The story about Douglas, the absentee father, teaming up with her controlling mother to use their financial situation as a weapon to force her into agreeing.

Too much…it's just too much to share, she thought.

She was getting more nervous and needed to do something to keep her hands busy. She reached for the cheese and knife, then recalled her attack at the hospital. She hadn't told Parker about the scalpel. Maybe because she wanted to limit the bad.

Trust.

She had to stop keeping her fears and the bad things a secret. Not wanting those she cared about to know of pain was a problem she had most of her life. But friendships required sharing both, she decided.

Holding up the knife, she said lightly, attempting to play down the situation, "This reminds me of the little episode at the hospital."

"How so?" he said.

"He had a scalpel. Can you believe he swung at me with it? Luckily, he missed, but in the darkness, the scalpel looked pretty menacing." Chi took a bite of cheese and bread before continuing; her nervousness was subsiding.

It was because Parker was listening and not judging. She watched him lie on his back looking up at the stars. "But I keep forgetting, I wanted to talk about us." She watched him stand and look out into the distance. She recognized his behavior. He was walking away to gather his thoughts. He had done that when she had told him about Anthony's illness.

Chi thought of the easiest way to finish her story. There wasn't one, so she got to the point. "Mama was right when she accused me of being a fool for Douglas. I got pregnant to keep him. It was stupid. And Mama has been holding her disappointment against me ever since. I think I have a way now to correct all my past mistakes. Douglas can help. He told me he's moving to Atlanta. He says we should share custody of Anthony."

"Chi, were there flashing lights in the room?"

Taken aback, it took Chi a moment to catch on. "With the criminal? Yes," she said uneasily, "in a way. The equipment has red lights and makes all sorts of beeping sounds, too."

She was telling him about his nightmare! Parker thought. It was happening again! He'd had a premonition about her, just as he had about Cynthia!

Parker heard very little of what Chi said after that. If this was his nightmare, she would end up dying. And soon.

No! his mind screamed. *Not again!* "Please tell me that didn't happen, Chi!" Parker was asking about the attack, but Chi interpreted it to be about the statement she just made about Douglas and his plan for them to share Anthony after he moved to Atlanta.

"Yes, it did," Chi said reluctantly. She stood and faced him, seeing pain, apprehension, and dread on his face.

I've said too much! she thought. I shouldn't have said anything about Douglas until I worked out all the details. "I'm just trying to find a way to have my son with me."

Parker looked up to the darkened heavens. The navy sky blanketed with stars hid what he wanted to see. Was God looking down and laughing at the fact that Parker was in so much pain? Was *He* playing a cruel joke on him? In the nightmare, Parker had seen himself watching the woman he wanted to love and the son he wanted to help raise taken away from him.

Just then he admitted the truth to himself. He was falling in love with Chi. And it would hurt immeasurably when he lost her.

"Maybe I shouldn't have said anything," Chi said sadly, fearful of what Parker was thinking. Maybe she should have left her secrets in the private corners of her inner world.

Why is this happening to me? I can't watch someone else I care about die! Parker was caught up in a world of disbelief. He hadn't heard much of what Chi had said in the past few minutes.

Chi was talking about Anthony's father wanting to move to Atlanta to be near her. "Parker, I don't know how to say this. I was afraid to tell you before." She stood and walked toward him.

"You should have been afraid." Parker finally said, listening to Chi again. "I knew I shouldn't have done this again. Fall for you. Want to love you," Parker said.

The statement was so powerful it almost made her stumble. "And..." Chi held out her arms. "I want that too."

Then Parker remembered that Anthony was crying in his dream. It was probably because Anthony had lost his mother, Parker concluded. Then he remembered seeing himself in the dream. Something about a car, no, a truck accident. He'd watched it happen. Just like he'd seen himself with Cynthia. That meant he would be there when it happened to Chi. "No," he said to that awful thought. As long as he was around Chi, she was at risk. "Chi, we can't do this."

"Parker?" Chi whispered as tears welled up in her eyes.

In his mind, Parker was organizing more of the nebulous and incoherent pieces of his nightmare. Looking around, he realized it was dark and murky, as in the dream. Was it going to happen tonight? Was her mentioning the one part of his nightmare he just recalled some twisted spiritual warning? He had to get out of here. Get away from Chi.

He abruptly backed away from her. "Chi, this is wrong. We can't be together."

"Parker, please, don't hold the past against me."

He stared at her. *How did she know!* How did she know about his past? Mom? Pats?

"I can't go through this," he said. "I can't be with you knowing what I know."

"Why can't we..."

Parker interrupted. "I must think about this! Something's wrong with this." He shouldn't be yelling at her, it was making her cry, but he needed to make her understand. "Chi, I don't want to hurt you…" he ended lamely, as anguished tears wet her cheeks.

She knew he would never forgive, never understand. If he didn't understand, no man would. She should have left her secrets in the deep, dark, ugly corners of her past. They were like cancer eating away at the healthy and wholesome aspects of her life. She shouldn't have said anything, but she thought he would understand and accept her despite her flaws. Now, all was lost, he was leaving her. "I thought you would understand…"

He shook his head before saying, "No. I don't want to deal with this right now."

Even before Parker voiced the words, she knew what he was going to say. She stood there waiting for him to reject her.

He was saying, "Let me take you home. I think we shouldn't see each other for a while."

Heartbroken and defeated, she managed to straighten her spine. "Don't worry. I'll walk." She knew better than anyone did that they would never see each other again. After retrieving her purse, she headed down the dim path toward her apartment.

Through tear-filled eyes, the brilliant stars ran together into a dull, unclear cluster of misery.

THE RYAN FAMILY

CHAPTER Eighteen

Harriett watched her only son stalk by her and around the corner leading to his bedroom. "Hello, Parker," she said to his retreating back.

"Hi and good night, Mom. I'm tired and headed to bed."

Parker was in a bad mood again. The last time she saw her son smile was the night she helped him pack a picnic basket for a date with Chi over a week ago. She had baked bread for him to take. If his mood since then was any indication of how well that evening had gone, it must have been a miserable experience.

"Good night, Son."

Harriett reached for her smartphone. She worriedly explained to Patricia the recent change in Parker's behavior and how she felt about the saga of his life that was unfolding before her eyes.

"Momma, are you sure?"

"Your brother's spirits are in the dumps. He was on the road to becoming the old Parker again. Like he was before Cynthia died." Harriett exhaled miserably. "But I think something is wrong between him and Chi. Whenever I mention her name, he changes the subject. My next checkup isn't until next week, so it would be too obvious to just call her without reason and ask her directly. He's been like this all week. What can we do?"

Patricia looked over her shoulder at her husband, Mac, who was sitting on the patio entertaining their daughter. Patricia considered posing the question to him but knew Mac would only warn her to stay out of Parker's affairs.

The last few months had been the first time in a long time she had seen her brother content and truly enjoying himself. Chi had brought that about. If her mother was correct, something bad had happened between Chi and Parker, and he wasn't handling it well.

"If they argued, let's hope they'll have resolved it by the time I get there this weekend. Or else I'll try to get him to talk to me."

"He looks so depressed, Patricia. I'm worried."

"I know, Momma. Just do what you can to keep his spirits up." Patricia said.

"He's very distant. Rarely talks to me. And only comes home at very late hours, if at all. Like he's avoiding me."

"Don't worry too much. I'll talk to him about all of this."

"Tell Mac and Courtney that I send my love."

"I will. Love you, bye." Patricia hung up the phone.

"Momma say hello."

Mac, seeing the worried expression on his wife's face, asked, "Baby, is something wrong?"

"Parker and Chi are having problems. It's upsetting Momma."

"If you are worried about Harriett, why don't you fly to Atlanta tomorrow and stay through the weekend?"

"I'm more worried about Parker. You never had a chance to spend a lot of time with him before Cynthia died. You don't know the old Parker. He was becoming his happy-go-lucky self again. I know it was because of Chi. He had become so reckless and careless after Cynthia's death. If it hadn't been for the opening of the second restaurant to keep him busy, I'm not sure if he'd be here today. He was so depressed and bitter. He blamed himself. I think he still does. Since Chi came along, though, he's been the old Parker again. I hope things aren't over between them."

As Mac balanced his daughter in one arm, he caressed Patricia's cheek with his free hand. His thumb rubbed across a worried brow. He leaned forward and kissed that brow. Mac didn't think it was any of Patricia's business, but he remembered the misery he had gone through when she left him. If he could help save Parker from that grim experience, then so be it.

His whisper was deep and comforting, "I'll call Mrs. Williams to come over and stay the week. She would love it now that her grandchildren have moved away. I'll have her watch Courtney while you're in Atlanta. You can fly there tomorrow."

Patricia linked her arms around her husband. She had been lucky to find a man so wonderful. Always supportive, always understanding. She knew her brother could be the kind of husband Mac was if he found the right woman.

Parker would resent her interfering, but if there was something she could do to help save her brother from falling back into that miserable existence, she would.

Patricia hated not being able to see her daughter for days, but it was better to leave Courtney in the comforts of someone else's care, while she helped her brother.

THE NEXT EVENING, PATRICIA PULLED THE RENTAL CAR INTO PARKer's driveway. Her mother had left the lights on for her. According to Harriett, Parker wasn't coming home most nights. He might not be home tonight, but she would wait for him.

Patricia had called him to ask if he could pick her up from the airport, but he claimed the restaurant needed his attention, and he couldn't come to get her. Another sign of the destructive behavior: avoiding family.

The front door of Parker's house opened as Patricia neared it. "Hi, Momma," Patricia bent over to hug her mother seated in the wheelchair. "I'm sorry, I got here so late."

"I'm just glad you came as soon as you did. Haven't seen Parker yet. He knows you're coming tonight. Claims he's busy."

"That's not like Parker," Patricia said, attempting to hide her concern.

"I told you he hasn't been himself," Harriet confirmed.

Patricia didn't think it had gotten to this point so soon. If Parker was avoiding those who loved him, he was avoiding Chi. What could have happened to destroy their relationship so quickly?

Patricia could see the anxiety behind her mother's typically comforting eyes. "He's throwing himself into his work?"

"I don't think so. I called the restaurant, he's not there."

Patricia set down her luggage and turned to push her mother's wheelchair into the kitchen. "Let's make some tea."

Over tea, Harriett told Patricia that Parker began avoiding her when she started asking about Chi and the change in his behavior. Patricia promised her mother she would get to the bottom of it. If nothing else, she would approach Chi.

"Parker will never forgive us if we go behind his back and speak to Chi," Harriett said.

"The way Parker's acting, he'll be lucky if *we* forgive him," Patricia said. "You head on to bed, Momma. I'll leave Parker a note to wake me when he gets home."

"*If* he comes home."

After helping Harriett to her room, Patricia went to Parker's room to leave him the note. At the very least, Parker should be watching Momma, she thought. That's why their mother was staying with him in the first place.

Entering Parker's room, Patricia felt along the wall for the light switch. To her surprise, the room was clean. The last time he'd been depressed, he'd paid little attention to his surroundings. Momma did this, she thought. At the dresser, she found a pen. She looked about for something to write on. Shredded papers near the end of the dresser caught her eye. The print on the paper reminded her of something familiar. Curiosity led her to rearrange the torn pieces of paper so that she could read it.

A Barbados trip!

Patricia recalled a conversation she had with her brother about romantic places to visit. Parker had said, "The Ivory Coast of Africa at any time, any tropical island but particularly the Cayman Islands, Tahiti, and Barbados."

Either Chi had refused to go, or he changed his mind about taking her. Either way, it was proof of a problem.

Patricia straightened. "What's going on?" she whispered. What had turned Parker away from Chi? If Parker was miserable, how was Chi feeling?

"What the hell are you doing!"

Patricia whipped around and saw an angry Parker standing in the doorway. Her first inclination was to ask him that same question in the exact menacing tone that he used, but she stopped herself. He was in pain. He needed understanding.

"I was about to write you a note asking you to wake me when you got home." She headed toward Parker, and he moved away toward his bed.

"It's late, Pats. I'm tired. Make it quick. What did you want to talk to me about?"

She walked toward him again. The smell of alcohol mixed with a woman's cologne almost made her sick. He's drunk, she thought. She ignored his tone, his intoxication, and the reek of cheap cologne. She recognized the smell but couldn't place it. Chi didn't wear it, she knew. It had to be another woman's cologne. Why did men turn to other women when they had relationship problems? She would broach that discussion later, but for now, she couldn't attack. It would get her nowhere. His attitude and behavior were a defense mechanism.

Getting to her immediate point, and one that Parker would respond to more civilly, she said, "Momma's worried about you."

"*Momma*," he said mockingly, "should be concerned about herself."

Maybe not, Patricia thought. He was hurting and wanted everyone around him to feel it. "Parker, it's obvious something is wrong. We just want to help. What's wrong?"

Go away, Pats. I don't want to talk about it, he thought to himself before saying aloud, "You can help by letting me sleep." His patience was running out, mostly because of a cognac-induced disposition. "Keep standing there, and you'll get to watch me undress." He snatched off his jacket and tossed it into the chair next to the bed.

"Don't take your anger out of me," Patricia said patiently.

"Understand this. I'm tired. I'm drunk. I've had a rough day. The drive home was the pits. The weather's hot. And I just want to sleep, but *someone* won't let me." Parker's speech, although flimsy and meaningless, got more offensive in tone with each word.

Patricia wasn't letting him run her off. She knew he didn't want to deal with the issue. Based on his angry tone and actions, she also knew it was better to leave him alone. But if she did, she suspected he would leave before morning and not return until she had left for Florida.

She would just have to take his foul attitude. She wasn't leaving until she got Parker's side of the story. It involved Chi, and she wasn't going to talk to Chi until she knew what was going on with her brother.

Since Parker was getting angrier by the second, Patricia decided to get to the point. If he was going to explode, she might as well get it over with. She watched him fight to unbutton his shirt. "I noticed you and Chi aren't going to Barbados. Is she the reason for this nasty attitude of yours?"

Glaring at her, he asked, "Did Chi tell you that?"

"Your actions told me that. Plus, I saw the torn brochure on your dresser." Patricia tilted her head towards the dresser.

He looked over at the brochure that had previously been a pile of ripped-up pieces of paper that now were reassembled back, like a jigsaw puzzle, into its original form. That caused a disapproving grunt from him.

Nosy! he thought. *My damn sister is just too damn nosy!*

He stormed over to the dresser and snatched up the pieces of paper. Then, he strode across the bedroom, down the small closet-lined hall into the master bath, and threw the papers into the trash can.

"Mind your own damn business!" he shouted from the bathroom, then slammed the door. The five-too-many glasses of alcohol were taking their toll; he had to use the bathroom too. Hopefully, his sister would hear him relieving himself and go away.

Parker washed his hands and splashed cold water on his face. He needed a bath but didn't feel like it. He would crash and shower in the morning. Looking in the mirror, watching his drunken gaze attempt to focus, he cursed his image silently.

Disgusted with both his reflection and guilt, he stormed out of the bathroom. He didn't like looking at himself. It reminded him of all the mistakes he had made in life. As he emerged into his bedroom, he was relieved to see Patricia wasn't there. He sent up a prayer to whatever so-called God who took on the role of making his life miserable. "Thanks, for nothing."

"You're welcome," Patricia responded from the corner on the other side of his bed.

Parker swung around. That was what he got for wishing and praying. The same as always, nothing he wanted. "Damn." *Go away. Just go away.* "I was hoping you were gone. No matter. You can watch me sleep." He sat on the side of the bed and began removing his boots.

"What happened between you and Chi?" Patricia asked quietly.

"Nothing," he said flatly.

"Why aren't you two seeing each other?"

"Because we don't want to."

"If that's the case, why are you so bitter now that you aren't seeing her?"

"I'm not bitter."

"Yes, you are!" Patricia was tired of talking to his back. She rounded the bed and stood in front of him. "You're angry. You're argumentative. You're drinking too much. You smell like cheap perfume which means you're screwing around."

Patricia looked into bloodshot eyes. "You're wallowing in self-pity. Nothing can be this bad, Parker. Life's too short to waste away in misery," she pointed to him, "like this."

Parker sat staring down at his boots and socks littering the carpet in front of him. He stood. His words came out like rattlesnake venom. "You can take that dime's worth of psychology and shove it. Do you think you know all about me? About life! *You*," he pointed a finger toward her, "don't know one damn thing about my situation!" As he spoke, his tone got louder, and his arms became expressive.

Patricia had never seen her brother act like this. Fear told her to run, and get out of his way. But he was drunk and in pain. She stood perfectly ill, allowing him to continue to spew vile statements at her and about himself. He was like a wounded animal cornered and trying to escape from pain but not knowing how. She bit back her fear and struggled not to cry. Seeing him hurting this badly made her agonize for him.

"How in *the hell* can you talk to me about life?" Parker shouted. "Everything I've ever wanted, I've lost. You haven't! Don't expect me to be happy just because you are. Screw happiness..." He continued to derail himself.

Unshed tears covered his bloodshot eyes.

Oh my God, Parker. I didn't know you hurt this much. I just didn't know. I'm sorry. I'm sorry. I should have been here for you sooner. You hid your pain so well.

When his shouts dwindled to dejected statements of woe, she finally said, "I'm so sorry."

He was completely dispirited as he sat back on the bed. "I just don't understand how some people get everything they want in life. Everything handed to them."

He sounded as though he wanted to just give up. She couldn't let that happen. Life was what you made it, and he was making a mistake by not trying. "Parker, you've gotten most of what you went after. So, I guess you must be talking about Chi?"

"We can't be together anymore."

"Did you tell her why?" Patricia asked.

"Drop it, okay?" he yelled. "I just can't, Pats."

"Why not?"

When Parker stormed by Patricia and closed his bedroom door, Patricia concluded he didn't want their mother to overhear.

"It's over between us," he said flatly. "So just drop it!"

"Is this why you're acting this way?" To his stare, she added, "Is this what not having her is doing to you?" She pleaded, "Please tell me what happened."

"I'm tired, and I don't want to talk about it."

"Tell me!" She would listen to every word and respond with understanding. "It can't be that bad, can it?"

His eyes pierced her. Parker moved to open his room door. "Get out!"

CHAPTER Nineteen

It had been nine days since Parker had rejected her. Chi had not heard from him, nor did she expect to. Chi stood at the bottom of the stairwell that led to her small, lonely apartment, dreading the night that lay ahead. Being alone meant having to ponder the misery of her life. At work, she had patients who wanted and needed her. She could bathe herself in their need and wash away her own emptiness and pain. During the weekend, she could be with her son, who truly loved and cherished her. Every moment with him replenished the void in her heart. Here, at home though, she couldn't escape the truth. No one was there inside her apartment to love her. And no one wanted to be.

Every step she took seemed to sap her energy and kick her spirits a little harder. Home, the place that once provided tranquility, had become instead a place of torment. She had been so involved with mastering her medical skills that building relationships with other people hadn't been as important. Maybe if she had made more friends, she could depend on them to help her through her time of loneliness.

It was Thursday night. At least, she would not have to be there tomorrow night. When tomorrow came, she would be with her son.

Inserting the key, she opened the door and entered the dark apartment. So much of the room resembled her mood: dark, lonely, lacking life. Walking deeper into the pit of darkness, Chi picked up her iPhone, thinking of calling Sarah. She noticed multiple missed messages appear. The first was from a number she did not recognize.

As Chi removed her lab coat, she found herself straining to hear as the message played.

What? she thought.

She pressed the replay code. There was silence for long seconds followed by the rustling of papers. A long, deep exhale. Then nothing. She replayed the message. Then again. Before she knew it, she whispered, "Parker, is that you?"

Not a word was uttered. She heard a deep sigh that reminded her of the sounds Parker made when he placed his mouth to her ear. Memories of the night they made love on her porch flooded her mind.

She replayed it again.

Then she turned and headed for the porch. Opening the patio door sparked a swirl of emotions: the serenity the porch offered, the ecstasy of when Parker had made love to her there, and the pain of Parker's rejection in the park below it.

Peaceful thoughts were elusive of late. Just painful ones. Sitting down in the chair, she listened to the sounds of the night; watched a navy sky bedazzled by brilliant twinkles; smelled the hint of wilderness from bark, leaves, and grass; and tried to enjoy the warm caress of the breeze on her skin. These small treasures were reminders that something more powerful often blessed the world. At least, she had that to hold onto.

But it wasn't enough. It wasn't what she wanted. Chi wrapped her arms around her waist and leaned her head back against the chair. She thought about the recorded message. "Oh, Parker."

Before she could enmesh herself in the pleasing thoughts that followed the uttering of his name, her iPhone rang. She bolted from the chair. *Maybe he was calling back.*

She smiled at the number. A rustling sound followed by silence.

"Hello," a soft voice, a child, said. "Mommy?"

"Anthony," Chi brightened somewhat.

"Hi, Mommy. Grandma said I could call to say good night."

"I'm glad you did," Chi said. "How was your day?"

"Okay, fine," Anthony explained. "I got some more toys from Mr. Douglas. He says I can start calling him 'Daddy' if it is okay with you."

Douglas was entangling himself into her son's life. "I'll talk to Mr. Douglas. Remember to say your prayers tonight and to brush your teeth."

"Okay. I will. Grandma wants to know what time you will be here tomorrow."

"Around seven." Chi heard Anthony relay the message.

After saying good night to Anthony, Chi hung up the phone. Rubbing her fingers across it, she whispered, "Let it have been you, Parker." It had to be him calling. She needed it to be him calling. "Please come back…forgive me."

She once more wrapped her arms around her waist and rocked gently. She needed to be in more pleasant surroundings. As she reached the patio doorway, she looked back over at her phone and willed it to ring again.

It didn't.

Chi returned to the porch. After about thirty minutes, she decided to take an active role in improving her disposition. She couldn't wallow in her misery forever. Getting up out of the chair, she reached for her phone.

"Hello?"

"Hi, Sarah. I hope I haven't called at a bad time."

"Of course, not. Just pouring myself a glass of wine."

Sarah, her closest friend, could help her. She needed to be with someone now. "Feel like company?"

Sarah heard something like depression in the request. Wineglass suspended in air; she considered the reasons for it. "What's wrong?"

Chi paused to consider what excuse she could give. Considering the truth to be the best thing to say, she exhaled slowly. "It's over between Parker and me. I'm not handling it well."

Sarah's medical experience kicked in. Before she knew it, she was corking the bottle of wine and grabbing some stuffed mushrooms from the refrigerator. Chi probably hadn't eaten a thing, she figured. "We can finish this wine off together."

In less time than it should have taken for Sarah to drive over, there was a rap at Chi's door.

As Chi opened the door, Sarah rushed through carrying a grocery bag and a bottle of wine. "You got here fast," Chi said.

"I was half-packed before I hung up the phone. I brought dinner," she offered, heading for the kitchen. "Come on."

In the kitchen, Chi watched Sarah search the cabinets for the dishes and wine glasses she needed. As Chi was about to offer help, Sarah said, "Grab us some utensils."

A half-hour later, the living room table was littered with the remains of a meal and a half-empty bottle of wine. Chi sat Indian style on the floor as Sarah lounged comfortably on the sofa. The conversation had been neutral.

Sarah, reaching for another cracker, said philosophically, "Isn't it amazing how the human species has survived for so many years?"

"We've been here awhile," Chi offered, suspecting this was Sarah's way of broaching the topic they had been avoiding.

"Think about it. Life forms ranging from the smallest things such as bacteria to the largest of things like dinosaurs to…hell, whale sharks, have coexisted with humankind and through all of our evolutionary changes, *man* has made it through. Do you know why?"

Chi thought about it. "Because we can reason and rationalize?"

"You're a doctor. That's why you would say that. Men have made it this far because of *women*."

"Actually, I was going to say it was because humans had thumbs. Imagine how hard it would be to attempt to drink away your problems without thumbs to hold your glass."

Both laughed at the lameness of Chi's reason. It was the first good laugh for Chi since Parker left her.

Sarah watched several expressions wander across Chi's face after the laughter stopped. "It's because of thumbs and because women can overcome. We always do."

Chi brought the topic close to home. "I'm not sure if I'll get over Parker that easily though."

"You hide pain well, Chi. I don't know how I missed this last week. I think you'll get over him…just continue to fake until you make it. In time, you'll think differently."

"I never knew loving someone could hurt this much. When I lost my father, I was devastated." She tugged at her lower lip with her teeth. "I didn't think anything could hurt that badly again until Parker walked away from me."

"What happened between you two?" Sarah asked more softly. "I knew from Marcus that Parker was gun-shy with relationships, but you two seemed to be doing just fine. What went wrong?"

"I went wrong," Chi explained what had happened. "I guess I've always known that it would end between us. But we were so close to having something wonderful that I thought I should share my past with him."

"Let me get this right. You told him about Anthony and Douglas?"

"Yes."

"And he left you because of that?"

"Yes."

"I consider myself a great judge of character even though I'm a lousy one to make judgments since I only want superficial lovers, but I never would have imagined Parker to be so insensitive. I mean, good God, everybody makes mistakes."

"Mama was right."

"Why do you continue to allow your mother to run your life?" Sarah watched disagreement forming on Chi's face.

"Sarah, she needs me."

"Like a frog needs more warts. And you didn't answer my question." Sarah sat up. "She blames you for everything that has gone wrong in her life and yours. And sadly, you believe she's right. You have this big heart that you want to use to save everyone. And you want everyone to love it."

Chi didn't agree. "Mama has high expectations, and I let her down. She watched Daddy die and doesn't want to spend the rest of her life watching her grandson suffer."

"That's what I mean. Here you are working on becoming a successful doctor. You take care of her, your son, and two households, but Agnes still doesn't acknowledge your accomplishments. Or seem grateful."

Chi didn't want to discuss her mother's merits or lack thereof. She had enough misery in her life right now. She sat forward. "Sarah let's change the topic. I asked you over to nurse my broken heart. Parker caused that, not Mama."

"I disagree. Your mother has been telling you how difficult life will be with a sickly child and how people won't accept you for it.

So, the minute there's strife in your relationship, you accept it. No questions asked."

"I tried to explain to Parker. He wouldn't listen."

"So, try, try again," Sarah said softly before taking another sip of wine. "Based on everything you've said, I'm surprised you've given up so easily. Chi, you allowed him to walk away without ever asking for an explanation. Especially knowing how he avoids painful discussions. And the only excuse you have is that your mother said it would happen. Who made her the expert?"

Chi became defensive. "That's not true." She stood up.

"Okay, then explain to me how a man who pursued you as hard as Parker did would stop all of a sudden."

Chi's eyes began to mist.

Sarah didn't let that stop her. "A few days ago, I got a call at the hospital. It was a man. He asked if you were on duty. He didn't want to page you. When I suggested he leave a message, he refused and hung up. It was Parker. I know his voice, Chi. If your suspicions are right about the strange call you got tonight, then I think Parker wants to talk to you."

"You're guessing, Sarah."

"And you're being stubborn." Sarah was angry now, "I can't believe the two of you are afraid to mend whatever's wrong between you. Chi, call him."

Chi contemplated that. Could Sarah be right? But why the calls without the messages? She watched Sarah move to sit next to her. As Sarah opened her arms, Chi leaned into them. It was comforting, providing much-needed strength.

"Thanks, Sarah," Chi whispered.

"Chi, he told you he was falling in love with you. Something powerful is keeping him away. And forgive me, but I don't think it's Douglas. You owe it to yourself to make sure." Sarah blinked back tears. Good gracious, she was acting like an emotional teenager, she thought.

"Okay."

Sarah leaned back and looked at Chi through a blurry gaze. "I didn't mean to be hard on you. Chi, my relationship with my ex-husband would have lasted if we had communicated more. Prove me right about you and Parker."

"Okay," was all Chi said.

Sarah wasn't sure if she would ever call Parker. Determined not to be pushy about the issue, she said, "Let's clean up dinner and go for a walk. I think the exercise would be good for both my hips and your heart."

SARAH WAS RIGHT, CHI DECIDED.

Pulling into the side parking lot of Parker's Place, she turned off the ignition and gathered up her vanishing bravery. The last time she chased after a man, it had proved devastatingly wrong. But she had fought several personal demons over the past month and was getting good at overcoming them. Chi felt she owed it to herself to remove the remaining demon of doubt keeping her away from Parker.

She had left the hospital early to give herself extra time to be with Parker before she made the Friday drive to Macon. If things went her way, by this weekend, she and Parker would be in bed enjoying each other's company and discussing ways to make sure they could continue to.

Chi had called earlier, but when he didn't return her call, she decided on the direct approach. The closer she got to the entrance, the more confident she became. She would mend this piece of her fragmented life as well.

"Hi, Kevin," Chi said, walking up to the bar.

"Hi." Kevin smiled brightly, removing his apron. "This is a surprise. Parker typically tells me when you're coming by."

Kevin didn't know about their breakup. "I'm surprising him tonight."

"I love it when my woman surprises me," Kevin winked. "I'm leaving now to go see Annie."

"Do you know where I can find Parker?"

"No. I haven't seen him since lunch. He's been locking himself in his office. The man's working too hard. Been that way lately. Try looking for him there."

"Have a great night," Chi said, getting off the barstool.

"I'm planning on it." Kevin winked again.

Outside Parker's office, Chi took several deep breaths. She placed the palms of her hands against the door. *I can do this*, she told herself.

Chi planted an inviting smile on her face and opened the office door. She stopped cold, trying in vain to figure out how to best excuse herself for the intrusion. Since Sheila was wrapped in a close embrace with the man Chi loved, she had no idea of what to say. Sheila smiled back at Chi before closing her eyes and kissing Parker.

They were still that way when Chi turned and stalked away.

If someone had chosen that exact moment to punch her in the stomach, it wouldn't have felt half as bad as the stab she'd just taken to the heart. It was a struggle to keep her head and her chin up as she practically ran to her car, but she had.

It didn't take him long to forget me, Chi told herself. She willed herself not to cry, but trembling hands caused her to fight with the car keys. Frustration worsened her disposition and tears fell despite it all.

Parker didn't care about her.

THE RYAN FAMILY

CHAPTER
Twenty

"Patricia, it's because I don't give a damn!" Parker said.

"Yes, you do!"

"I've got to go," he said.

"Parker, you never go into the restaurant on Sundays," Patricia said from the other side of the kitchen.

You've never been here on Sunday mornings just to harass me, he thought. "New brunch menu today. I want to be there to check out the crowd," Parker said, opening the refrigerator.

"Having a beer for breakfast?"

"Give it a rest, Pats."

"I was planning on leaving today, but maybe I should stay with Momma since you're working so hard."

"Bullshit," Parker corrected.

Patricia pleaded softly, "Parker, we've always been able to talk to each other about everything. If this wasn't worrying Momma, I wouldn't be dogging you."

"You're not going to let up, are you?" To her obstinate stare, he shook his head in disbelief. When his sister got this way, it was easier to just give in than argue for hours. She would never let up. Besides, he didn't have the energy to continue arguing with her.

"I'm not leaving until you open up to me." Patricia placed her hands on her hips and took on a stance of defiance.

"My business is growing." He went to the cabinet to get some chips.

"And?"

"And I don't have much time for something else."

"Including Chi?"

"Especially Chi."

"Parker, you two are good for each other. Why are you doing this? Is it because of her son's illness?"

"Of course, not. I'm crazy about Anthony." Parker sat at the kitchen table, and his sister joined him. "If I stay with her, something bad will happen."

"Are you talking about intentionally hurting her with your womanizing?"

"No!" he defended. "I wouldn't do that to her. She's too special."

Patricia contemplated that revelation. "So, Chi broke it off?"

"I called it off."

This was getting confusing. "Damn it, Parker, you're not making sense."

"As I said, I don't give a damn about your confusion over Chi and me. Believe me, when I tell you, it's over between us."

"You are not going to scare me off by getting angry," Patricia said. "So, talk to me."

Wanting to end the discussion and his frustration, Parker finally spoke about the root of his problem. "It's my fault Cynthia's dead. I don't want the same thing to happen to Chi."

Patricia sat dumbstruck. The man had to be even drunker than she thought. That was the most ridiculous statement she had ever heard. But, based on the serious look on Parker's face, he thought it a completely rational statement. Calmly and slowly, she asked, "Why do you think that?"

"Because I saw it."

Searching for an understanding she could not find, Patricia asked, "Please, explain that last statement to me."

Parker inhaled and exhaled. "I ran into Marcus."

"Marcus? The last time you saw him it got nasty. You punched the man at the funeral."

"I was angry. I know I was wrong about that," Parker said. "I didn't cause any problems this time, I'll tell you that whole story later, but seeing him a few weeks ago made me realize something."

"What?"

Rubbing his hands across his head, he added, "The visions." Seeing a look of confusion on her face, he tried to explain as best he could. "It doesn't make any sense. I have these crazy dreams. I don't know how to explain it. But I can somehow see death before it happens."

"I know you've always been able to sense pain with me and Momma. But what is this death thing you're talking about?"

"I somehow blocked out most of my memories about Cynthia's death. Especially the dreams I had before she died. But when I saw Marcus, the memories started to return."

"What does that have to do with Chi?" Patricia was completely confused.

"I didn't put two and two together until Chi told me about an incident that I'd dreamt beforehand. Only I'd seen myself in the dream. Watching her die." He took a longer gulp of beer. It wasn't strong enough. "I'm having them again. Just like before."

"Like when, Parker?"

"I've never told anyone this, but a week before Cynthia's death, I dreamt about it. I saw myself and Marcus watch Cynthia die. I didn't make the connection until Chi's dream. I never wanted to believe I had seen Cynthia die beforehand and didn't do anything about it. I guess that's why I still feel guilty about her death. Blaming Marcus was an easy out for me, too."

"How would you know something like that could be real?" Patricia asked. "You never had those types of visions with me and Momma."

"I think it's only for people that I'm in love with. The stronger my feelings for them, the greater the connection maybe? At least, that's the only thing I can come up with."

"Are you sure about the visions of Chi?"

"Everything she mentioned to me, I'd dreamt about. Maybe I only get visions about the death of someone I fall in love with. Or maybe it's because of me, that they die."

No wonder her brother was drinking so heavily. After hearing that statement, she needed a drink herself. And he needed a shrink! That was the most irrational thing he could have said to her. Either he was drunker than she thought, or Parker believed what he'd just said.

"I think I need a drink," she said wearily.

Patricia had seen many shows and read numerous articles on people having a psychic connection to others. She paid attention to those shows and articles because of the connection Parker had shown with her and their mother. But Patricia had never challenged her beliefs on the validity of such things. Patricia asked more for proof than for understanding. "What visions have you seen with Chi? How often? I mean, how do you know these visions are valid?"

Parker rubbed his hands up and down his face before leaning forward to rest his elbows on the table. "Just the one," he said with a rush. "It only began to make sense to me when Chi was attacked."

Concern registered. "Attacked? Is she okay?"

"Yes, yes." He recounted the disconcerting dream and actual attack. After watching his sister digest that, he compared it to the dream he had of Cynthia's accident.

"I don't understand why this caused you and Chi to break up. Are you embarrassed about this extra sense you have?"

"I dreamt of Chi dying in front of me, Pats," Parker said in frustration. "Knowing the other parts of the dream were real, then the death must be real, too. If I stay away from her, she'll be okay."

Patricia took a deep breath. This was bewildering to her. No wonder her brother was acting the way he was. How would she handle knowing someone she cared about was going to die? She, like a lot of people, had déjà vu, the sense of encountering something previously. But nothing as powerful as this!

"Couldn't Chi still be hit by the truck as you dreamt even if you aren't there?"

The nightmare he had of Cynthia's death flashed in his mind. He had awakened frightened for her and reached over and found Cynthia sleeping peacefully next to him. He had blocked that part out of his mind until the nightmare about Chi. Then, he thought of the dream of Chi, and it angered him. Could she still be killed?

"How should I know!" Parker spat out. "I don't know how this thing works. The only thing I know is that I witnessed it happening just as I did with Cynthia. That I *am* there. I figured as long as I'm not around, she'll be okay. I thought maybe *this time*... this time I could do something about it."

Patricia asked, "So, these visions only come as dreams? When was the first time you had these psychic dreams?"

"I don't know!" he spat angrily. Parker linked his fingers together and stared as if in deep thought. Hell, he really didn't know. He'd never thought about it. Then something came to him, remnants of thoughts long past surfaced. But it was so long ago. He looked up searchingly, dissecting his thoughts. Softly he said, looking at nothing in particular as the pictures played in his mind's eyes, "I remember when we were kids, I'd awaken thinking you and Mom had been crying. Then, I had found you in Mom's bed crying along with her. She did that a lot after my dad died and especially after yours left her. I used to wake up thinking that the sobs were what woke me, but sometimes I would wake up knowing you two were hurting even though I couldn't hear you cry. I saw myself coming to check on you in my dream. That's about as far as I can remember. Sometimes I've had flashes of images when I'm relaxed."

He sat there trying to think of other episodes or dreams. He pondered long, brows furrowed in concentration, but frustration came first, "Hell, I don't know," he stammered. "I can't remember."

Patricia processed that information. She stood and stared into the distance before turning back to him. "I don't know enough about this kind of thing to advise you on it, but I do know that you and Chi care deeply for each other. And if you left her without explaining your concerns, I can only imagine how hurt she must be. It must be painful for her not knowing what caused you to run off. She's probably blaming herself."

"I can't tell her this nonsense. It doesn't make any sense. Not even to me," Parker said.

Patricia walked to the sink and stared out the window above it. This wasn't something she could help her brother with after all. She could only be a sounding board, but she wanted to share one last thought.

"Parker, I see things a little differently than you do. I know you don't know enough about these visions to determine exactly what they can or can't do for you. But the way I see it…," Patricia looked lovingly at her brother who sat looking partly drunk, partly beleaguered, and said, "You can let them corrupt your life like they're doing now, or you can use them to better control your life."

"How?" he sounded hopeful.

"It's true you saw Cynthia die before it happened and couldn't stop it. So, you feel responsible. But Chi's alive, and you're alive. And being without her is killing you, and I suspect it's doing the same to her. You need each other. You care about each other. We can't control what's planned for any of us. So, you shouldn't feel responsible for the outcome. What you *can* do, though, is enjoy life to its fullest. You've been given a chance to do that with Chi. I can't remember ever seeing you as happy as I've seen you with Chi."

As Parker sat listening to his sister's speech, he couldn't help appreciating her openness. She had always been there for him. "Thanks, Pats."

She smiled warmly, "One other thing. If you can foresee things, maybe you can use that to control the outcome."

"How?"

"Use that smart brain of yours. If you've seen what will lead to Chi's accident, maybe you can use that knowledge to change the outcome." Patricia walked away. "I'm going to check on Momma."

The feelings of impending doom about Chi had subsided. He had assumed those premonitions had diminished because he wasn't around her. Now his sister had just asked him to think about seeing her again. Could he do it, knowing what might happen to her?

All Parker wanted in life was an education, a successful business, some good friends, close ties with his small family, and to start a family of his own. He had accomplished all except the latter. And every time he got close to it, life snatched it away from him. Maybe it was meant to be that way. He had asked for too much out of life, and this was life's way of telling him he had enough.

Then, Chi Addams appeared. When he first saw her, she was just another pretty face. Yet being with her felt so right. Parker rubbed his index finger along the edge of the table as visions of Chi's lovely face came to mind: smiling at him, looking reassuringly at him, nodding confidently at him, winking seductively at him.

Was she the woman who could take away his pain and replace it with joy? Was she the woman he could love deeply and meaningfully?

But Chi was gone. Gone from his world, gone from his life, gone from his arms. And he'd caused it. Yet no matter how hard he tried. Chi wasn't gone from his thoughts. Or his heart.

Standing, Parker walked out of the kitchen to get dressed.

"Hi, Parker," Sheila said, standing in the doorway of his office. She had been there at the main restaurant all week, relieving him of the day-to-day issues he hadn't felt like dealing with. "I've been reviewing the inventory list. You were right, we are going to need more supplies sooner than planned. I'm sure it's because of Mellow Moods playing. It's a good idea of yours to keep them for a few extra weeks. It paid off."

"Sheila, it's time we purchase another dishwasher for the other restaurant. Repairing it won't do any good. The thing is destroying more dishes than it cleans. Would you take care of that as soon as possible?"

"Sure, Parker," Sheila said. "Is everything okay?"

"Why wouldn't it be?" he said, returning his gaze to the papers on his deck.

Sheila recognized the pain she saw in Parker's eyes. She had seen similar pain after Cynthia's death. It was fortunate for her that she still had been inside the restaurant when Cynthia was hit and didn't have to experience the emotional trauma of watching someone she knew die.

She had always been attracted to Parker and afterward did everything she could to let him know it, but Parker would always brush her off. Sheila had waited too long. She had given him too long to get over Cynthia. Just when she was about to make a full assault on him, Dr. Chi Addams stepped into the picture and began to heal him of the pain she'd wanted to remove.

But things had changed again. Sheila had recognized the loneliness behind Parker's smile. Others noticed, but no one else cared about Parker as much as she did.

A week ago, she had casually asked Kevin, the bartender, about Parker's doctor friend and was told Parker hadn't mentioned her in days and was abrupt toward anyone. Maybe things were over between them.

Sheila still wanted him and was determined to get him this time. She'd been aggressive in her approach, but it still wasn't working. Every night that he worked late, she was practically all over him. He tolerated her but had not submitted to her charms.

It was a convenient coincidence when Chi had walked into Parker's office and had seen them embracing. Hugging Parker goodbye had become second nature to her, and when she saw Chi, Sheila couldn't help kissing him on the cheek to give the appearance that it was more than what it was. It worked. Chi had run off and was out of the picture.

Now, looking at Parker's fake smile, she knew it was time to make her move. She will be there this time.

"Sure, no problem," Sheila said. "I've already started looking." She paused, then asked, "Parker, what about having a late lunch with me?" When she saw him getting ready to disagree, she placed her hands on her hips knowing it would pull her blouse tight across her hips before saying, "I'd like to discuss some issues about the other restaurant."

Parker responded, "That sounds good. I haven't eaten yet. And I want to test the baked salmon on the new menu."

As Parker rounded the desk, Sheila added, "I suspected you were going to get another machine soon. Just so happens, that there's a hotel auctioning off some equipment today. I was thinking of going by to see what they have. Ride with me to the hotel after lunch. Maybe we can find something we both want." If Parker picked up on her double entendre, he hid his reaction. At least, she thought, he looked at her chest when she placed her hand on her hip earlier.

Sheila decided she would call the hotel in advance to reserve a room. If she played her cards right, she would have him in bed, right after buying the dishwasher. It would be a way of celebrating a new find. For both of them.

As Parker neared her, she reached out and caressed his arm, then said teasingly, "Come on. You've been working too hard. We're gonna have to get you into having some fun."

CHAPTER *Twenty-One*

Chi opened the door to his smiling face. She had to admit he was a good-looking man.

"Chi, I've missed you."

"Douglas," Chi stepped back. "Come on in."

"Thanks for letting me stop by to see Anthony this afternoon."

"Actually, Douglas," Chi led the way to her mother's living room, "Anthony is taking a nap. I was hoping we could talk privately."

"Is your mother here?"

"She's at church." Chi sat on the sofa.

Douglas sat next to her and stared into her eyes. "Our son has your eyes," he said.

Our son. She would have given her right arm to have Douglas say those same words four years ago.

"Yes, he does. And he has a lot of other wonderful characteristics." She placed her hands in her lap and looked at them. *These hands held Anthony when he cried. When he laughed. When he slept. When he hurts.* Chi thought of the best way to tell Douglas her feelings. "Douglas," she said softly looking back at him, "I'm glad you want to be a part of Anthony's life."

"I hoped you would agree," he said.

"Mama's also glad."

"She's told me that."

"I know," Chi said. "I'm going to ask you to not discuss the welfare of Anthony or any other issues involving him with my mother any longer."

Douglas' laugh held indifference. "You're kidding, right?"

"I mean it, Douglas. I think the reason you approached Mama first is because you know how indebted I feel toward her. I know that I allow her to control too much of my life, but that's my issue. I realized that I need to deal with that, too."

"What does that have to do with us?"

"Everything." Chi reached out and touched his arm. "You see, there is no us. And there won't ever be an us."

Douglas leaned away from her touch.

"I need you to accept it. And I want you to know that going to Mama to get her to change my mind will not work."

"What does Agnes have to say about all of this?" Douglas stood.

Chi needed to make him understand. Her life has been dysfunctional for too long because Chi has avoided the truth about her mother. It was time that she corrected that as well, but for now, she needed to deal with Douglas.

"That's my point, Douglas. I will decide what happens in Anthony's life. And only me." She stood and walked toward him. "If you want to be a part of his life, I will allow that. But on my terms. I will not allow you and Mama to decide our future."

"I take it, you've decided against my plan to share custody after I move to Atlanta?" Douglas asked.

"You can visit Anthony when I decided to move him back to Atlanta. I'm not going to have an arrangement that allows you to have him most of the time just because you can afford a live-in sitter."

"Agnes doesn't want to continue to keep him."

"That's my problem."

"I'm not letting my son live in poverty just because you've decided to stand up to your mother."

"You gave up all your rights a long time ago. I suggest that you work *with me* and not against me if you truly want to spend time with Anthony."

Douglas threw his arms up in exasperation. "Why can't we stick to the original plan, Chi? What has changed suddenly?"

"I never agreed to your plan. And I'm not interested in rebuilding a relationship with you."

"We can be good together," Douglas pleaded. "This is my only chance."

"What do you mean by that?" Chi frowned.

"Chi, I was so angry when I found out that Anthony was born with sickle cell, I had a vasectomy, so I'd never get someone pregnant again. Now I can't have children. He's the only child I will ever have."

"Reverse the operation," Chi said. "The procedure isn't that difficult."

"I've tried. Something went wrong, Chi," Douglas said softly. "But with you, I have a son. I can be a father."

No wonder he was so interested in being a part of Anthony's life, Chi thought. It made perfect sense to her now. He wasn't searching for a son, but for a means to reclaim his masculinity. His own selfish need to feel manly forced him to work so hard at slithering his way back into her life. And no wonder, he was interested in Chi. Who else would willingly agree to not have any more children with him?

Douglas the Conniver, Chi thought.

"When were you planning to share this with me, Douglas?"

"That doesn't matter," he smiled, hoping to change the topic. "I'm still Anthony's father. And I want to be."

"True," Chi agreed. "But I might want more children."

Douglas' smile faded. "Get real! And bring another sick child into the world?"

And there was the real Douglas.

"I didn't say with you," Chi said. "I have a sickle cell trait. You know as well as I do that if the other parent is normal, then the offspring may just as well be normal."

Douglas forgot about being cordial and his frustration was beginning to show, "Oh, and you think Parker character will want to father a child with you?" he shouted. To Chi's surprised look, he added, "Anthony told me a lot about him. It seems you don't mind flirting in front of my son with other men."

Chi refrained from being argumentative. This was the old Douglas she knew. He was always combative when he didn't get his way.

When he finished pacing, she said, "I'm willing to allow you to visit Anthony, but only on terms that I agree to."

"Does that mean the trip to Chicago to see my parents is out?"

Chi's knees weakened. This was news to her. Her Mama was again making plans without her. Chi hid her surprise behind a stoic look. "Correct. He cannot go on any trips without me."

Douglas stormed toward the front door. He marched out without even saying goodbye. And Chi couldn't figure out a reason to care. Or to remind him that he forgot to visit with Anthony.

Chi stood there looking at the closed door. In less than an hour, her mother would be walking in that same door. Chi would have to calm herself to deal with the other dysfunctional part of her life–her relationship with Agnes. And it was time that she did.

Chi was in the kitchen washing dishes when Agnes arrived home.

"Hi, Mama. How was Service?"

"Not as interesting as your afternoon," Agnes said. "Douglas was waiting for me when I got out of the church."

Chi hadn't expected this and was unprepared to deal with an upset mother. Attempting to delay the inevitable confrontation, she said, "Do you want me to fix you something to eat?"

Agnes ignored the question. "I think you need to talk to Douglas. I can't believe you treated him the way that you did. You're being completely unreasonable. Douglas wants to be the father you always wanted him to be."

"Mama, I told Douglas he could be. Just not the way that he wants."

"I don't see why not."

"It's not us that Douglas wants. He's discovered he can't have children."

"He has Anthony."

"Let's just drop this discussion for now. It's not going to end in agreement." Chi headed toward the doorway leading to her bedroom.

"Douglas told me you just want to chase this Parker guy," Agnes said to her back.

"That's none of your business, Mama."

"You think Parker is going to stand by you and a sick child? The others didn't. You are walking away from a good man who's trying to correct his mistake. Why don't you do the same and forget Parker!"

That was more than Chi could take. "Mama, please stop this!" Chi shouted. Her visit with Douglas, the struggle to keep her spirits buoyant, and her mother's arguing were getting the best of her. "What I do with the men I meet is my business. Douglas didn't want us when we needed him. And Parker isn't any of your business."

Agnes wouldn't stand for this kind of treatment. "Don't you dare disrespect me!" Agnes placed one hand on her hip and pointed the other at Chi. She hated Chi's ability to accomplish the things she wanted despite her advice. "You will apologize to Douglas. You're going to let him be a part of Anthony's life. He wants to be, so let him! And he has money."

"Mama, let's not forget that I've been able to bring home the money for the past few years. I've repaired this old house to make it livable. I'm taking care of Dad's bills because you can't afford to. I keep money flowing into this house and your bank account. All without Douglas!"

"It's not enough, Chi!"

"You're being greedy and selfish, Mama!"

Agnes was infuriated. "If your daddy hadn't left all the money to you so that his 'little princess' could go to medical school, I would have had all the money I needed. You took that money from me. You're just paying me back!"

That stung, but Chi withstood the bite. "Face reality, Mama. I'm self-sufficient and you just can't stand it. Nor can you make it without me."

"You want to bet?" Agnes shouted.

"I will take care of Daddy's bills. Since this house is paid for, you should be able to maintain it going forward. It's your responsibility."

"And Anthony is your responsibility."

"You know, Mama, all this time I've been accomplishing my goals because I thought it would make you forgive me. I guess I was wrong." Turning, Chi headed to her son's room. This was the Lord's Day, and her mother had forgotten about that and his preaching about forgiveness.

As she entered the room, she saw Anthony quivering in the center of his bed. She recognized that fear in his son's eyes. *Mama's shouting caused this.*

How could Chi have overlooked how this would affect her son? Seeing his reaction evaporated the rest of Chi's spirits.

Chi spoke softly to her son because she didn't have the strength to speak any louder. "It's okay, sweetie. We're going home. Mommy's taking you home."

Chi pulled together the scraps of her pride and tied a knot strong enough to give her the strength to do what she'd always wanted to do. She would find a way to raise her son without her mother. Grabbing as many of Anthony's belongings as she could stuff into his suitcase, she picked him up and headed for the front door.

Agnes met her halfway down the hall. Anthony immediately wrapped his arms tightly around Chi's neck. Chi's body stiffened. For the first time, Agnes looked as though she was about to hit them both.

"We're leaving, Mama. Get out of the way."

"You will do what I tell you to!" Agnes screamed.

Chi just stood quietly, not wanting to provoke her mother any further. Thankfully, the phone rang, and Agnes headed for it.

"That's Douglas!" Agnes said hurrying to the phone. "Just wait till I tell him about this!"

THE RYAN FAMILY

CHAPTER
Twenty-Two

Sheila and Parker were headed toward the back exit of the restaurant en route to the hotel auction.

"Hey, Parker, Sheila." Kevin said as he adjusted his bow tie. A tuxedo shirt, pants, and tie were required attire for Sundays.

"Running late from returning from your vacation, huh? Glad to see you made it back." Parker's smile was laced with an inquiring look.

"Barely," Kevin said as he adjusted his cummerbund. "We celebrated until dawn. Only the best for Annie."

"I'm going to need that updated list of things to order for the bar as soon as possible, Kevin," Sheila said before turning her attention back to Parker.

"I'll get right on it," Kevin said.

Just as Kevin turned to head to the bar area, Parker asked, "You give Annie my suggestions for honeymoon places?"

"I sure did. But she likes your lady friend's suggestion more." Kevin turned to walk away, and Sheila let out a pent-up breath.

Parker, who was leaving because Sheila was tugging at his arm, froze. He whipped around and said to Kevin's retreating back, "What did you say?"

Kevin gave Parker a puzzled look. "Chi...," he started, but the murderous look on Sheila's face made him pause, "suggested a cruise for our honeymoon. So, we're making plans for it. She called here Friday afternoon and left you a message to call her at her mother's. She left the number." Kevin looked at Sheila since he'd given her the message to deliver to Parker. "I also saw her Friday night when she stopped by looking for you," Kevin finished, his gaze turning from Sheila to Parker.

Parker was also looking at Sheila. She stared at the ground.

"Thanks." Parker turned to her. "Do you have the number Chi left?"

Sheila reluctantly and busily flipped through the papers on her clipboard and found the small piece of paper she had intended to trash. "It must have slipped my mind," she said, handing it to him. "I assumed you'd probably have talked to her by now," Sheila added in her defense.

"You pulled several messages off that clipboard for me over the last two days. I'm surprised you forgot this one," Parker said in an accusatory tone touched with an undertone of disgust.

Sheila refused to look at him. "You know how busy it's been. Must have slipped my mind."

"Things never slip your mind." He began walking away.

Sheila didn't want to lose Parker. "I just wanted you for myself," she wailed.

Parker stopped and looked down at the floor for several seconds before turning to face her. "It wasn't like that between us, Sheila. Never has been. I told you so in the beginning." He watched her eyes glaze with unshed tears. "I'm sorry you thought differently." He walked away.

As Parker sat at his desk, he replayed the last few minutes in his mind. This was the reason he'd never acted on Sheila's flirtatious yet subtle advances before. If things ended, someone would be hurt. He might lose a damn good manager out of this. He cursed his carelessness. Hurting women's feelings was becoming an unhealthy pastime for him.

Chi had called and come for him. While he had been trying to forget her, the idea of her reaching out to him was immeasurably pleasing.

Leaning back in his chair, he slid his palms against the front of his jeans before rubbing both hands up and down his face. He needed a drink. Hell no, he didn't, he corrected.

He needed Chi.

Standing, he looked around his office. Was this all his life would be? It was a big lifeless room. True, expensive furnishings were there. Relics of his football career and proof of his business acumen surrounded him. But these were all inanimate, trophies of the past. What value did they have without someone he loved to share them with?

Maybe his sister was right. Could he control destiny if he approached it knowing the downside beforehand?

He thought of all the people he admired and respected. People who knowingly approached adversity without flinching. People who put their pain aside to confront a difficult predicament. Strangely, he thought of his African American ancestors who struggled so bravely to ensure a better future for their descendants and all people of their race. He thought of his father, who died in the War defending a country that didn't necessarily defend all his human rights. He thought of people he knew that struggled every day just to make ends meet. Then, he thought about the friend who used to make him laugh. Marcus Allan. He would have to apologize to Marcus and try to mend that friendship.

Then, he thought of himself.

Self-pity was a sonofabitch, he concluded. He had plenty of reasons to feel accomplished, yet he didn't. For the past year, he had believed he was being punished for being a success in life, that he didn't deserve love. The funny thing was, since he believed he didn't deserve it, he allowed his self-deprecating beliefs to dictate his future.

Negative thinking was sonofabitch, too.

He visibly shook himself to get rid of the weight of his misery. Those thoughts had caused him to walk away from the woman he wanted. But no longer. He would find her, hold her, confess his fears to her, and make her take him back.

Then a feeling, more intense, more debilitating twisted at his gut and swirled through his being. Grabbing his throbbing temple, he realized the source of his distress.

Chi was in trouble. He could feel and sense it.

CHAPTER
Twenty-Three

When Agnes picked up her home phone, she was still shouting vile epithets as Chi walked out of the front door. "Well, go home then, Chi." Agnes' vileness switched to the caller. "Hello?"

Agnes heard the concern in the man's voice. "Mrs. Addams, is everything all, right?"

"I thought this was you, Douglas. If you're looking for Chi, she just stormed out of the door with Anthony. If I were you, I'd forget about her. She doesn't want to do the right thing. I told her you were the best thing for them, but she won't listen to me."

"Mrs. Addams, please stop Chi from leaving."

Agnes finally realized it wasn't Douglas she was talking to. "Who is this?"

"This is Parker Ryan. Can you put Chi on the phone?"

"You're the man she's been seeing in Atlanta. If it wasn't for you, this would have never happened!" Agnes was angry all over again and took it out on Parker.

Parker had enough of this woman's abrasive attitude. He didn't give a damn about her anger. All he wanted to do was stop Chi from getting in the car. The awful feeling inside had multiplied since hearing Mrs. Addams tell Chi to go ahead and leave. Parker concluded the premonition about her dying in a car accident was about to happen. He could feel it.

"Don't let Chi drive off in her condition!" Parker commanded.

Agnes heard Chi's car backing out of the drive. Walking over to the window, she watched the car pull away. She directed her wrathful attention back to Parker. "Don't you raise your voice to me! That's the problem today. No one respects their elders anymore!"

"Listen, Mrs. Addams, if Chi drives that car in her condition, she's going to have an accident. Anthony's in the car with her," Parker said hoping that would soften her resolve. "For your grandson's sake, stop her."

"I can't!" Agnes heard Parker exhale quickly. "She's already gone."

"No," was the last thing Agnes heard just before the distinctive sound of the phone hitting the cradle.

Parker dialed Chi's cell phone, and it went straight to voicemail again. It was a habit of hers to turn off her phone to limit distractions when with her son.

"Damn it!"

"PLEASE," PARKER BEGGED. BEHIND THE WHEEL OF HIS SECOND VEHIcle, a Jeep Cherokee, an older vehicle used when needing to pick up restaurant supplies. He tightly gripped the steering wheel as the other fought with the jangling assortment of keys as he unsuccessfully attempted to shove the proper key into the ignition. "Damn it!" he breathed desperately. "Go in!" Parker had to get to Chi before it was too late. He had tried to page her, but there had been no response.

Radial tires ate at the pavement after he slammed the gear into reverse. Wheeling out of the parking lot, he slammed his foot down on the brakes, narrowly missing a passing car. His heart was racing. His mind was racing.

"Please, take your normal route home, Chi." Parker didn't realize he was talking aloud until he heard himself say her name. "Let her make it home to me," he pleaded. Parker's first thought was to go to her apartment and wait for her arrival. The nagging, aching premonition in the pit of his stomach wouldn't let him sit back and do nothing. If she traveled her usual route, he could meet up with her in another forty-five minutes or so and he could get her off the road. Then, he could make sure Chi was safe. And Anthony. The son he would love to watch grow up.

He reached for his iPhone and tried to call her again. Straight to voicemail, she must not have turned it on. "God, don't let this be a warning." It was all wishful thinking if he didn't get to them in time.

As he traveled I-20, he found himself staring at every car traveling toward Atlanta in the hope one would be Chi's. Some parts of the interstate had dividers, and he couldn't see the other side. That heightened his frustration, and he reached for his cell phone. His rational mind told him he hadn't been traveling long enough, so it was too soon to expect her. His heart and soul argued he had to make sure he didn't miss any passing car.

Out of the corner of his eye, because his head was turned looking over his left shoulder, he noticed red brake lights from the cars in front of him. Looking ahead quickly, he realized he was gaining too fast on the car in front of him. He jammed the brakes, all the while checking his mirrors for tailgaters. His car wasn't stopping fast enough! He was going to hit the car in front of him!

Parker cut the wheels to the right onto the shoulder of the road. Thankfully, he had driven his Jeep today instead of the Corvette. That car would be scrap metal by now with all the bumps encountered in the shoulder. Several cars in front of the one he'd almost bashed were hitting their brakes for some unknown reason. As he roared by them on the shoulder, Parker tried to see the other side of the highway for Chi's car. One looked like her Honda.

Stopping, Parker jumped out of the Jeep and ran back along the shoulder attempting to see. He couldn't tell if it was her car or not.

"Damn!" He debated driving across the grassy median to confirm if it was Chi. His mind wrestled between backtracking and losing valuable time or continuing to plow forward. Checking the time, he realized she couldn't have made it this far this soon. He cursed himself for not using reason. He had just wasted valuable minutes. He ran back to his Jeep.

"Where are you, Chi?" he growled worriedly to the empty inside of his vehicle.

TEARS OF PAIN BLURRED THE ROAD IN FRONT OF CHI, TEARS OF LOSS, tears of devastation. Her attempts to stop crying only caused her insides to ache more intensely. She didn't want to wail in front of Anthony because it would upset him. But try as she might, Chi couldn't prevent the tears and sobs. Thankfully, her subconscious had taken control over the drive because her conscious mind was filled with murky thoughts of the arguments, she had with people she thought loved her. More thoughts, dismal and uncontrollably painful, ran their course.

Chi never suspected the anger ran as deep as it did with her mother. Chi had spent most of her adult life trying to make her mother love and forgive her.

Chi's father used to hug her when she was sad, and it always made all her pain go away. She never knew how much she missed those hugs until this moment. She needed one of those hugs just then.

Chi also realized that her relationship with Douglas was her attempt to replace the love she had lost with her father's death. That had been a mistake, but she'd learned from it. What she didn't learn in time was that those aspects of her past had governed her relationship with Parker. She'd kept Parker at arm's length because of her past. Why was it just now becoming clear to her? Chi wondered.

She had lost all the hopes she had clung to. Hopes of winning her mother's love. Hopes to have proud parents to see her achieve her career goal. And the hope of having Parker.

No one was there for her. Not even Douglas. He didn't want her or Anthony. He was just feeling desperate because of his impotence. And Chi knew that when, not if, he got over his self-pity, he'd leave again.

Parker, she thought. He didn't want her either. His actions had shown how repulsed he had been the night he walked away from her. Of the two men, she'd loved Parker more deeply and more unconditionally. If she had just had faith in herself by not being open and honest with him initially. It was an expensive and painful lesson that she did not like and would repeat.

All Chi wanted now was for the pain to stop. The blurry, unfocused highway was filled with speeding cars all around her. Closing her eyes to blink away the tears, she caught clear snippets of since-past, wonderful memories. They came through clearly. She kept her eyes closed to get a better look at the pictures painted in her mind.

Her car veered out of her lane, almost grazing the fender of the vehicle next to hers. The honking horn interrupted her thoughts. Automatically, she jerked the wheel to the right back into the original lane and almost into the Bronco gaining on her rear end. Instantly, she sped up her car to avoid an accident.

As the Bronco zoomed around her, Chi saw the angry driver shaking his fist at her. She didn't care. The only thing she wanted now was for the wonderful thoughts to return.

IF NOT FOR THE HONKING, PARKER WOULD NOT HAVE SEEN CHI'S CAR at all. She had almost sideswiped the Bronco passing her. Other cars and a trailer truck hit their brakes. *Didn't she see them,* he wondered. He found himself yelling at Chi to be careful. It was a fool's demand, considering she couldn't hear him, but he had to do something.

The fifty-foot, grassy median looked dry and hard enough for his Jeep to manage. Parker also debated traveling to the next off-ramp and making a U-turn.

"The hell I will." He slowed considerably to cut over into the left lane in front of a fast-moving car before veering onto the grassy, bumpy median which dipped at its center. His tires struggled to cut through the grassy ground; Parker gunned it, hoping not to become stuck. The Jeep lurched across the valley and onto the shoulder.

"Thank you," he said looking up.

Flooring the gas, Parker raced past several cars. Two trucks, traveling close together, blocked his view of the right lane. Several cars in the left lane, traveling the same speed as the trucks, prevented him from passing.

Parker's patience was long gone. He sharply cut the wheel to the right onto the shoulder and illegally passed the trucks. Zipping back onto the road, he spotted Chi's car several hundred yards away with a few cars between his Jeep and her car. Based on the other cars' flashing brake lights, Parker assumed Chi's driving was causing the cars to slow down.

"What are you doing, Chi? Pay attention to the road!" Parker screamed, pushing harder on the gas pedal. He began blowing his horn, hoping to get her attention.

Parker sped up as the cars began to pass Chi. Now, he was behind her and the two Semi Trucks behind him. Cutting over onto the shoulder again, he drove alongside Chi's car, still honking his horn. He rolled down his window, but her windows were up. Either she did not hear him, or she was ignoring him.

"Chi, pull over!" He got no response. She looked dazed and withdrawn. "Chi!"

Anthony was strapped into his child's seat in the back.

Chi must have said something to Anthony because he began to point. Parker noticed Anthony's index finger pointing at him. When Chi looked over, Parker saw the slightly puzzled look on her face before it slowly shifted to surprise. Her car began to slow down again as Parker spied one of the two semi-trucks moving quickly to get from behind Chi. Which meant the second truck probably didn't see her car.

Quickly looking back, Parker saw the truck approaching fast. "No, Chi. Don't stop!" Parker's hand signaled for her to get off the road. He started blowing his horn.

Chi, forgetting to check her rearview mirror, slowed while reaching to scroll down the passenger window.

Parker quickly looked back at the truck behind her.

The truck driver jammed on the brakes. But it was too late. The massive truck slammed into Chi's car.

Parker's nightmare became a reality.

He watched helplessly as the truck sent Chi's car spinning wildly out of control. The last thing Parker saw before he slammed on the brakes was Chi's car heading into the other lane as other cars darted this way and that before her car was hurdled over the embankment toward a patch of trees.

CHAPTER
Twenty-Four

As the passenger side of Chi's car smashed into a tree, Parker's heart almost stopped. "Nooooo!" he screamed. "Not again!" In a flash, he was out of his vehicle and running toward her car.

Fear gripped his heart, and he willed himself not to be overtaken by panic. This couldn't happen again! He couldn't watch someone die again. Approaching the car, he heard Anthony's cries to his mother, with no visible injuries. Parker yanked open the front passenger door. Chi's head was lying limply against the steering wheel, eyes closed.

Please, don't take her away, too, his mind screamed.

The truck driver who hit her car had made it to Chi's car. Standing next to Parker, he said, "I wouldn't have slowed down if not for your honking. Otherwise, I'd have smashed into that car much harder! Oh, God, I pray they're okay."

Parker didn't have time for this man. "Go call for help!" Parker snapped.

Carefully, he laid her back against the seat. Pressing his fingers against her neck, he felt a pulse. A weak pulse. Then, he noticed the large bruise across her forehead and saw blood.

"Chi," Parker croaked, his mouth dried with fear. "Chi, don't leave me." To stop Anthony's crying, he said, "Your mommy will be okay." He hoped he was right. "Be a big guy and stop crying, okay? I'll come get you in just a minute."

CHI WAS IN A COMA.

The ER trauma had examined her for broken bones and internal injuries. She had suffered a brain contusion and was in intensive care being monitored closely. The doctors had no estimate of how long it would be before she would recover. Such head injuries could sometimes take hours or years to recover if the person regained consciousness at all. The doctors informed Parker to notify her family members and hope for the best.

Five hours after she was admitted to the hospital, there were no signs of change. Anthony had been examined and pronounced free of injury. They kept him under observation, however, concerned that the stress could cause a Sickle Cell crisis. Parker had finally reached Chi's mother, and she was en route to the hospital.

In the waiting room, Parker sat despondently, staring at a wall. Patricia sat next to him holding his hand. "Parker?" Patricia said. "I'm going to get you something warm to drink and check on Anthony."

That brought him out of his stupor, "Yeah, Anthony's been alone too long. I'll go with you."

She looked at her brother's downcast head. "You saved them, Parker."

He glared at her, "Did I? Chi's unconscious, and they have no idea if she will ever recover. Anthony may lose his mother."

"The driver of that truck said if it wasn't for you, it would have been much worse. They were lucky you were there."

"Maybe I should have done something else. Maybe if I had driven ahead of her, she would have followed me to safety."

"Stop it," Patricia said. "I won't let you do this to yourself again, Parker. Because of you, she has a chance. You changed the outcome of your dream." Patricia wrapped her arms around her brother. "You saved her. Remember that."

"I can't lose her, Pats."

"The doctors will make sure you don't. Chi is strong-willed. She has everything to live for."

As Parker was about to voice his disagreement with that, a pecan-colored Black man and an older woman walked up to them.

"Are you Parker Ryan?" the man asked.

"Yeah."

"I'm Dr. Douglas Carlson. Anthony's father. This is Agnes Addams, Chi's mother. We've just left Chi's room. Her doctor said you were here."

Anger flicked in Parker's eyes and Patricia touched his arm to halt him from doing something foolish. Parker had told her about the first call he'd made to Chi's mother. Patricia knew her brother respected elders, but it was a question of respect being earned.

"Mrs. Addams, I hate meeting you for the first time under such circumstances, but I begged you to prevent this from happening. All you had to do was call out to her. Was that so hard of a task for you?" Parker asked.

"Parker, this may not be the best time to discuss this," Patricia said. "I'm Patricia, his sister," she said to them.

"My daughter and grandson are all I have," Agnes said in her defense. "I was angry."

"Chi's so easy to love," Parker responded. "Was it that hard for you to overlook your anger knowing the state she was in?"

"Don't blame her," Douglas interjected, "Chi's headstrong."

Parker gave Douglas a look that said if he opened his mouth again, Parker would make sure nothing else came out of it. He looked back at Chi's mother. There was guilt and shame in her eyes. But also, pride.

Parker took a step closer to her, and she straightened her spine as if ready to defend herself. There was too much defensive anger in this woman, Parker thought. Tenderness was needed. He reached out and embraced Agnes. "Let's hope for the best. Chi needs that right now." Her stiffness melted into trembling. After several moments, tears came.

"I'm so sorry that I didn't listen to you," Agnes said with a sob. She hadn't cried in so many years she thought she'd forgotten how. "I love my daughter. And my grandson…so much." When her tears turned into sniffs, Parker released her.

He stepped back, holding her arms. Trying to look reassuring, he said, "Mrs. Addams, we were just going to see Anthony. He needs a familiar face. Join us." During the walk, Parker gave them a recap of the accident and the latest on Anthony's condition.

As Agnes and Patricia entered Anthony's room, Parker noticed Douglas' hesitation. Douglas looked as if he was about to walk into a pit of snakes. Was the man stalling in giving comfort to his son?

"I wonder if the both of us should go in there," Douglas said to Parker. "I don't want my son getting confused about my role."

What an asshole! He should be leading the way! "I'm not going to interfere with your newfound fatherhood," Parker stated flatly.

"Good," Douglas said, "because that's what I plan to be."

"Frankly, man, I think it's a little late in coming," Parker added.

"You don't know the circumstances," Douglas defended.

That was true. Parker didn't know the whole story. But he didn't have to. Both he and his half-sister, Patricia, were raised in a fatherless home. Parker could justify his upbringing because his father died in a War. Unlike Patricia's father, who just up and left them. Their mother struggled her entire life to make sure they were cared for. That struggle as well as the feelings of abandonment Patricia had experienced could have been avoided if the man had done his part as a supportive father.

In Parker's mind, there was no justification for a man abandoning his child. If he didn't want children, then he should take necessary precautions to prevent a child. In a matter of seconds, Douglas had lost any hope of gaining Parker's respect.

"I don't give a damn about your version of the circumstances. There's a frightened boy in that room who doesn't even understand the concept of having a father. Right now, he needs comfort." Parker took a menacing step toward Douglas, "But Chi is another matter. When she comes out of the coma," Parker pronounced each of his next words clearly to remove any misunderstanding, "I'll be the man by her side."

Douglas spat out an angry retort, "So, be it! Just be careful when you screw her. She's quite fertile."

A short temper was the direct result of worrying about Chi and dealing with this spineless Black man. Before Parker could stop himself, he grabbed Douglas by the neck and slammed him against the wall. Since he stood a few inches taller than Douglas, Parker glared down into very surprised, frightened eyes.

"That's a lousy excuse for being an absentee father. But pricks like you always find excuses to justify your mistakes. My advice to you is to try condoms. And grow a backbone." He dropped Douglas, not caring that the man was gasping for air. He turned and walked into Anthony's room. Douglas didn't follow.

When Agnes asked where Douglas was, Parker said, "Hopefully, in orthopedics. Ordering a spine."

Agnes didn't respond to that, but Patricia did. "Good!" she said before leaning over to caress Anthony's forehead. "The wimp needs it." Parker had told Patricia that Douglas hadn't been around his son for over four years. It was inexcusable, she thought. Patricia knew better than anyone the pain of growing up without a father.

After an hour, Anthony decided he had enough entertainment. The boy turned and said, "Nightie night, Grandma," He looked at his other guests. "Night, Miss P'teecia and Mr. Parker."

As they left the room, Agnes reached for Parker's arm. "I was wrong about you," she said. "His real father hasn't been to see him at a time like this. Yet I thought he was the best thing for my daughter. You've only known my Chi for a short time. And you're here."

"This is where I'm supposed to be, Mrs. Addams," Parker said.

"Yes, I believe you're right." She squeezed his arm supportively.

CHAPTER
Twenty-Five

Chi looked so lifeless.

Parker had been sitting next to her hospital bed for about thirty minutes. There were no signs of change in the past twenty-four hours. Patricia had taken Agnes to the cafeteria while Anthony slept. Douglas had long gone, only calling to claim he needed to attend to a personal matter.

Yeah, Parker thought, a personal matter that involved him perfecting his ability to be a spineless worm. How could he leave? Parker wondered.

Parker reached for Chi's hand. It was cold, so he began rubbing his warmth into her. "Chi, I was thinking." Parker stood up. "When we leave for Barbados, we should consider extending our stay there. Say for a month? That warm climate is good for Anthony's condition. Once Mom is up and moving again, we can start planning the trip." He held her small hand in both of his. "Of course, you're going to need to spend more time at my place to speed up her healing."

Healing. The doctors informed them that familiar touches and voices could stimulate Chi's recovery. Coma patients often responded favorably to it.

Please heal, Chi. Don't leave me, he prayed. *Come back to me, Chi. Let me help heal you.*

Then Parker said aloud. "Chi, what do you think about … the three of us in Barbados for a month?" He looked at her closed eyes, closed mouth, expecting an answer.

She didn't move.

Only the slight rise and fall of her chest indicated life. He needed to feel her move. He willed her hand to squeeze his. It didn't.

He leaned over and gently placed his face against her chest. Rubbing his forehead against her, he took comfort in feeling her steady breathing against his skin. His ear listened to her heart beating. It was beating for him. He needed it to beat for him.

Closing his eyes, he sent up a heartfelt prayer to the Heavenly Father he had reluctantly talked to over the past year.

Then he spoke to her. "Chi," he said softly, "I've spent the last year forgetting how to love. Including myself. You gave me the desire to believe in love again." He squeezed her hand. "Did I ever thank you for that?" He pressed his lips against her heart. With each rise of her chest, he kissed her. He lovingly caressed the heart that had opened to him and made his life livable again. "Thank you, Chi."

He straightened. Reaching, he stroked her cheek.

"The doctor says you might be able to hear me. So, there's no reason you can't come out of this deep sleep. I know you were upset with me for leaving you the way that I did. Is that why you won't talk to me now?"

She just lay there. Breathing.

"You had every right to be angry. I was foolish. No, I was afraid. I was afraid to lose you like I lost Cynthia. I allowed my demons to run me away. If you let me, I promise not to let that happen again."

The emotions inside Parker were threatening to spill down his cheeks. His eyes misted and he willed that shameful action away. The next time he spoke, it was difficult to maintain any calmness.

"Damn it, Chi! Don't make me do this alone. Talk to me. Please, show me that you hear me."

He listened for sounds. Silence.

He looked for movement. None.

He was becoming an emotional basket case, traveling from sorrow to anger in a matter of seconds. He wanted to also shout at her to stop making him hurt this way!

Talking to her as the doctors had suggested wasn't working. She couldn't hear him. Or didn't want to hear him. Then, he thought of the one thing that she would never deny. Talking about her son should get a response.

"Your mother says she's sorry about the argument. Since the hospital kept Anthony for overnight observation, Agnes stayed with him so he wouldn't be afraid. He's just an elevator ride away. I'm going to go check on them. Come with me."

Silence. Stiffness.

Parker turned and walked away. Before exiting, he turned back, half-expecting, half-hoping Chi would wake up asking to go with him. To her resting form, he said, "Sweet dreams."

CHI COULDN'T SEE. COULDN'T MAKE OUT HER SURROUNDINGS. SHE WAS *trapped somewhere deep inside a black hole that kept her hostage and in pain. But there was warmth in parts of the emptiness that enveloped her. Parker's warmth. She could feel him all around her but couldn't touch him, see him, talk to him. He was saying that he believed in love again...didn't want to lose her…was afraid…wanted her to go with him. She attempted to call out to him. She sensed he was leaving her again…going away. She tried to call him, but something was preventing her from talking. Did Parker say Anthony was hospitalized? Not another sickle cell attack! She couldn't see Anthony either. The pain. She was in pain.*

Parker don't leave me again! Please… Then, the darkness came back. It beckoned her to give in to it. The darkness wasn't so bad when you didn't fight it. It made the pain stop. She listened to the call of darkness. And went to it.

CHAPTER
Twenty-Six

"How is he doing, Mrs. Addams?" Parker asked, worried.

Agnes Addams was sitting next to Anthony's bed. She looked up at him. Parker, she thought, was a man much like her Tony had been. Tony had the attitude of a stallion. Fierce. Mighty. Withstanding.

"He's still sleeping," Agnes said.

"What have the doctors said?"

"I know my grandson, Parker. He's strong, like his grandfather. Tony could withstand a lot and come out on top. The doctors are not concerned. And I can't be."

"Chi mentioned that Mr. Addams died before Anthony was born," Parker said.

"If Tony had ever heard you call him 'Mr.,' he would have given you a mouthful of trouble." She smiled weakly, "Unfortunately, he didn't get a chance to be with Anthony, but he would be proud. Because our grandson is strong. I believe the reason my husband lived so long with the pain was because he refused to give up. He fought the disease to the end."

"Chi told me the same thing."

"Her condition hasn't changed?"

"No. I've been talking to her like the doctors suggested," Parker stated. "But she's being stubborn."

"I've been talking to her also. Maybe I'll take Anthony to say something to her. She's strong, Parker. I trust in God that she'll be okay."

Parker had to stop himself from questioning her belief. He'd questioned his own constantly over the past year. Then, he said almost guiltily, "I said a prayer for her."

Agnes Addams, for the first time tonight, smiled warmly and deeply at Parker. "Thank you." She nodded. "For everything." Agnes looked back down at her sleeping grandson. She could see the rapid movement of his eyes. Then the twitching of his arm. With concern, she reached out and patted the arm. She rubbed her hands up and down his arms, then legs.

"What's wrong?" Parker questioned.

"He's not sleeping restfully. I hope that doesn't mean a crisis is coming on."

Parker moved from the foot of the bed to the side opposite Agnes. He placed a hand on Anthony's resting form. For the first time in his life, he willed thoughts and ideas to stop. Closing his eyes, he envisioned peaceful, restful times in his life. He slowed his breathing and concentrated.

Concentrate on the serenity, he told himself.

He moved his hands to other parts of Anthony's body.

Concentrate.

Then, he felt it.

Opening his eyes, he looked at Agnes, who was staring at him in confusion.

"He's fine, Mrs. Addams. A little soreness, but okay. I'm sure of it."

THE RYAN FAMILY

CHAPTER Twenty-Seven

Three days and nothing.

Parker stood at the window of Chi's hospital room looking at a clear sky filled with puffy clouds. All he wanted was a sign. Something. Anything.

When he touched her, he felt nothing. With Anthony, he had sensed peace, but he couldn't connect with Chi. He'd never understood his ability to feel things about those he cared deeply about. And not until now did he want to try. Why could he sense Anthony's being at peace so easily? Was it because the potential pain was always there, just dormant at times? He didn't know. Nor did he know how much longer Chi would be in a coma.

"Parker…"

Spinning, he rushed to the bed and looked down at Chi's face. "Chi?" he took her hand in his.

Nothing. She didn't move.

Had he imagined it? Was the stress causing him to lose his mind? Now he was hearing things. Maybe it was time to leave. This was becoming too overwhelming. He had prayed for the past three days just to hear her call out to him. And now this.

As he turned to leave, he felt a slight squeeze on his hand. He didn't dream that!

"Parker…" It was barely audible.

"Chi." He leaned down close to her face and her eyes fluttered open. She was awake! The doctors had said this would be the first major step! "I'm right here." He wanted to sweep her up into his arms and spin her around. Instead, he forced himself to calm down. "Welcome back."

Chi took in her surroundings. She didn't recognize the room, but she knew it was a hospital room. Then fragments of confusing images flickered in her memory. It took too much effort, so she concentrated on his gaze, his warm smile, his touch, lips against her forehead. They gave her so much comfort.

"I've missed you, Chi."

Chi leaned into the underside of his neck. His closeness was just what she needed. The soreness in her body, ache in her head, and dryness in her throat all ebbed a little. He was like an elixir, healing her. "You're here." Her whisper was raspy.

"I'm here," he said. "And I'm not going anywhere."

It was difficult to talk but she managed just above a whisper to say, "It was so dark. You were there…coming to…save me." Her eyes misted.

Parker was thinking the same thing. She had rescued him from a black hole that was absorbing his soul and draining his life away. Because of her, he had climbed back up from the depths of the hell he'd been in for the past year.

"You saved me first." Parker rubbed his lips across her forehead. "I didn't know I needed saving, Chi. And then came you."

EPILOGUE

Six months later...

The best remedy for a broken heart was a potent mixture of tenderness, willingness, and love. Chi was sure of it.

Not only had she healed completely from the car accident, but her heart had also healed.

The tenderness Parker had shown her, her mother, and her son, was the solvent that helped to wash away some of the tension between Chi and her mother and allowed them to begin to build a healthier relationship. There was still more mending to be done, but Agnes's love for her grandson and the near loss of her daughter forced her to change her attitude. Agnes was still living in Macon, but since Chi had moved her grandson to Atlanta, she occasionally traveled to visit.

Parker's willingness to accept Chi, flaws and all, removed the last vestiges of fear that surrounded her heart and allowed her to give it completely to him. They talked about their past fears and current issues. And through that, they grew closer to one another.

And the most important ingredient to their relationship was love. It was complete, it enabled them to mend the battered portions of their inner selves and allowed them to openly give and receive. That moment had started on the day Chi had awakened from the coma and found Parker waiting for her. She hadn't known how long she had been unconscious. Seeing him then, she knew immediately that all her concerns about their relationship could be resolved. Just before he left her room that night, she asked how long he had been waiting for her.

Parker had said, "Since the moment I lost my faith in love."

She, too, had lost her faith in herself and her relationships. But no longer.

Parker had confided that he had a special connection with her and her son. She didn't completely understand its meaning until the onset of a sickle cell crisis for Anthony. Just before it happened, Parker had told her they needed to get him to the hospital. He could sense Anthony's attacks before they happened. It lifted a world of burden from her mind. Whenever she was concerned, she could turn to Parker, and he would assure her that as well.

Harriett was up and about, walking with a practically unnoticeable limp. She had returned home to Florida but visited often, refusing to go to any doctor except Chi.

Parker had invited both their mothers to visit to celebrate their wedding arrangement. During their visit, Parker, Chi, Anthony, Agnes, and Harriett were having dinner at Parker's Place.

At dinner, Harriett nagged both Chi and Parker to finalize the date of their trip to Barbados, suggesting it was the perfect place for a honeymoon. They didn't respond when she added, "Mothers know best."

Surprisingly, Agnes corrected Harriett, saying, "No. We just want to believe that we do."

"You're both right," Chi said, smiling. "But regardless, the trip will be scheduled by us." She looked lovingly at Parker.

Chi reached up and cupped his face with her left hand. The finger adorned with an engagement ring rubbed under his lips. Her heart swelled with love and longing and desire. "Can you feel this?" she asked about the emotions that she was experiencing.

He kissed her finger and arrogantly said, "Yeah. And give me more of that," he winked, "late tonight."

And Chi thought just then that attitude was the one flaw she loved the most about him.

The End

THE RYAN FAMILY

THE RYAN FAMILY SERIES

The Ryan Family Series will make you cry, make you laugh, make you cheer.

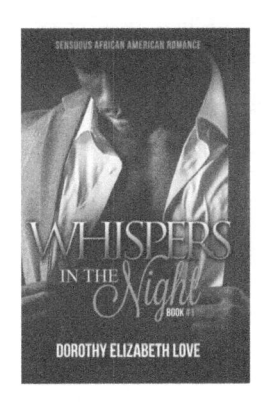

Patricia Ryan is the board president of a center for at-risk kids. The expansion plans of the Mackenzy-Duran Company require demolishing the center and with it, the hopes and dreams of the kids who attend. Mac Carter, owner of Mackenzy-Duran, finds that he wants to win Patricia's heart, but risks losing his own heart during the battle over the center's property. Winning her over will mean losing a great deal more.

"Ms. Love has written an exceptional novel." – RT Magazine

Parker Ryan enjoyed two things love and happiness… but hasn't experienced any of that since the day his fiancé was killed. Dr. Chi Addams, a woman who spent her career healing others, but didn't know that same passion would heal the heart of man needing it most, Parker. Chi's secrets and not-so-previous relationship will rekindle Parker's past pain. Will he run or try love again?

A top-notch page-turner that has everything without overdoing it." – RT Magazine

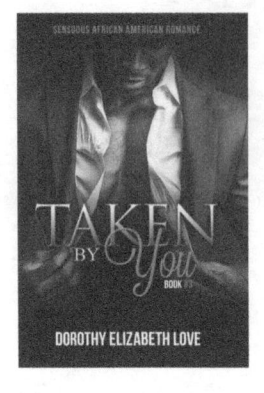

The Ryan family reunites in **TAKEN BY YOU** for the wedding of Parker Ryan and Chi. Leila Chamberlain is Chi's best friend and Reese McCoy is the Best Man. A troubled marriage left Reese reserved and hurt. Leila finding happiness with this man she barely knew meant jeopardizing more than she bargained for. When Leila gets too close to Reese, his ex-wife, Suzette—who's still in love with him—will do whatever she can to eliminate the competition… including murder.

"Ms. Love's writing was flawless." Brenda M. Lisbon

AUTHOR'S MESSAGE TO READER

I HAVE THIS UNYIELDING BELIEF THAT LOVE CAN CONQUER JUST ABOUT all. My goal is to provide a form of entertainment that allows readers to transcend their current situation if only for a moment, to be pleasantly entertained and emotionally moved. Although I write to entertain, I also believe in awareness. Social issues that impact African Americans and women are also addressed in my novels. My characters are flawed yet constantly strive to overcome as most of us do… their story, however, is enhanced with a dose of sexiness.

Thank you for allowing me to share a part of my passion with you. Until we meet again; look for the latest below! What's next for me (and YOU):

The Ryan Family Series

- The first novel, WHISPERS IN THE NIGHT
- The second novel, AND THEN CAME YOU
- The third novel, TAKEN BY YOU

The TLC: Travel and Love Collection.
Romance in exotic places
- WHEN DREAMS FLOAT
- CROSSING PATHS, TEMPTING MEMORIES
- EVERLASTING MOMENTS

YOU ARE MINE – is my foray into suspense

UNDENIABLE – more scintillating romance

DL

Visit my website
www.DorothyElizabethLove.com
for release dates and other juicy updates. Would love to get your thoughts and feedback on my novel!

Made in United States
Cleveland, OH
22 July 2025